Before and After

by

The Fairfield County
Creative Writers Co-op

Cover and interior design by
Sue Finch Photography and Design LLC

[signatures, handwritten]

ISBN: 9781790977574

Introduction

You are holding in your hand the very first (and certainly not the last) collaborative work from the Fairfield County Creative Writers Co-Op. Our group began in early 2017 as an infrequent set of meet-ups between a few budding authors starved for someone to share in the craft of writing. Just over a year later the group had grown to include over a dozen writers in various stages of their journey. The ad-hoc get-togethers were now monthly informational meeting where those with skill and knowledge in an area would share with the rest of the group. The mid-month meet-ups were held at a local eatery for fun, games, writing sprints, and relaxed conversation. Despite how far our group had come, it was wanting more. We needed a project.

The ideas of providing a showcase for our members was met with gusto. An anthology was considered and rejected – anyone could group short stories together – but, what if they collectively told a story. Thus, the idea of the collaborative project came into existence. It would be a book in which each chapter told the story of a different character, all contained within the same framework – the end of the world. It sounded like a lot of fun, and a lot of work.

Two members, the science fiction writers of the group, were tasked in crafting the end of the world. A catastrophe so big and so sudden that no one would survive. The rest who wanted to join were divided into pairs, becoming writing buddies who helped each other work their narratives. It was exciting, it was fun, and it was work.

Our collaboration became a great teaching tool for less experienced writers. Deadlines were set, and missed. Ideas flowed. Storylines were rejected. Revisions and edits were made, helping to develop the thick skin all writers need. Some received their first critiques ever from a professional editor, and the rest cheered them on as they worked through the pain of killing their darlings. In the end, we had a book. You have it now.

Please read this collection of stories in the spirit in which they were created. Have fun. Search inside yourself for the answer to who you truly are, as our writer's characters had to do. But above all, enjoy it for the effort of growth and learning that it was. In tackling this story, we not only learned how to write, but we also learned how to live and enjoy our lives and the people in it.

Happy reading.

Mike Ghere
Dec. 2018

Table of Contents

Part 1 (November 7th)

Part 2 (November 8th)

Acknowledgements

The Fairfield County Creative Writers Co-Op would like to thank the following individuals for their contributions to this project:

Many thanks to Jane B. Night, who developed the original concept for this collaborative effort. Without her enthusiasm and tireless effort in herding the clowder of cats we call a writing group, the project would never have crossed the finish line.

And a special thank you to Michael Wilson for taking on the near-Herculean task of proofreading and suggesting improvements for all the stories in this collection. He has been a fantastic coach to our writers of all levels of experience.

Before and After

by
The Fairfield County
Creative Writers Co-op

Part 1
November 7th

BC Winters
NASA, Goddard Space Center, Maryland

"All satellites show positive connection." The technician looked up from his screen and grinned as the room erupted in celebration. "All satellites are holding position well within project parameters. Great job, Freedom. Thanks for working the night shift."

The sudden, exuberant cheer delivered directly into BC's ear was so loud it drowned out Captain O'Neil's response and made her wince, but she shrugged it off. This was a truly momentous occasion, one for which she had called in every favor she was owed, and some of Anton's as well. Perks of dating an astronaut, she told herself. She shook off the tension now that Anton's spacewalk was over and grinned at her friend, Rebecca.

Although she wasn't a physicist, Rebecca Murphy was a damn good science journalist and a NASA, SpaceX, and all things space-related geek. She understood the tremendous difficulty of tethering seven satellites together far past the moon. Rebecca grinned and slugged BC in the shoulder. "That was awesome, Winters!" Her eyes darted to the older man, busily clapping NASA engineers on the back, and her smile faded. "It must be rough to see him succeed, but think of the science. Gotta be a professional, Business Chick. Forget about the old jerk."

BC ignored the good-natured jab at her name. It was rough, but she wouldn't have missed it. This was what years of graduate and post graduate research had been for. As much as she disliked the over-stuffed ass in charge, she was excited for the project. It may have been his dream first, but it was hers, too.

As if he could feel her glare on the back of his neck, Professor Montgomery Beachum turned to face the gathered press. He smiled broadly and extended an arm toward the wall of displays.

"In a moment," he said, "we will be making history." He grabbed the lapels of his suit coat and puffed out his chest "For the first time ever, we will be able to directly observe dark matter." He jabbed the railing that separated them with a finger. "Dark matter. One of the fundamental building blocks of the universe, yet so different from normal matter that, until now, we have only been able to sense its presence by its feeble interaction with gravity."

The assembled journalists and science writers nodded and made notes as he continued. BC fought for enough professionalism to avoid rolling her eyes. Dark matter might be her area of expertise, but everyone knew why they were there. This was just Beachum's self-aggrandizement.

"Until now, I say, because once the sensor array is on-line the mystery surrounding this material will finally be solved." He pointed to the display again, where a string of commands crept up the right side of the monitor, slowly turning green as an engineer called them off. "In a moment, we will be the first humans to actually see dark matter. To actually see it!" He grinned again. "You all are part of history today! Aren't you glad I invited you?" He gave an exaggerated wink. "You can thank me later."

BC sighed and tried to keep the scowl off her face. He was such a pompous ass. A charming, pompous ass, to be sure, but he never got tired of patting himself on the back. She scanned the monitors and tried to focus on the activities of the combined NASA and SpaceX crews. The sense of déjà vu was overwhelming. She was transported back six years in the past to the previous dark matter experiment. Her foul mood deepened and settled deep in her belly. She turned her gaze back to Professor Beachum and felt some small satisfaction at the disapproval in his eyes. Her editor had kept her name off the list until the last minute. After all, she was only a freelancer, not from the website's stable of journalists. He turned away to hide his fading smile and clapped the nearest engineer on the shoulder.

"How is it coming along, son?" Beachum leaned over the young man's shoulder and squinted at the screen in front of him. "Are we on track?"

"Yes, sir," the engineer said. "The Q-E will be on-line in a moment."

Beachum swung back to the journalists, a smile back on his broad face.

"And once the array is on-line, we can begin." He placed his fists on either side of the expanse of his wide belly. "While we have some time, are there any questions?" "Why seven satellites this time, and why are they so much farther away?"

BC glanced at Phil, a "journalist" from a popular science-ish website and suppressed a sigh. Really? Did he ever do his homework? He never wrote anything besides "Top Ten Reasons" pieces, but he had been around long enough one would think he would have a clue by now.

"Glad you asked." Beachum drew himself up into his lecturing pose and BC prepared herself. "This is the second attempt at this particular experiment. The first test was with three satellites in order to try out the tethering system. As you know, of course," Beachum winked at Rebecca, evidently Phil's reputation extended out of the journalistic world. "The tethering lines," Beachum continued, "form a literal satellite dish, a focusing array for the particles we are transmitting. Unfortunately, a series of miscalculations by a former team member caused the first Quark-emitting collider to fail ..."

Beachum's eyes flicked ever-so-slightly in her direction and BC immediately looked down at her notebook. She could tell by the subtle shifts in posture that her fellow journalists were watching her. She felt the heat rise in her neck and ears, but kept tight control on any other outward sign of her anger and embarrassment.

It had not been her fault! Beachum had needed someone to take the blame, so he had placed it squarely on her shoulders. She had fought the accusation, but he was too well established, and she had made a reputation for being difficult — if by difficult you meant refusing to blindly follow authority and willing to argue your point. She had been lucky to get out with her Doctorate. Even luckier that another lab would take her in. At least she had been able to continue her research. BC felt Rebecca lean into her slightly. As close to a hug as she could get right now.

"However." Beachum had continued. "The engineering on the tethering and transmission systems was perfect, so the project was not a complete loss."

BC took a deep breath and let the anger pass.

"So why seven satellites now, Professor?" Phil still looked puzzled. He evidently hadn't realized Beachum was only taking a breath. A flash of annoyance crossed the scientist's face, but he cleared his throat and continued with a broad smile.

"Well, this is the second generation of this experiment, and we have learned from the mistakes of the first." He chuckled, and BC gritted her teeth. "We salvaged enough success from the first to warrant another try, and this time we will get it right." Beachum's arm swept out to point at the 3-D rendering of the satellite array. "A hexagon formed with six satellites at the vertexes, ten kilometers across."

The professor strutted across the room to the model and began tapping the wires that made up the web of the "dish". BC wondered how much NASA had paid to have it built, and whether they would charge Beachum for bending the wires.

"Transmission cables connect them along the edges and across the width of the hexagon," Beachum continued.

"The central point is anchored by a seventh satellite located fifteen degrees below the plane of the other six." He tapped the central, and largest, piece of the array. "And the seventh is the most important of all."

"Why is it so important?"

BC winced at Phil's interruption. Either he was oblivious to the fact that Beachum had only paused for a breath again, or Phil was intentionally baiting him. Either way, it wasn't very smart. She could see the red creeping up Beachum's neck. She suppressed a grin and silently wished she had some popcorn to accompany the show.

"It is important," Beachum's words grated from between clenched teeth, "because it is the world's first, operational, space-borne particle collider."

He turned, and his eyes bored into BC's. She hadn't imagined the stress he placed on the word 'operational', and he was making sure she realized it. BC felt her own jaw clench and rise a fraction of an inch in defiance. Beachum pivoted away with a smirk.

"It is a fully functional, and remotely programmable, highly specialized, quark emitter." Beachum's face was flushed as his finger jabbed at the model. "The Q-E, ladies and gentlemen. The future of astrophysics!"

As if on cue, the scroll of commands on the monitor halted and the screen flashed green.

"The Q-E has finished self-testing and is on-line," the engineer announced. "Proceeding with initial energizing of the emitter."

BC lost herself in the celebration. This was what she had dreamed about these several, long years. It hurt that she was no longer at the forefront, but when she was honest with herself, she knew no one could have pulled this off better or faster than Beachum. He was a charming, driven, persistent ass, but he bent the ear of every politician and private space company he could find. He was a master at obtaining funding, and he wasn't above playing dirty. She knew from several friends still within Beachum's camp that when Congress began to drag their feet, he went straight to the European Space Agency and the China National Space Administration. It wasn't a bluff, and it paid off. Beachum was about to make history.

"What will we see when the array is in operation?" Rebecca's question pulled Beachum away from his celebration. "Will there be a flash of light? A beam?"

The professor chuckled. "Unfortunately, nothing of the kind, my dear. The energies we are dealing with are beyond the scope of mere human vision. But never fear, the array is a transceiver. It both emits and senses. What it picks up will be analyzed and rendered on the display as an image suitable for the eye." He stole a quick glance at the screens and smiled. "Now, if you will excuse me for a moment or two, we are about to begin."

Rebecca switched off her recorder and sighed. "What sucks is that I'm going to have to reduce hours of his going on and on into a thirty second sound bite and fifteen hundred words that only a handful of science geeks will read." She shook her head. "This isn't nearly as interesting to the average Joe as he thinks it is."

Phil leaned in with a conspiratorial smirk. "If SpaceX and Musk weren't involved there wouldn't even be any cameras. Quark, shmark. No one cares."

"I care." BC had meant to say it under her breath, but Rebecca's ear pricked up.

"Of course, you do." She looked up at BC with hungry eyes. "Let me tell your story, Winter. You know I'll treat you right!"

"I know, but that ship sailed a long time ago. I just want to get on with my life. You know? My research and freelance gigs like this."

"If this thing works," Phil said, "won't it make all the theoretical work obsolete?"

"Of course not. Don't be absurd." They all turned toward Beachum, who was frowning at Phil. "You are a reporter of science, sir. Do you not understand how it works?" He advanced on the hapless journalist as the rest turned their recorders back on with evident glee. "Every scientific advancement begins with an observation that is immediately followed by a question. 'That is interesting. Why does it behave in such a manner?' From that question, a hypothesis is formed. 'Maybe this thing makes it happen.' Then experiments are made, tests are run, data is analyzed, all in a loop until the hypothesis can be proved or disproved." Beachum shook his finger in Phil's face. "We would not be here today without the questions and the testing. Very often the only tests possible in this field are mathematical in nature. Research and theoretical mathematics are the fundamental building blocks of science. As Sir Isaac Newton once said, 'If I have seen a little further it is by standing on the shoulders of Giants.'"

"Professor, we're ready."

Beachum turned and nodded directly at BC, then turned to the bank of instrumentation.

BC stared numbly at Beachum's retreating back until a nudge from Rebecca broke her from her paralysis.

"Did Beachum just stick up for you?"

BC shrugged. "I don't know. Why would he start now?"

~

"Q-E at seventy percent target power."

The entire room was tense as the engineers slowly brought the DMI collider up to full power.

"Eighty percent. All systems nominal."

"Good. Very good." Beachum was positively beaming. "Are we ready for injection?"

"All systems go for injection, Professor. Ready on your signal."

"Ninety percent target. Systems are nominal."
BC forced her fingers to unclench from around her pen. The scene in front of her was bringing back all the stress she had spent years trying to shed. She took a deep, calming breath. It wouldn't be long now. One way or another the tension would break. She rolled her shoulders and wondered if she was rooting for the project or against Beachum. She couldn't tell.

"Quark emitter at full power. All systems green-lined and ready to go." The engineer swiveled his seat to look at Beachum. Though his voice had remained steady, the excitement on his face was impossible to miss. BC jotted a quick note and flexed her aching fingers. "The DMI is ready for operation, Professor."

Beachum straightened and threw his arms as wide as the smile on his face.

"Excellent job, everyone. Excellent work!" His arms fell to his sides and he gave a dramatic shrug. "What say we turn it on then, eh?" He pointed to the operator. "Release the hounds!" The assembled journalists gave a polite chuckle, while BC rolled her eyes and stifled a groan. The man was simply full of himself.

"Yes, sir," the operator replied. "Injection interval set at three seconds."

Phil smirked. "The old guy is certainly full of it today," he whispered. "How long has he been planning that cheesy line?"

"Six years," BC said. "Ever since the first experiment failed. I'm sure he's been practicing."

Phil's chuckle changed to a gasp that was repeated around the room, but quickly turned into a roar of celebration.

"Yes!" Beachum threw his hands in the air in celebration and ran closer to the main screen like a child whose favorite television show has started. "Amazing! It's wonderful." His voice broke and he coughed, apparently speechless for once. He rubbed at his eyes as the project scientists and engineers congratulated him.

BC could understand. She felt a tear run down her face and wiped at it as the screen continued to fill with complicated crystalline structures. Like the view of a radar screen, the twisting ropes of dark matter were painted bold as the sensors picked up the reflected burst of quarks, then faded until it saw the next burst three seconds later. It was nearly too much. Her research the last several years had showed this would work, but seeing it was awe-inspiring. Dark matter was theorized to be the structural support of the universe, the underpinning that fixed normal matter into place. And here it was. Though only a small bit of nearby space was affected by the DMI, it was absolutely incredible.

"It's beautiful," she breathed. "How big is it?"

Beachum turned from where he peered into a monitor, grinning broadly. "At least ten thousand kilometers across.

"Um, Professor? We have an anomaly." One of the engineers had turned in her seat, concern creasing her forehead. "Could you take a look at this please?"

"What is it?" Beachum waved impatiently from his seat. "Just put it up on the screen."

"Uh, yes, sir. Okay."

The woman's voice was tight with tension, but she only hesitated a moment. The view on the screen changed.

Phil pointed at the screen. "What the hell is that?"
"A piece of dark matter," BC said. "Like the rest."

"Why is it moving, then?"

"Because it's an asteroid," Rebecca said. She scribbled frantically in her notebook. "This is great stuff!"

BC watched the jagged chunk of matter pulse with the green glow of the sensor display as it tumbled. It was craggy and sharp with spikes of multifaceted, crystal-like protrusions.

"What is the problem?" Beachum asked. "It stands to reason free-wheeling bits of dark matter would exist, just like normal matter."

"It is very large, Professor. About one hundred and sixty kilometers across."

Phil leaned toward Rebecca. "About a hundred miles," she hissed, and waved him away.

"It, um, appears to be getting closer, rapidly, sir. There isn't much data as we only have the one sensor array, but the director should be notified."

Beachum chuckled. "This is dark matter, my dear. It has no interaction with normal matter. The stuff has been passing through the earth since the beginning of time itself. There is nothing to worry about."

BC saw the engineer's eyes narrow at the words "my dear" and inwardly cheered the woman on. Don't take his crap. Stand up to him.

"I understand, sir," the woman said. "However, there are protocols and levels above this project. I thought you should know before I made the call."

Beachum's face purpled, but he nodded. "Of course."

"Professor?" one of the project members called from across the room. "Were you expecting this?"

"Expecting what?" Beachum snapped. He shot a glance at the press box and made a subtle, but visible, effort to control his temper. He pushed himself out of the chair.

"Expecting what, Ben?"

"Expecting the dark matter to be visible in normal light?" The main screen changed again, and the green-traced picture was replaced by one of bright, flashing multi-hued light. "This is the view from the Hubble. The crew of Freedom confirms."

Flashes of blue, green, and gold flickered briefly and were gone. In their absence, a faint trace, like an afterimage, of something remained.

BC stared in fascination. "That isn't possible," she said.

"Why not?"

Rebecca's laugh was a short bark or derision. "Because physics, Phil."

"Look, that doesn't mean anything to me and you guys know it. If it isn't Bitchy Chick over there making fun of me it's you, Becky," he spat. "I'm just a guy that works for a magazine. Excuse me if I'm not a damned particle physicist."

BC stepped in before Rebecca could start in on him. She knew Phil and others used the nickname, among others, for her, but she wore it as a badge of pride. Anything was better than the Buffy Cordelia her far-too-nerdy parents had saddled her with, and everyone she knew had come up with at least one play on her initials. If Phil expected to upset her, he was mistaken. Besides, the view on the screen was far more upsetting than some ass-hat calling her names.

"The dark matter should only be visible with the sensors, Phil. The quarks bounce off it, like radar, and the sensor sees that reflection." She gestured at the screen. "This just isn't possible. Well," she amended, "it obviously is, but nothing in my research, or anyone else's, shows a quark will interact with dark matter in this way. Hell, only about one in a million should interact with it at all."

"So, what's going on then?"

"I don't know," BC said. She was watching Beachum as he studied the screen intently. He was holding it together well, but she knew the signs. He was perturbed. He didn't care for the unexpected. He was stalling, wracking his brains, as he studied the monitors around him. "I don't think Beachum knows either. Our research really isn't all that different, he's just better funded. There's nothing to suggest this is even a possibility." She let out a long breath. "He hit the jackpot with this one. He'll get a Nobel for sure. And he knows it."

Beachum straightened as if on cue.

"Absolutely fascinating!" he said. "No one expected this, and that is what makes science so wonderful. Record everything! And thank you to whomever decided to watch with the Hubble. An inspired action!"

The room descended into barely controlled chaos. Technicians and engineers jumped onto the phones and, like magic, the project doubled in size as other instrumentation and telescopes from around the world were brought to bear on the new discovery. It was an awe-inspiring act of scientific cooperation that was rarely seen, let alone recorded.

BC wrote furiously as she tried to make sense of the nearly incomprehensible rumble of overlapping conversations. Her mind was in a whirl. This was what she had hoped for years before. This was what over a decade of research had been leading to. And once again, it was Beachum ending up on top. She wrenched her thought out of that track with a physical shake of her head. None of that mattered. What mattered was the impossible had happened. How did a chunk of the most undetectable substance in the universe suddenly turn visible? Beachum was right, no one expected this. Nothing in her years of research, or anyone else's, had even suggested it. What were the implications? Was it some sort of energy emission? A reflection?

As her mind worked the problem over, BC scanned the room, taking note of the growing level of excitement and the growing number of people in the command center. Word of something big was spreading, and the excitement was contagious. Everyone was happy, and they should be. This would make their careers for years to come. Even her own would get a boost. All this data, all the observations, the new theorizing, it would energize the field for decades. It would see Beachum into the history books and maybe even carry herself to retirement. A second fiddle, of course, but that didn't matter. She would happily work away at building on whatever had been discovered today. She would make her own mark on the field.

As that thought crossed her mind, BC's scanning eyes landed on the lone person in the room that was not smiling. The engineer that had put Beachum in his place earlier was speaking rapidly into a phone, a furious frown on her face as she studied the monitor in front of her. BC began pushing her way toward that side of the room and eventually came up against the railing that separated the journalists from the working scientists in the room. She leaned as close as she could. The woman's conversation was hushed, muffled by the phone at her lips, but the urgency of her tone and alarm in her eyes spoke volumes. Something was wrong. BC was about to catch the woman's attention, but the engineer turned instead to a tall, suited man who entered the room and made a beeline to the terminal. The engineer hung up the phone as he approached.

"Thank you for coming down, sir. I thought you should see this first hand."

"Of course, Sheila. Show me what you've got."

The pair bent over the computer monitor and BC's mind was whirling once again. She recognized the man, and his presence added a completely different flavor to the chaos in the room.

"That is Marc Justus, the Planetary Defense Officer." Rebecca's voice at her elbow made BC jump. "The guy in charge of tracking asteroids." She scribbled in her notebook.

"And what brings Director Justus down here from his air-conditioned office?"

With the influx of people and heightened excitement, the ventilation system was struggling to keep up. BC brushed the back of her hand across the sweat beaded on her brow and shook her head.

"I don't know," BC said. She cocked an eyebrow at her friend. "Listen in?"

Rebecca nodded and they both leaned closer.

"The data is fairly incontrovertible, sir. Additional observations are confirming the original track and refining it." Sheila, the NASA engineer, wiped a shaky hand across her forehead. "It's a code black, sir."

"Oh, shit!" Rebecca hissed. The look of stark fear on her face and the sharp look of disapproval by Justus sent a jolt of adrenaline through BC's system.

"What is it? What's a code black?" She had to physically take Rebecca by the arm to get her attention away from the rapidly retreating backs of the two NASA employees.

"What is a code black?" she repeated.

Rebecca brought a shaky hand up to rub at her forehead. "A planet killer," she whispered. "A rock big enough to end everything." Her eyes were wide as she turned to stare at Beachum's beaming face as he rattled off instructions.

"Beachum's killed us all." She suddenly turned and began elbowing her way through the throng of the press corp. "I've got to get to a phone!"

~

An hour later the control room was a very different place. The air of celebration was long gone, and the only person in the room who was not grim-faced or outright distraught was Beachum. He was positively apoplectic.

"And I'm telling you," he shouted, spittle flying from his mouth, "there is absolutely nothing to worry about!" This is dark matter. It has no effect on normal matter at all!"

Beachum was a big man, and tall in stature, as well. He towered over the NASA Director, red-faced and so angry that everyone else had drawn back from the two men. Director Justus stared, unblinking and calm, into Beachum's fury. BC wished she had been able to do the same all those years ago.

"Bringing back memories?" BC jerked her attention back to Gregg Smith. He was former NASA, now SpaceX Communications Liaison for the project. He had pulled her aside at his manager's request as the only unaffiliated person in the room with dark matter experience. She noticed he said unaffiliated and not neutral.

"Yeah," BC sighed. "Memories I had hoped to forget." She glanced at Director Justus. "I wasn't quite so calm."

"Well," Gregg said, "he's had politicians yelling at him for years. He's used to it. Besides, you did pretty well. It moved you from Brainy Chick status to Badass Chick for most of us." He caught her eye. "You stood up to him and anyone else would have just taken it." He winked. "That's what clinched the deal for Anton, you know."

BC shook her head. "What clinched the deal for Anton was that I was the only girl not swooning over Scott O'Neil at the time. And since Hinata wasn't interested in him, my attention did wonders for his ego."

"Ha!" Gregg caught himself and stifled his laugh. "Don't sell yourself short, BC." He took a deep breath and his mood changed. "Seriously, though, I need Brainy Chick right now. Is he right? Is there nothing to worry about?" Gregg shot a worried look at the argument, still in full swing.

"If it weren't for all the connections the man has, he would have been shut down forty-five minutes ago."

BC rubbed the back of her neck and heaved a sigh of exasperation. "I just don't know, Gregg." She waved a hand at the tumbling, crystalline body on the monitor. "We can see it, but it's reflecting crazy wavelengths. We can analyze it with spectroscopy, but the results are screwy. We can hit it with a laser, but it absorbs it instead of reflecting it, which makes absolutely zero sense, by the way." She shrugged.

"Brainy Chick is more like Blatantly Confused at the moment, but I would say Beachum can't be as certain as he is letting on. Or at least he shouldn't be. This is all new, all different physics now. No one is an expert."

"I thought you might say that," Gregg said. "Most of us feel the same, but no one has the credentials to debate him on the science." He took a deep breath and BC watched him shift from good friend to SpaceX official. "You know I have to report what you have said." It wasn't a question. "It will probably mean another showdown with him." He jerked his head in Beachum's direction.

"I know," BC sighed. "The sad thing is that he already has made history here. He is just too full of himself to back down."

As Gregg stepped away, Rebecca filled the empty space he left behind.

"Dish, Girlfriend," she whispered. "I'll show you mine, if …" She cocked an eyebrow expectantly.

BC filled her in on the conversation. It wouldn't matter. It would be in the open soon, anyway.

"Wow!" Rebecca said. "Head to head with the big man again. BC must stand for 'Big Cojones'."

"You know, the name jokes are growing a little old."

Rebecca chuckled. "Well, here's some new news." Her voice dropped and gave a conspiratorial glance around.

"We're cut off now."

"What?"

"We're locked in. No contact with the outside. They're using a cell scrambler to boot." She shot the director a dirty look. "The only news getting out is official NASA reports. I was in the middle of briefing my editor when they cut me off." She looked wistfully at a nearby terminal. "You suppose that thing gets the internet?"

"What are they telling people?" BC smacked her thigh with her fist. "Damn it, I had the SpaceX Communication guy right here. He didn't say anything!"

Before Rebecca could respond, Sheila, the engineer from earlier, pulled the Director away from Beachum and spoke quickly into his ear. BC took note that his calm demeanor turned positively icy.

"Must be bad news," she whispered. "He clenches tighter every time he gets an update."

"Hey!" Phil tapped Rebecca on the shoulder. "Is your cell working? Mine's on the fritz."

"Attention, everyone! Quiet please! The Director has an announcement." Sheila's voice was surprisingly loud and commanding for someone who murmured into a throat mike for a living.

"Ladies and Gentlemen," Director Justus said. "I have just been told that analysis of this Dark Matter object's trajectory has it on a collision course with the Earth. There is a slight chance that it may impact the moon first, but either outcome is catastrophic due to the object's size and speed." He turned to look directly at Beachum. "There is no room for supposition, Professor. We need to know what this is and what to expect. In the meantime, I am ordering that the Dark Matter Initiative project be powered down for the time being."

"What?" Beachum surged forward. "You can't do that!"

"I can, and I have." Justus nodded to the engineers at their terminals, and they began to speak into their microphones.

"You —" Beachum took a deep breath and BC recognized the look that came over his face. Bluster wasn't working. Time to bargain.

"Director Justus." Beachum forced a smile onto his face. "Please. Hear me out. I know I am a tad upset, but seriously, why shut down the only instrument capable of truly examining this phenomenon?"

"Professor, this is no longer the only instrument capable of that. Telescopes all over the world are trained on this 'phenomenon' and the panic it is causing is gaining a frightening amount of momentum." His smooth veneer developed a slight crack and his voice rose. "We now have a planet-killing asteroid, aimed at the Earth, and only hours away. There is nothing that can be done to stop it or deflect it. So, pardon me if I step on your toes as I turn off the damned machine that created it!"

His shout was practically a snarl. The room was dead silent for a tick, then the engineers went back to work. Justus stretched his neck to one side, then the other and took a deep breath. The veneer was back in place, but his voice still seethed.

"Feel free to figure this thing out, Beachum. Everything we have is at your disposal. Everything but the DMI. I suggest you cross your fingers and hope that rock disappears when it powers down." Justus smoothed his tie as he stalked across the room and out the door.

The room erupted in pandemonium as the press lost their minds.

"Did he say planet killer?" Phil looked worriedly at his dead phone. "What do we do?"

"Calm down! Calm Down!" Beachum's roar cut through the noise like a knife. "There is nothing to worry about," he said. "The Dark Matter will pass through the moon as if it were not there. You will see. This is an anomaly. Nothing more."

"How can you be certain, Professor?" BC was surprised by the sound of her own voice. She hadn't meant to speak until she actually did so. She just found it impossible to take anymore bullshit or baseless optimism. "Do you have any data to support that claim?"

18

The look of pure hatred Beachum shot at her turned BC's stomach sour.

"What I have, Ms. Winter, is over forty years of experience in this field, the last six spent with the brightest minds in modern physics. I believe I know what I am talking about!"

BC seethed at the dig, but reminded herself that she was here as a journalist. "Even so, Professor Beachum, you stated yourself that the results of the quark beam were unexpected. How can you extrapolate from that to nothing has changed?"

"Because nothing has shown me that it has not." Beachum's teeth were clenched so hard, BC thought he might crack a molar. She was getting to him. The thought filled her with a dark joy. Brave Chick indeed! She opened her mouth for a retort, but Beachum turned his back on her.

"Are there any other questions?"

BC clenched her own jaw shut. Pride warred with professionalism and ultimately lost. There was nothing she could say. She had no data of her own. Soon they would all know the answer to the question.

Beachum spent the next hour vacillating between lecturing the room on why there was nothing of concern and raging at the walls about the stupidity and close-mindedness of anyone who did not support him. She half expected to see him claw at his chest at any moment. His cardiologist had been concerned years before about his weight and stress, and if BC were a Betting Chick, she would put money on Beachum ignoring his doctor. Regardless, his anger and outrage did nothing to change the Director's mind. The DMI was powered down. But, in the end, it did not matter.

Everyone had been so focused on the Moon and the Earth that no one had noted anything else in the way. A kilometers-long spur of the tumbling asteroid snagged the edge of the DMI array like a whale in a fishing net. The assembled scientists, engineers, and journalists gasped as years of work and millions of dollars of hardware was flung into space as a tangled mess of debris.

Three hours later the asteroid clipped the moon.

~

BC poked at the half-eaten cup of yogurt in front of her and watched the scenes playing out on the silent television mounted high in the corner. She was all alone in the cafeteria. There had been no one to take her money, so she helped herself and put a buck in the cash register. Nearly everyone was gone. NASA was practically a ghost town. Once the jagged asteroid clipped the moon and blasted debris into space, they all left to be with their families.

The reporter on the television mouthed silent calls for calm as the frame floating by his head showed a mob destroying an electronics store. The scene flickered and changed to one of a group of young people with linked arms preventing a man from jumping from the Golden Gate Bridge. Another flicker and the screen showed a closeup of the shattered face of the moon. The debris spread out and away, while the dark matter asteroid flickered like a celestial diamond in the middle of the cloud. The reporter began to sob, and the station went to a commercial.

BC didn't know what was worse. The defaced moon, or the depths humankind sank to in their panic. There were scenes of hope and joy, to be sure, but they were offset by anger, anguish, and hopelessness, played out across the world. She wondered what she would do if she were out on the street. There was no tomorrow, only now. It could be liberating to let one's self go and give in to their secret inner being. What would she do? What could she do?

A different reporter was back on the news, and the cycle started again. Despair, hope, and then the moon. Lawlessness, inspiration, and then the moon. BC rubbed at her cheeks with the palms of both hands, desperate to remove the rictus grin of horror frozen on her face. It was all too much. She had secretly wanted to see Beachum fail, but not like this. Not taking the entire damned world down with him. Her hands fell to the table, knocking over the yogurt, as she stared back at the TV. That was what was missing. His face.

There was no mention of the man responsible for it all. It wasn't the asteroid that clipped the moon, it was his ego.

BC shoved to her feet, galvanized with purpose. The reporters had fled NASA. There was no one to force Beachum to face the music for his arrogance and vanity. No one but her.

She stalked the halls and offices of the nearly deserted building unopposed. No one cared that she was there. The few that remained clung desperately to telephones or were too busy trying to do four jobs to even notice her. Where was he? She was certain he had not left. Where would he go? He had no one close, no family, no loved ones.

"Oh, God!" The sob escaped her clenched jaw, and just like that her fury was replaced with the earlier anguish.

"Anton!"

Tears blurred her vision and BC braced herself against the corridor wall, legs too weak to carry her any farther. She would never see him again. Never feel his touch, his kiss. There wouldn't be any gentle teasing of her name. She was stuck here, completely alone, and he was floating in a tin can, either about to be pulverized by moon debris, or fated to watch the earth die as he slowly starved to death.

Her stomach heaved, and she slammed through the bathroom door, clawing the tears from her eyes.

"Aah!"

The shout of alarm was followed by the patter of falling rain. Beachum stood at the sink, a handful of tablets bounced off the counter top along with the bottle he had poured them from. BC snatched the bottle as it bounced and peered at the label. Flexeril. A muscle relaxant.

"You fucking coward!" BC hurled the empty bottle at him and Beachum backed away, arms raised in front of his face. "Suicide? Since you've got no one to throw under the bus you're just going run away from all of this? Just go to sleep and pretend it never happened?" She raised her fist as Beachum backed against the wall. He broke into tears and slid to the floor.

"What would you have me do?" he cried. "Wait for incineration?"

"Face the music, you bastard. Tell them it was your fault. Take responsibility for once in your miserable life!"

"How was I supposed to know?" Beachum glared up at her, anger burning away the tears. "How was I supposed to know this would happen?" He used the urinal to pull himself to his feet and BC realized she had barged into the men's room. "It wasn't in the research," he said. "Not in mine. Was it in yours? Why didn't you stop me?"

BC lowered her raised fist and shook her head.

"No, you're not dragging me into your mess this time. You couldn't have known this would happen, but you swung your ego around the room like you owned the place. You should have shut down the experiment earlier when it started going off the rails. This experiment is a catastrophe of your making."

"This is my life!" Beachum roared. He stopped and heaved a sigh. "This was my life." He wiped his face with a shaky hand and stooped to begin picking up the scattered pills. "This could have taken me to the end of my days." He grunted as he straightened and fixed her with an appraising eye. "Yours too. This was the first new data on dark matter. More would come. The next generation of experiments would be your design. The most wonderful opportunity of a lifetime." He looked sadly at the pills in his hand. "But now, nothing."

"You're not going to take those!"

"Why not. Am I supposed to sit quietly in some sort of forced penance while the world is destroyed around me?" he barked a bitter laugh. "You know me better than that."

BC shook her head. She did know him that well. Without his work he had nothing. It was one of the only things she admired about him. His dedication to the science. Better this than wandering the streets trying to decide what to do with his last hours. She walked toward the door as he turned on the tap. She stopped and began to chuckle.

"You find this amusing?" Beachum growled. "Seeing me reduced to this."

"No. It just struck me that we are the country's preeminent experts on dark matter, in one of the top research facilities in the world. We have nowhere to go. No one waiting at home. What else is there to do?" She shrugged. "You said the research could last us the rest of our lives. Well, that's a pretty safe bet." BC turned back to the door. "What do you say, Professor," she called over her shoulder. "Want to come solve some equations?"

~

The arguments began almost immediately, but BC had known they would. She was far too cynical to think staring at a fistful of pills would change Beachum in any way. If anything, he seemed determined to make up for the faltering of his iron will. BC remembered those days. She had lived through several long years of never being good enough, constant questioning of her methods and result, if not her intellect, and being pushed harder than she ever had been in her life. Now six years later, she found her perspective had changed.

"I don't care what your friend at the LHC told you, if it isn't published and peer-reviewed it's worthless. You should have left hearsay behind in your undergraduate years, Winter." The finger Beachum had been pointing in her face dropped to rest on the table as he shook his head. "I expected better of you."

If he expected the sour look of disapproval on his face to affect her it did. BC leaned back in her chair and burst out laughing. His expression quickly slipped to confusion and then to anger, which was evidently the ground state of his emotions.

"Do you find your lack of professionalism amusing, Ms. Winter?"

"No," she chuckled. "It's just —" BC leaned forward and smiled up into his scowl. "Do you really think any of this is getting published? Peer review? Really?" She threw her hands in the air. "We've been through the data a couple of times now and nothing either of us has read or published has any bearing on what has happened. My friend at the Large Hadron Collider designed his experiment based on your own papers that led to the DMI. The results were very intriguing and might have some bearing here. I'm sorry if he hasn't published yet, Beachum, but I don't see it happening before we're all vaporized." She shrugged. "Do you want to hear about it or not?"

BC settled back in her chair as he continued to scowl. She didn't care, and the thought surprised her. For years she had tried to fool herself into thinking that, but she still carried the scars of Beachum's blacklisting. She in turn had carried a morbid fascination and burning hatred for the man. Today it was gone. Maybe she had grown. Maybe it just didn't matter in the face of a giant space rock aimed at her head. Maybe Beachum's inability to set aside his ego was just too ludicrous to take seriously anymore. Whatever the case, she didn't care. And with that baggage out of the way she found something else. Confidence and surety in herself.

"I suppose if wouldn't hurt to consider these premature findings," Beachum said. "But if they were based on my own work, I take offense that he shared them with you before presenting them to me."

"Whatever," BC waved him back from where he loomed over their ad-hoc work table. They had commandeered the conference room just off the control center in order to have easy access to the data gleaned from the abandoned experiment. A single NASA engineer remained at his post. He watched them through the open doorway, obviously as confused by their presence as they had been at his. "Here is what he had to say about the makeup of the quark cloud during the experiment."

It was in the third hour of their debate that things took an unexpected turn.

"Wait a minute," BC said. She stepped back from the table and fought for control of her whirling thoughts. Beachum ground to a halt mid-spiel and he watched her with expectancy. "What if the quarks aren't decaying? What if this phenomenon isn't due to the quarks, per se, but because of their makeup? What if there is a greater percentage at the higher energy state? What if it's got something to do with strangelets?"

"Impossible," Beachum scoffed. "The quark decay is too rapid. The energy provided by the reactor is insufficient for such a thing. It has never been seen before. You've gone off into science fiction."

BC grinned and pointed at him. "You're right. This is sci-fi turned real life. I propose that we have never seen this before because we have always performed the experiment on the Earth. Space is full of high-energy radiation and particles. Cosmic rays, gamma rays, neutrinos — the list goes on. Did you consider their effects on your quark beam?

Beachum opened his mouth, then closed it with a click. BC slammed her hand on the table. "Ha!" she said. "You didn't."

"Of course not!" Beachum Huffed. "The extra energy would be inconsequential."

"But if it's not," BC argued, "then you just bombarded the dark matter with strangelets. What if this is a dark matter and strange matter reaction. It might explain why the asteroid is interacting so weirdly with normal matter. Why it seemed to phase deep into the moon. And," she spun in place and jabbed a finger in Beachum's direction, "if that is true, by bombarding it with charm quarks, which would break down the strangelets, you could possibly reverse the reaction!" her heart hammered in her chest. This was it. It had to be. It felt too right.

Beachum sat slumped in his chair, and as she spoke, he began to nod. When she finished, he leaned forward with his face in his hands.

"That is brilliant," he said. His words were muffled, but he repeated them. "You always were brighter than anyone gave you credit for, even myself." He looked up at her with a sad smile. "I believe you have solved it." Unfortunately, we are a bit too late. I'm afraid we won't need to fight over whose name is first on the paper."

BC felt too sick to acknowledge the professor's attempt at humor. She had thrown herself into the work as a way to make herself feel better. Actually arriving at a solution was completely unexpected and made her feel a thousand times worse than before.

"I need some air," she said.

Beachum nodded. "Of course."

He looked as defeated as she felt, and despair welled up in her chest. It was all she could do to take a breath. It was over. It was her last day on Earth and she was alone. BC squared her shoulders and headed out into the hollow corridors of NASA. She needed to talk to Anton. There was no way in hell she was going to die without saying she loved him one last time.

~

BC raced down the deserted hallway, her mind whirling with the implications of her conversation with Anton and the crew of the Freedom. Tom Higgins, Freedom's ground control liaison, was close on her heels.

"Can you. Really. Stop this. Thing?" he wheezed.

"I don't know, Tom, but we have to do something." BC Rounded a corner and shot a glance over her shoulder at the engineer. He was out of breath, but intent on keeping up with her. She grinned and slowed her pace a bit. "Too much desk time, Tom?" she asked.

"That and the donuts," he laughed. "A percentage of every project budget goes into keeping the conference rooms stocked."

BC chuckled. "Seriously, though, thank you for sticking around. We wouldn't have this shot if I hadn't been able to contact Anton."

Tom shrugged. "It's my job," he said. "I'm single, an only child, and my parents have passed. The best thing I can do right now is my job. The crew deserves to have someone on the ground to help them, and … it helps me, too. You know?"

"You're a good man, Tom. Without you patching me through to Anton, Captain O'Neil wouldn't have come up with this crazy idea. What is it with rocket jockeys and their addiction to adrenaline?"

"I wouldn't know," Tom panted. "I prefer eclairs."

"Ha!" BC put on a burst of speed. "Let's find the professor. We don't have any time to spare."

~

Beachum wasn't hard to find. He had not moved from the chair he had collapsed in. For a moment BC wondered if he had finally taken the pills, but he glared at her as she ran into the room.

"Go away!" he growled. "Leave me in peace. I had planned a quick and peaceful death and now I don't have the courage for it."

"That wasn't courage, Beachum, it was despair and self-loathing." BC continued before he could argue. "But that doesn't matter. There might be another way. The first collider. What if it could be fixed? What if the crew of the Freedom could get it running?"

"Impossible," Beachum scoffed.

But, if they could?" BC insisted.

"Even if the collider still has power there is no way to configure it. Besides, your program-"

"My program had nothing to do with the failure of the damned satellites! The collider wouldn't power up. Not. My. Fault." BC leaned across the conference table and jabbed a finger at Beachum. "I might have been too young, naive, and devastated by your treachery to fight back, but those days are long gone." She sat in the chair across from him and crossed her arms. "If they can fix it, they can load a program to change the emitter output. It has a one in a million chance of succeeding, but what else can we do? I'm not ready to give up, and I don't think you are either." BC leaned forward. "Now, are you going to help me do this? Or are you just going to sit on your ass while I do it myself?"

Beachum flinched away from her defiant stare and looked instead at his hands, folded on the table top. BC was struck by how very old he looked. Following that thought was the realization that she would try with or without him, because it came down to one thing. What did they have to lose?

Beachum sighed and closed his eyes. "Well, since you won't let me kill myself ..." he muttered.

"That's the spirit. Besides, if it works, you can always kill yourself tomorrow!" Her chipper sarcasm earned her a death-ray glare. She laughed, because she just didn't care anymore. Nothing mattered more than this.

They threw themselves into the work, and in the end, there was hope. Hope that rested on the shoulders of three brave astronauts hurtling toward the earth in a battered tin can tied to an experimental rocket engine running far beyond its test parameters. Where, BC wondered, were the reporters? Where were the cheering crowds they deserved?

She gave the program she had written and Beachum's installation instructions to Tom to transmit to Freedom's crew. Two other engineers had joined him, and the three operated a dozen workstations among them. BC wanted to stay, she wanted to watch, but she couldn't bear to hear Anton's voice and know each word could be his last. Maybe Beachum wasn't the only coward.

She found an abandoned office with a comfortable chair and began writing their story. Hers, Beachum's, the loyal NASA engineers, and the brave crew of the Freedom. If the sun rose in the morning her editor would be screaming about deadlines and crowing about her scoop. If not — well, it was the right thing to do.

Rachel
Yellow Springs, Ohio

For as long as she could remember, Rachel was different. The usual games and activities of her peers didn't interest her. Rachel had this creative spark in her that wouldn't be squelched. She herself had a hard time controlling it. As a young girl she would bring home things, trash to most, but treasures of infinite possibilities to her. She'd gather broken bits of glass, scrap pieces of wood, discarded bits of twine or wire and before long she'd make the most fascinating pieces of art. In school crayons opened up whole new worlds to her and were not a passing phase, but a way of expression that touched her soul.

Those predictable artistic endeavors became another way to feed the beast within her, this almost alien 'thing' which needed an artistic outlet. She was different, special. To the teachers who if they didn't quite understand her gift could at least appreciate it, she brought this beam of light that expanded the walls of the minds of her classmates. To others, she was odd, a rebellious non-conformist who disrupted carefully laid out, controlled lesson plans. Her out-of-the-box thinking in their classrooms led to numerous parent teacher conferences with concerns that she'd never fit in, that there was no place for her.

Thank goodness for high school and Ms. Madison, the art teacher. She saw Rachel as the prodigy she was and the amazing artist she could become. She encouraged and taught her and gave her permission to apply what she learned in her own unique way. Young artist awards would follow and a scholarship to the Cleveland Institute of Art where she entered into a whole new world that fanned the flames of her creativity. She learned, absorbing her teaching like a sponge and realized her creative approach could support her, albeit meagerly. So, armed with a degree she settled in Yellow Springs, Ohio, a quirky, non-conformist town where she could have a base of operations from which to unleash her art to the world, or at least Ohio and surrounding states for a start.

All of this history mattered to her. Rachel had been making a comfortable living for her and her cat for the last several years. To some she was barely getting by but to her the chance to create made up for a small apartment and studio and some less than wholesome meals. What mattered was being able to create, on her own terms. That was a satisfying life. She was currently absorbed in a series of paintings, edgy, abstract canvasses of light and color that seemed to be trying to leap off their two2-dimensional stretched fabric prison. She was happy. In fact, her happiness would have been beyond description were it not for her inexplicable inability to embrace her most organically creative offering yet. Her hands absentmindedly went to her huge belly where her 39-week-old infant waited to make an appearance.

Rachel was torn. She had wanted to love this child, this flesh and blood gift of self, but she just couldn't let herself. Perhaps it's more accurate to say, she wouldn't let herself love it. She wouldn't and couldn't love it enough. Her life was one that simply wasn't enough for a baby. There was not enough money; not enough time; not enough stability; not enough structure; simply not enough to enable her to keep her soon-to-be delivered offspring.

At first, she didn't know what to do. The child's father was a chance encounter, their time together spent in a whirlwind of uncharacteristic feelings and actions. She'd met him at a coffee shop. He'd been passing through. She was lonely. An artist's life, especially when in a creative lull can be lonely. Their night spent together was glorious and filled her with a never before kind of rapture. It filled her in ways she never considered possible. And then 20 weeks later she realized had filled her with something else—this child.

After he left, she had been filled with such energy, such creative power she didn't notice the upset stomach, the tiredness, the lack of monthly flow. After all this had happened before. She simply didn't listen to the signs of her own body.

November 7th

When she realized something was different and finally went to the doctor his news of her condition was totally surprising. Once the shock wore off there was lots of sobbing and many sleepless nights before she realized she had to make a decision. By now she was 22 weeks pregnant, the odd sensations she'd passed off as indigestion now know for what they were, movement inside her womb. By this point she basically had two options, keep the child or give it up for adoption. When she made the decision, everything seemed to fall into place. She loved the couple she'd chosen to adopt her child. Ken and Rebecca had a 3-year-old girl, Elly. Rebecca's difficult, life-threatening pregnancy made birthing another child impossible. Rachel felt good about her decision for the most part. There was this small part of her that couldn't quite accept this was happening to her and would always wonder, what if.

All of this and much more went through her mind as she watched the news that morning. She had awakened earlier than usual and had a modest breakfast after which she spent some time considering her painting. Her heart just wasn't in it, perhaps because she spent most of the night tossing and turning, never getting comfortable, her back aching intermittently probably due to her enormous belly which made sleep these days difficult. She ended her studio session early with a cup of tea and turned on the television. That's when the Emergency Broadcast alarm went off, the relative silence of her living room shattered by its foreign, clamoring insistence.

A LARGE, CRYSTALLINE METEOR IS HEADING TOWARD THE EARTH. THERE DOESN'T APPEAR TO BE ANY WAY TO STOP IT. AT THIS POINT, PLEASE STAY IN YOUR HOMES AND DON'T PANIC.

Rachel went through several emotional responses in a few moments. Disbelief, denial, sorrow, desperation, to name a few. Rachel's parents had died years earlier and she was an only child. Her thoughts went to friends, her cat and her unborn child. Again, her hands went to her belly and at that moment the flutter of movement was like a beacon, telling her what she must do.

The news report said that in twelve to eighteen hours it would be over. The world would end. There was no hope. The planet was history. There would be no survivors, the end of humanity. As the finality of all of this echoed in her mind she grappled with endings—her end, the cat's end, her child's end. Would he or she even be born? If the birth did happen, how long of a life would it be—minutes, hours, a day? And as the child's conception happened in a whirlwind, so too did Rachel's decision. She thought to herself: I have to keep my child. I cannot abandon him or her with the end so near. She paused and let out a deep exhalation and knew she had to call Ken and Rebecca right now. Straining to hoist herself off the couch, her back really bothering her now, Rachel went to the table to get her cell phone. She was just about to pick it up when it rang. The Caller ID said, Ken and Rebecca

"Hello" Rachel said. "I was just going to call you."

"Can you believe what's happening? It's surreal," Ken tersely replied. "It's so horrible there aren't any words…" he continued in a voice heavy with sorrow and regret. "Listen Rachel, I know we said we'd drive up at a moment's notice to be with you during delivery, but we just feel like we have to go to be with Rachel's parents. It's only a few hours from Cincinnati to Louisville, and if we leave now we will have some time with them, before… They must be so scared and we want Elly to see them one more time, to be together when the end comes. We're so sorry. We hate leaving you alone, but we can't be two places at once."

"It's alright. I totally understand," Rachel replied. She tried to keep the tears out of her voice when she said, "I really love you guys but I had decided, given everything, I needed to be with whoever this is I'm carrying. Even if he or she isn't born, I owe it to him or her. It's something I feel I have to do. I didn't want to disappoint you, you've been so great. But you need to be with your family. I'll be Ok, especially if these pains in my back let up."

Rebecca broke in, urgency in her voice, "What kind of pains? How long have you been having them?"

"They kept me up off and on all night. The last couple of hours they have been worse, especially the last hour. I figure all the anxiety is making them worse."

"How often have you been feeling the pains?" Rebecca was even more insistent this time. "I don't know, about every 5-10 minutes or so I guess."

"Rachel, you have to get to the hospital. I think you may be in labor. Can you get there?"

"I think so." Rachel bit her lip to keep from crying out the pain was so bad.

"Well, go now. Text us. Good Luck." Rebecca turned to Ken, "I hope she gets to the hospital ok."

"You too," Rachel replied and immediately hung up the phone. She doubled over in pain. The pain subsided after a little while so she grabbed her keys and went to her car. The hospital was only 5 minutes away.

Rachel arrived at the hospital safely without too much drama. She had one more episode of pain but was able to pull over until it passed. The scene at the hospital was confusing. She had been there before with a friend who sprained their ankle and the ER was busy with activity. When she walked in the ER was practically empty. This made it seem even more sterile and foreign. With activity you could imagine you weren't alone in all of this. The unnatural silence only heightened Rachel's feelings of anxiety, driving home the fact that she really was all alone. The only people in the waiting room were folks with obvious wounds. And there didn't seem to be many staff people. It was understandable she thought, given all that was happening. She made it to the desk just in time for another wrenching pain, this one radiating from her back around to her stomach. As she began to speak a gush of water streamed out uncontrollably and her clothes and the floor were soaked. "I think I'm in labor," Rachel managed to spit out in between gasping for breath.

"I can see that," the nurse said and he immediately went to get a wheelchair while simultaneously calling the maternity floor on his cell phone. The next few minutes went by very quickly as she was rushed upstairs, gowned and hooked up to a fetal monitor, and given an IV. Here, in the hospital's designer birthing rooms the comfy atmosphere meant to calm her seemed surreal. What I am experiencing is anything but comfortable or controlled or peaceful, Rachel thought. The pains kept coming with increasing frequency and not much time elapsed before a resident who seemed to be about her age came in to examine her. The resident's name was Tammy and she was all business, checking the monitors and doing a physical exam. She came to the side of the bed and told Rachel in a pleasant, yet serious voice, "There's not going to be enough time to give you an epidural so I am afraid you will be in quite a bit of pain. This baby is almost ready to be born. I think you will need to start pushing in about half an hour. The nurses will keep watching you and I'll be back."

Rachel instinctively looked up at the clock. It was 2:15. She first heard the news around 11:30, spoke with Ken and Rebecca at about 12:45 and was now about to deliver. Within a span of less than 3 hours she had made a decision that would affect the rest of her life. Good news, it was going to be a short life. Bad news, it was becoming all too real. And yes, the pain was becoming quite intense.

Her delivery went pretty much the way Dr. Tammy predicted. By 3:15, tired and sweaty, Rachel held an 8 lb. 4 oz. baby boy in her arms. He felt deceptively heavy while at the same time making her feel lighter somehow. She couldn't take her eyes off him. This child, the creation of her own self, was here, in her arms—a place she never thought he would be. When she decided to give him up for adoption, she had told herself she wouldn't hold him. Now, inexplicably he was snuggled in her embrace and he was the most beautiful creation she had ever seen. The joy she felt was beyond description yet when it seemed as if she couldn't contain it, the crushing doom of the world's impending end tried to envelop her in its devastating wake.

Here she was, happy beyond belief and part of her wanted to go with the wave of emotion. But like waves, there were ebbs of joy and flows of despair, coming at equal intervals, with similar intensity. Time stood still yet the grains of sand were steadily slipping down in the hourglass image which was in her mind. "I wish I could stay here, holding him forever," her heart ached with the impossibility of that desire.

At some point her child was taken from her. She needed to rest. Her mind fought against it. There's no time. I have to stay awake. But she needed rest. She needed food. Soon her son, she had to think of a name, would want to nurse. She needed to be ready. She woke a few hours later. It was a little after 6.

His first feeding, successfully, albeit awkwardly (who knew your body could do that?) completed, Rachel's thoughts went to when can I get out of here? I don't want to spend my last minutes on earth here in the hospital. She started to cry at the thought of her son never meeting her cat. Names swirled in her head and she was having a hard time concentrating, her emotions totally out of control. She finally settled on Benjamin David.

Rachel was amazed at the care and concern she was receiving from the staff. Everyone was under such a strain, but from her perspective it seemed as if Rachel and Benjamin were the most important people in the world. She finally got up the nerve to ask if she could go home. Her nurse said she would talk to Dr. Tammy and see. A few minutes later Dr. Tammy came in. "Normally Rachel, you would need to stay here at least 24 hours. But things aren't normal, are they? Let's see how well Benjamin nurses and let me check you for any bleeding and maybe we can get you out of here by midnight."

"Thanks," Rachel sighed. "I just want to be with him in my own home, if only for a little while."

True to her word, after Benjamin's feeding at nine, Dr. Tammy came in and checked Rachel out. "Given the circumstances I don't see why you can't take Benjamin home. "Do you have anyone to pick you up? Do you have a car seat?"

"Oh, no," the words streamed out of her mouth. "I drove myself here I am not prepared at all. I wasn't going to keep him. I don't have anything."

"Let me see what I can do" Dr. Tammy reassured her.

Rachel, emotions reeling, once again found herself alternating between sobs of despair and moments of happiness as she gazed at her sleeping son. In what seemed like hours, but in reality, was minutes, Dr. Tammy, several nurses and other staff people came into her room. They carried a car seat, some onesies, blankets, an 'I was born at Yellow Springs Community Hospital' t-shirt and other items. Some were part of the normal welcome package. Others came from the hospital gift shop. One of the nurses stepped up. "I'm off at 10, so I can drive you home after I finish my report. One of the other nurses can follow me in my car. We usually carpool." Once again, Rachel was overwhelmed, tears of gratitude streaming down her face. "I don't know how to thank you," she said.

After they left, it all started to hit her. How did I get here, Rachel thought to herself? This time her thoughts didn't go back to the whirlwind of conception, but rather to the last day or so. Rachel shut her eyes, willing back the tears, and tried to move beyond the shock of it all. She tried to pull herself out of the emotions and logically, rationally consider how she was going to spend these last 24 hours with Benjamin, her son. Benjamin, son—words she hadn't conceived of, a concept which was foreign to her even as she carried him for 9 months. Now, for twenty-four24 hours more or less, she was responsible for this tiny human part of herself. Funny, she mused, the world is ending and all I can think of is how to spend time with my son. I'm not as sad and panicked as I should be, but rather scared and excited for these few hours. Maybe this was meant to be. I'm not sure I could do the whole parenting thing for more than 24 hours. Rachel set about making a mental list of what she wanted to do with Benjamin, never considering how illogical most of it seemed. Introduce him to Vincent the cat, named after Van Gogh of course. Show him her work in progress. Watch the sunrise. With those few plans in place, she looked at her peacefully sleeping child and closed her eyes.

She awoke to the gentle prodding of Sue, the nurse who would take her home. "I'm going to give report. Anne will be here soon to help you two get ready." With a smile and a nod, Sue said, "It shouldn't take too long tonight." So, less than an hour later, Sue helped Rachel get Benjamin and all his newly acquired stuff (who knew someone so little could need so much stuff?) into her apartment and studio. After Sue left a loudly meowing Vincent made his appearance. "Hi Vincent, sorry I was gone for so long," Rachel put Benjamin and his car seat on her small table and immediately went to get Vincent the food. For once though, Vincent wasn't interested. He jumped to the table and began eyeing the foreign object that had invaded his domain warily. "Vincent, this is Benjamin." Rachel held her breath as Vincent cautiously began to smell the sleeping child. Benjamin stirred a bit and Vincent moved back, only to once again approach. "It's alright," Rachel urged. You two are going to be friends. At that moment, the futility of a transient friendship brought tears to her eyes, but Rachel pushed them back, having already decided that these last hours would be about life, not death.

Introductions made, Vincent jumped down and over to his food. Rachel wondered whether or not she should take Benjamin out of his car seat since he was content but reminded herself of her list and the ticking time bomb of the end of the world and unhooked him and cradled him in her arms. Again, these unexpected and unfamiliar feelings were overwhelmingly real. She caught herself holding her breath and let it out, wonder and awe seeming to fill the room.

She carried him to her studio, showing him the work she was currently creating. She poured out her feelings, her desires and hopes for a work that she simultaneously realized would never be completed. She was sad at this unfinished creation until a cute baby noise wafted up from her bundled

Rachel

child. At that moment she knew in her heart that Benjamin was the greatest thing she had created. She felt only love as she smiled down at him. Almost an hour had passed and Benjamin needed fed. That task completed Rachel was overcome with exhaustion. She took Benjamin into her bedroom and thought to herself, "we'll just sleep a little while, there's so little time." She closed her eyes, glanced at the clock. It was a little after 1 am. I wonder how much time we have. I wonder if it will hurt. I wonder …. Her unfinished musings drifted away as she slept.

Robert

Indianapolis, Indiana

Robert picked up the remote and turned off the TV. The news seemed at once incomprehensible and terrifying. Dark matter racing toward the earth, a killer asteroid, the extinction of all life on the planet. He had been watching for nearly three hours. Now he got up from the couch and started pacing back and forth. For years he had listened with skepticism as reporters hyped various crises, but this time the sky really was falling. If this was his last day on earth, he'd better do something, but what? Robert looked at his watch – 3:00 pm. Should he go in to his office or the lab? No, no point. All those unfinished projects, what did they matter now?

Robert walked into the kitchen, and opened the frig. Not much there, but enough to last one more day. Since his divorce, Robert had lived alone. His ex-wife had moved back to Minnesota. His son Ben, his only child, was in grad school, about an hour away down in Bloomington.

Robert looked out the window and saw his neighbors loading some suitcases into their car. He stepped out on the front porch and called over to them, "Tom, Jody, where are you going?"

"The fallout shelter. Looks like things will get pretty bad," Tom said.

"Are you OK?" asked Jody.

No, thought Robert. None of us are OK; we are all about to die. He shrugged.

Jody looked at Tom. "We better get going, before the shelter fills up." She turned back to Robert, "Maybe you should head over there too."

"OK, thanks," said Robert. "Good luck."

Robert

He went back inside. Should he be going to a shelter, or driving to the airport to try to get on a flight to New Zealand? No, the entire earth was about to be wiped out. The newscasters had made that quite clear. Emergency shelters, underground bunkers, other continents—no place was safe. Robert checked his phone for the twentieth time, but there was still no reception. All cell service was down or jammed with calls or something.

Why was this happening? Was it some sort of divine retribution for the sins of humankind? On TV they had shown scenes of people gathering in churches to pray. Robert had never been religious. He had always been dismissive of Christian evangelists preaching about the judgment day—turns out they were right after all. But no, he thought, this was not the hand of God. It was a random astrophysical event, an apocalyptic reminder that in the scheme of the universe, humans were nothing more than microbes crawling on a speck of dust. His existence, like that of all people, meant nothing, and now it was coming to an end.

Robert looked at his watch again—almost 3:30. He had to do something, but what? He opened the cupboard, grabbed a large bag of pretzels, put on his jacket, and headed out to his car. One more day to live; he wasn't going to spend it sitting at home. He started the car and glanced at the gas gauge—half a tank—more than enough to get across town. Maybe he should go over to Will's house. Will was a good friend and a sensible guy. Perhaps he would have some advice. But what could he possibly say? With the world coming to an end, how could anyone have any advice? Robert backed out of the driveway and started driving down the street. But he was not headed toward Will's house. No, he was driving south, toward Bloomington. Without really thinking about it, he knew where he had to go. He had to see his son Ben, one last time.

November 7th

Robert hadn't spoken to Ben in almost a year. After the divorce, Ben seemed to want nothing to do with him. He did not return Robert's phone calls. He never visited. When Robert called Ben on his birthday last January, he'd answered the phone, but their conversation was stilted. Ben talked a little about his classes, but not much more. Finally, Robert had said, "Well, maybe I could come down sometime this spring, and we could go out to lunch or something."

"OK Dad," Ben had mumbled.

Robert never followed up. He could tell his son didn't want to see him. Why was Ben mad at him anyway? It wasn't as if the divorce was his idea. His wife had left him. If Ben felt angry about it, he should take it up with his mother, though apparently he was hardly on speaking terms with her either. So, Ben was upset with both of them. And maybe they were both to blame. Robert thought of the phrase his wife kept repeating when she left him. "You only care about your work."

Robert was almost out of the city when he saw flashing lights up ahead. It looked like multiple police cars and a roadblock. Traffic moved ahead slowly, and Robert now saw that highway patrol officers were waving outbound cars through. Inbound cars, however, were being forced to turn back. When he reached the roadblock, an officer signaled for him to stop to allow several inbound cars to turn around. Robert put down his window. "Officer?" he began.

"Where you headed?" the highway patrolman asked.

"Bloomington, to see my son."

"OK, but be aware, you won't be allowed back into Indianapolis. There's been looting downtown. No traffic allowed into the city."

"Alright," said Robert. He put his window back up and waited in the glare of flashing red lights. When the officer motioned for him to go, he resumed driving toward Bloomington.

Robert

It was a mild day for early November, and the farmhouses and empty fields along the road looked surprisingly normal. The late afternoon sun shone through the clouds. No sign of the impending apocalypse. Then, headed the other direction, a convoy of five military trucks rumbled past—it looked like the National Guard. Maybe just as well he had left Indianapolis, thought Robert. What if the whole city were to go up in flames? His house, his lab at Lilly, his research—it could all be destroyed. Wait, why was he worrying about looting and fires? Everything would be wiped out tomorrow anyway.

All his research, his life's work, would be obliterated. He and his team had spent years on a new medication for diabetes, but it still had not been approved for use. Why hadn't he sought FDA approval sooner? He had been so cautious, wanting to triple-check everything, despite the fact that the drug would have been tested in clinical trials. All that work had been a waste of time. No one would ever take this medicine, no one would benefit from it. But even as he rued his failure to help people, he knew that diabetics' health had not been his main concern. He had wanted to become famous. He had sought the acclaim of doctors and fellow scientists who would have admired his great breakthrough. It had been his own vanity, and with the world about to end, all that counted for nothing.

Robert reached the outskirts of Bloomington. A lot of cars were driving out of town—probably students trying to get home. He had half expected to find a big party going on. After all, IU was a party school, and what better excuse to let loose than the apocalypse? But there were no signs of merriment. He drove past two students on the sidewalk, and they were walking quickly with their heads down.

For the first time, it occurred to Robert that Ben might not be home. In fact, he might not even live in the same house he had been in last year. He and his housemates might have found another rental. Robert looked at his phone again—still no service. Well, nothing to do but go to Ben's old house and hope to find him there.

Robert pulled up in front of the house and turned off the car. It was a two-story, white wooden house. Some of the paint on the side was peeling. As he walked up to the front door, Robert heard a television on inside. He knocked on the door. After a pause, the door opened, and there stood Ben. He looked at Robert for a moment and finally said, "Hi… Dad." He opened the screen door to let Robert in, but then turned and walked into the living room with no further greeting.

Robert bit his lip and followed his son. Perched on the couch in front of the TV was a young woman with short brown hair. She was looking at him and then looked at Ben.

"Dad, this is my girlfriend, Heather."

Heather said hello, but then turned back to Ben and asked, "Do you think he could take us?"

"I don't know," replied Ben. He looked at the floor.

"Is something…?" Robert stopped. Of course something was wrong, the world was coming to an end.

Ben cleared his throat. "Heather wants to see her sister up in Indy. But on TV they just announced a curfew. They also said the city is under martial law, and no one will be allowed in. Did you come from there?"

"Yes. There was a roadblock on highway 37, but we can probably get around that," said Robert. He turned to Heather. "Where does your sister live?"
"Raymond Street."

Robert nodded. Not far from his lab, he thought. "I can take you there."

"Are you sure, Dad?" asked Ben.

"I may not be Mad Max, but I know my way around the southside of Indianapolis."

Robert

Heather jumped up from the couch. "Let me grab my bag." She and Ben hurried out of the room. Robert overheard her ask, "Who's Mad Max?"

Robert glanced at the TV. All afternoon reporters had been waiting for some pronouncement from the White House—some words of hope or solace. Finally, the President had posted on Twitter, and his tweet was now displayed on the television screen. "Obama and Crooked Hillary did absolutely nothing to prepare the country for this calamity. What a couple of LOSERS!"

When they got out to the car, Ben and Heather hesitated before getting in. "It's unlocked," said Robert. Then he noticed they were looking at each other and holding hands. "You can both ride in back if you want." As he started the car, Robert felt a bit like a chauffeur, driving alone in the front seat with two passengers in back. He glanced at them in the rearview mirror. Ben had not shaven for several days; maybe he was growing a beard.

"Thank you so much for taking us," said Heather. "I haven't been able to call my sister, but I know she must be freaking out. She's a single mom, and her daughter is just four years old."

Robert told her he was glad to help. He wanted to add some words of reassurance, but he stopped himself. Given the circumstances, there was no way he could say that things would be okay. He didn't even know if they could make it past the roadblocks to her sister's house.

When they had driven halfway to Indianapolis, Robert checked the gas gauge—only an eighth of a tank left. He took the Martinsville exit and pulled into a BP gas station. But all the pumps were dark and the doors to the building were locked. They drove a couple blocks to the Marathon station up the street, but the same thing there. With no other gas stations in sight, they got back on the highway. Robert thought they might have enough to make it anyway.

November 7th

As they approached the south suburbs of the city, Robert turned off the highway and began to drive east on County Line Road. All the highways into the city would be blocked, he figured, so they needed to find another route. They turned north on McFarland Road. So far, no roadblocks or police. The sun was starting to set. It occurred to Robert that this would be the last sunset they would ever see. Ben and Heather were quiet in the back seat. He wondered if they were thinking the same thing.

Flashing lights up ahead. Damn, thought Robert, another roadblock. He turned right and headed farther east. There had to be some open route into the city. He turned north once again on Gray Road. Surely a two-lane road like this one would be open. But no, after half a mile there were more flashing lights up ahead. Worse yet, Robert saw a police car with its flashers coming up behind him. He pulled over, hoping the police car would continue on past, but instead it stopped right in front of him. It was now dusk, and as the officer stepped out of his car, he turned on a flashlight and pulled out his gun. He approached the car, shining the light in Robert's face.

Robert lowered his car window. "Excuse me officer, we need…"

"No one allowed into the city," the officer barked. "Furthermore, you are in violation of the curfew. You will have to follow me to the National Guard base at Camp Atterbury."

"But officer…"

"No exceptions. All curfew violators are to be taken there. It is for your own safety. Now turn your car around and follow me."

Robert put up his car window, did a U-turn, and waited for the police car to do the same. He heard Heather crying in the back seat. He looked over his shoulder. Ben put his arm around her and said softly, "I'm sorry we won't make it to your sister's."

46

"The hell we won't!" said Robert.

"But Dad…"

"Look Ben, we've got nothing to lose. If they shoot us tonight, it doesn't really matter, because we're going to die tomorrow anyway. Now I'm just going to follow this cop until we can make a break for it."

The police car started driving south, and Robert followed behind. He noticed that the policeman had three people in the back of his cruiser—probably other offenders he had apprehended. They drove about two miles, into the darkness of the Indiana countryside. As they approached a crossroads, Robert saw a car up ahead, apparently another curfew violator. The police car switched on its flashers and pulled the other car over. Robert slowed down and waited. This is our chance, he thought. His heart started to race. The officer got out of his car, flashlight in one hand and gun in the other. He walked over to the other car. Robert could hear him saying, "You are in violation of the curfew…"

Robert inched his car forward, turning onto the cross road as if to pull out of the way. But instead of coming to a stop, he floored the gas pedal. As the car accelerated, he heard the police officer shout. Then a gunshot rang out behind them. Robert switched off the car lights. They were now barreling down a back-country road in the dark. He strained to see as the car careened ahead.

"You guys okay?" Robert called to the back seat.

"Yes, Dad, but be careful!"

"Don't worry," said Robert, "country roads in Indiana always run straight."

A siren started up far behind them. Robert checked the rearview mirror; he could see police flashers in the distance. He pressed harder on the gas and gripped the wheel. He wanted to look back again but didn't dare. Hurdling into the darkness, he just tried to stay on the road. He heard the siren, still far off but getting closer.

Ben's voice sounded tight. "Dad, I don't think you can outrun him."

Robert saw the silhouette of a farmhouse on the right. It must have a driveway. He braked hard and swerved into a gravel entrance way. He coasted back between the house and barn and shut off the engine. "Duck down," he said. They all crouched down below the seats. Robert tried to quiet his breathing as the siren got closer. The siren's wail became louder and louder. It seemed like the police car was bearing right down on them. But then it zoomed past, the siren suddenly dropping in pitch. For some reason, Robert remembered the time he tried to explain the Doppler effect to Ben when he was five years old.

"We better lie low here for a bit," said Robert, as the siren died off in the distance.

"Will he find us if he turns around?" asked Heather.

"I doubt it," said Robert. "There are a lot of farmhouses along this road, and he won't want to stop and search each one. He'll probably go back to corral that other 'curfew violator.' "

Several minutes later they heard a car pass going the other direction. They saw the light of police flashers, but this time with no siren. Robert waited a couple minutes and then sat up. "It looks like the coast is clear," he said as he started the car. But the engine sputtered and then died. He turned the key again and cranked the engine but the ignition wouldn't catch. He switched on the overhead light and looked at the gas gauge—empty. "Hell. We're out of gas."

"How far would it be to walk from here?" asked Ben.

"At least ten miles," said Robert. "We'll do that if we have to, but first let me go ask at this farmhouse."
As he climbed out of the car, Robert saw streaks of light flash high up in the sky—it looked like a meteor shower.

The asteroid wasn't due to hit for several hours yet. These "shooting stars" must be the fragments of the moon that newscasters had warned would reach earth first.

Robert

Robert hurried toward the house. He was halfway there when a woman came out the front door. He couldn't see her face in the darkness, but he could see she was brandishing a shotgun. "Get the hell off my property!"
Robert stopped and held up his hands, but he did not back away. "Sorry to bother you…"

"I said, get the hell off my property!"

"Ma'am?" Robert heard Heather's voice behind him. "Ma'am, is there any way you can help us? We're trying to get to my sister's, and we ran out of gas. She is all alone with her little girl. I just have to see her."

The woman lowered her gun. "Was that you the police was chasing just now?"

"Yes," said Heather. "They said we're violating the curfew, but we can't wait until tomorrow. It will be too late by then."

"I hear you," the woman sighed. "I'm prayin' my own daughter makes it home. Drove up to see a friend in Zionsville this morning, and she ain't come home yet. Probably on account of this damn curfew."

"I'm so sorry," said Heather. "I'm sure your daughter would come home if she could. They set up roadblocks all around the city, and they're not letting anyone through."

"I ain't got much gasoline. The tractor runs on diesel. But I got a couple gallons for the mower—you're welcome to that. Come on."

All three of them followed her into the barn, and she switched on a light. Robert noticed that she was younger than he had thought, no more than 40.

"There it is." She pointed to a gas can along the wall.

"I'll get it," said Ben. "We're really grateful to you."

"Yes," said Heather. "Thank you so much." She went up to her and hugged her. The woman embraced her with one arm, still holding the shotgun in the other.

Robert kept his distance but thanked her as well. He added, "I really hope you get to see your daughter again."

With some difficulty, Ben managed to get most of the gas into the gas tank. When he got back in the car, he smelled like gasoline. Heather gave the woman another hug and then hopped in the car. Robert started the engine and backed out onto the road. He started driving farther east.

"How are we going to get there, Dad?" asked Ben.

"We'll try Shelbyville Road. It slants in from the southeast. Probably a roadblock there too, but we'll find a way around it. Heather, where on Raymond Street does your sister live?"

"Right across from Garfield Park."

"Good," said Robert, "If we make it into the city, we won't be far from there."

Robert drove about a mile and then turned left on Shelbyville Road. In contrast to the deserted back road, there were quite a few other cars here. Apparently, they were not the only renegades prowling about. As they approached the city limits, Robert saw a roadblock half a mile up the road. He veered onto a side street headed directly north. As they drove through a suburban neighborhood, he thought they might be home free, but then he saw police flashers up ahead again. He felt sick to his stomach.

As he slowed the car, however, Robert noticed something different here. There was only one police car, and there were six or seven "curfew violators" stopped in front of the roadblock. A number of people had stepped out of their cars and were yelling at the police officer to let them through. Fifteen yards away, the lone police-man glared at them from his car parked sideways in the middle of the street.

Robert pulled up behind an oversized pickup truck and shut off the engine. They couldn't afford to run out of gas again.

Robert

"Wait here," he said as he stepped out of the car. He walked around to the front of the pickup truck where a cluster of people had gathered.

An older man in a baseball cap half turned to look at Robert. He exhaled cigarette smoke and grunted, "He ain't lettin' no one through."

"Doesn't that cop have anything better to do his last night on earth," said Robert, his voice rising. "Shouldn't he be home with his family?"

"Yeah," said a tall woman in the group. "All we're trying to do is get home. We're not criminals."

"Look," said Robert, "I say we make a run for it. There's only one cop, and he can't stop us all. Whose truck is this?"

"Mine," said a burly, bearded man stepping forward.

"Can you jump that curb and get around him on the right?"

"Sure," he said.

"Good," said Robert, "I'll cut through this parking lot and try to get around him on the left. Everyone else follow either right or left. If the cop moves his car to chase one of us, just drive straight up the middle of the street."

"What if he radios for backup?" asked the older man.

"We'll be long gone by the time any backup arrives," said Robert. "Just don't hesitate. When we go, everybody goes. OK?"

"Let's roll!" shouted the woman.

Robert hurried to his car and started the engine. He glanced back at Ben and Heather. "We're all going to make a run for it. The cop can't stop more than one car. Just stay low in case he shoots."

The pickup truck in front of them revved its engine. Then with a screech of it tires, it bolted forward and to the right. Robert stepped on the gas and angled to the left. He heard the police car switch on its siren. Robert swung into the parking lot and accelerated, headed for the exit at the far end of the lot. They were almost there when he saw a wooden police barricade across the exit. No stopping now, he thought. He pressed harder on the gas. With a thump their car hit the barricade and knocked it aside. Robert turned up the street and floored it. "Is he chasing us?" he yelled.

"No," shouted Ben, "the cop started to go but then stopped. I think we got away."

After five blocks, Robert turned onto a cross street and slowed down slightly. He kept the car lights off and began to weave through town, sticking to side streets. After twenty minutes he said, "OK, we're almost there. Garfield Park is ahead on the left."

"Great!" said Heather. She sounded excited. He heard her whisper to Ben, "I thought you said your dad was kinda lame."

Robert drove to Raymond Street at the north end of the park. "That's Cheryl's house right across the street," said Heather.

Robert parked, and Heather jumped out and ran up the steps. Robert and Ben hurried after her. By the time they were on the front porch, Heather was already inside. She hugged Cheryl and they both started to cry. Ben went over and hugged Cheryl too. Robert was about to say hello when a little girl in pajamas appeared on the stairs.

"Nora," said Heather, as she went up and hugged her.

"Why are you crying?" asked Nora.
Heather wiped her tears. "I'm just happy to see you," she said, stroking Nora's hair.

"Who are they?" asked Nora, pointing to Robert and Ben.

"You remember Ben, my boyfriend. And that's his dad, Robert. He drove us here to see you."

Robert

"Are they going on the rocket too?"

"Nora, honey," said Cheryl going over, "I need to talk to Auntie Heather. Come on, let's get you back to bed." She took her by the hand and they disappeared upstairs.

Ben looked at Heather. "Rocket?"

Heather shook her head and shrugged.

After a minute, Cheryl came back downstairs. She started speaking quickly. "They were just saying on TV that Elon Musk is getting one of his rockets ready. If it can launch in time, then the people on board can survive, at least for a while. They were saying there would be room for a few passengers. Maybe they'll have a lottery or something. I need to try and get Nora on board."

"The next SpaceX rocket was due to launch from Vandenberg Air Force Base," said Robert. "It must be that one."

"Is there any way we can get there?" asked Cheryl, looking back and forth between Heather and Ben.

"Vandenberg is in California," said Ben. "It's a long way away…I mean, it would take like three days to drive there."

"Maybe we can fly," began Cheryl. She started to cry again. "I need to do something…"

Heather put her arms around Cheryl. She looked over her shoulder and said to Ben, "I need to talk to her alone for a minute."

Ben and Robert turned and went back out onto the front porch. They sat down on some porch chairs. The night was cool, but it didn't bother them. They still had their jackets on. They sat in silence for a few minutes. Robert suddenly realized he was really hungry. He went down to the car to retrieve the bag of pretzels and came back. He opened the bag, grabbed a handful, and passed it to Ben.

"Thanks," said Ben, "I guess this is our last supper."

"Yeah," chuckled Robert.

November 7th

The city seemed calm. No looting or rioting, at least not in this neighborhood. Apart from an occasional passing car, there was no one even out on the street. The last night on earth, thought Robert. He was glad that he was not alone. Robert looked out at the park across the street. It was dark and quiet. Many trees had already lost their leaves. He could almost see to the swimming pool in the middle of the park. "Remember the time I took you swimming at the Garfield Park pool?" asked Robert.

Ben nodded. "Yeah, that was fun. I think my friend Justin came along too."

"I wish I had done that more, Ben." He turned toward his son. "I wish I had taken you swimming every day."

"Thanks Dad," said Ben with a smile, "but I'm pretty sure the pool is only open in the summer."

"OK then, every day in the summer." They both laughed. After a moment, Robert continued more seriously.

"Those summer days are gone. And now they will never come back."

They heard a siren in the distance. Gradually it faded away, and the night became silent once again.

Heather opened the door and came out on the porch.

"Cheryl went upstairs to lie down with Nora." She paused, then said, "She knows we can't make it to California. At least she and Nora can have these last few hours together."

Robert and Ben stood up and followed Heather back inside. "Should we check the news again," asked Robert.

"No," said Ben. "I don't want to spend any more time watching TV."

Heather took Ben's hand. "I think I need to lie down. Cheryl said we could have her bedroom."
Ben hesitated. He looked at Robert.

"You two go ahead," said Robert. "I'll stay down here."

Robert

Heather came over and hugged Robert. "Thank you so much for driving us here. I am so, so grateful to you." Ben came over too. "Yeah, Dad, you were great."

"Well, Ben, I'm just glad I got to spend one more day with you."

Ben hugged Robert. "I guess we better say goodbye, Dad. I love you."

Robert swallowed. "I love you too, son."

Ben stepped back and smiled, then held up his hand to wave as he turned away. He put his arm around Heather as they went upstairs. Robert pulled out his handkerchief and wiped his eyes. He let out a long sigh and sat down on the couch. What now? The last few hours of his life—it seemed a shame to waste them. But he felt exhausted. He lay down on the couch and fell fast asleep.

Videl Corbin

near Leitchfield, Kentucky

"Hey Corbin, are you still digging that big stupid hole in the ground?" The man behind the counter asked. The coffee steamed as he snapped the lid on and shoved the cup toward the man in front of him.

"It's not stupid," Corbin said with indignation. "It's the chamber that will save the believers. It's finished. It's where you need to bring your smart mouth when the sign is given. Your salvation will depend on it." Corbin snatched the steaming cup from the counter and neglected to slide a tip into the jar by the register. The Angel didn't say anything about punching a barista, but he was sure it wouldn't be happy. He wasn't an expert on Angels. In fact, until this very year he had not thought much about them.

The coffee took the chill out of his hands and he was grateful for it. The four blocks he walked to the town square was covered with a fresh dusting of snow. The breeze blowing through the valley made the park unseasonably cold. Dirty paw prints tracked their way into the bushes. Corbin smiled and said, "Looks like the Barton's dog is loose again." He pursed his lips and made a sharp whistle. It was quickly followed by rustling and a deep woof from the brush.

He arrived at the empty fountain at the center of the park and turned his back on it. "May I have your attention," he addressed the empty walkway. "Y'all know me. Six months ago, an angel rose from the ground and gave me a message from God."

The Barton's dog trotted past the vacant town square. "Hey buddy," he said to the dog. The dog wagged and smiled in his direction. "You get on home now," he whispered to the dog. The dog decided instead to sit next

56

to Corbin. Corbin smiled and gave the dog a scratch on the back of the neck, "At least I have one buddy."

Corbin turned back to the empty courtyard and with his best puffed-up politician voice called out. "Prepare a chamber to receive the faithful. Fill it with the bounty of the earth to keep them. Save the souls of the believers." Corbin took a breath and the cold air made him cough. "I have prepared the chamber and I am here to bring you to safety. Believe in the word of God and you shall be saved." Nailed it, he thought to himself.

Corbin picked up his coffee and whistled to the dog. It stood up and trotted behind him. Corbin removed his belt and looped it through the dog's collar and walked from the park. "I bet you don't listen to them any better than you listen to me."

~

"Hey Corbin, I see you found Banjo," The overly thin woman said from the plastic sheet enclosed porch. She motioned for him to come in. The radio was playing Kentucky bluegrass that sounded like it was poured straight from the Appalachian hills. "Put him in the house and then come sit down next to me. I have tea." She patted the empty chair and smiled sweetly at him.

He was surprised to find that the porch was warm. He looked around and saw a glowing space heater on the porch. "You shouldn't be outside in this weather, and that thing can't be safe." He pointed at the heater and looked at her with exasperation.

She handed him a tall glass of tea and said, "Now, don't you worry none about me. Tell me about you. How's your chamber? Is it ready?"

"I finished last night. The last of the food and water are stored." He leaned back in the chair and smiled with contentment. "I have the animals penned outside and ready to go in when the sign comes."

"You save me a good spot," she said and took a sip from her glass. The radio made a siren sound and she reached over to turn it down. "What kind of a sign do you think you'll get?"

Corbin smiled, and knew that if the only person he saved was Mrs. Barton, then he was going to be grateful. "Mae, you'll have the best spot in the chamber," he answered. "The angel said I would know the sign. It'll have to be a big sign. I'm not very observant." Corbin winked and finished his tea.

The radio siren stopped and a reporter spoke. "It's being reported that an asteroid type object is headed directly toward the earth. Government sources confirm that the asteroid cannot be stopped. It will cause great destruction on a cataclysmic scale." There was a sound of paper being shuffled.

Mae looked up at Corbin, and then back to the radio as the announcer continued. "Is this real?" The reporter sounded incredulous.

"You need to get to the farm," he told his host and set his tea on the table. The ice clanked and settled in the glass. "This has to be the sign. The time has come."

The dead air ended and the reporter came back, "I'm being told that there is no escape. This is the end of the world?" There was another long pause and the reporter continued. "I am being told that this is 100% legitimate." There was the sound of a microphone being knocked over, "I quit, and I am going home with my family," the reporter said and the radio went quiet.

"Corbin?" Mae started but he was gone. The door slammed shut behind him.

Corbin ran for his truck. God had given him the forewarning to save the town and he was twelve miles away; Twelve miles, and three blocks by foot, away from salvation. He heard a woman scream. "This is my last day on Earth and I am not spending it with you." There was a shot. The sound ricocheted through the tree lined street and caused him to flinch like he was avoiding a ninja attack. He recovered and ran faster. "Don't be afraid. Salvation is yours if you believe!" he yelled and felt himself being hit from behind, His body slammed to the ground.

"What the hell is wrong with you?" The voice sounded familiar. "It's one thing to be the town character but I don't want to hear it. Nobody wants to hear your bull." Corbin tried to roll. "You have to believe me. Follow me to the chamber and you will be saved?" He looked into the face of the barista. The once familiar face of a jerk was twisted in anger and fear.

The barista planted his knee into Corbin's ribs. The sound of bones cracking brought a satisfied smile to his face. The menace, in coffee shop garb, finalized his point with one last punch and jumped up.

Corbin watched him run between houses and out of sight. With a slow rocking motion he rolled to his feet. Every movement was filled with pain. "Move," he ordered himself. "You'll have time to rest when the morning comes." He limped his way along the path to his truck and slid into the seat. A woman ran across the street, gun in hand. She made eye contact and dismissed him in one look. With the door closed he said a prayer. "God, help me to save them." He started the truck and reached for the shift.

There was a banging on the hood of his truck. The Barton's looked at him through the window. "Take us with you," Mae said.

"Get in," Corbin replied with a nod of his head.

"Thanks Corbin," her husband said as he threw a bag in the back. He ran around the truck and slid next to his wife. Banjo licked his face and smiled. "We've had our bag packed for two months.

"Corbin, the radio is saying that there is no escape from this asteroid thing," said the woman.

"God's angel said to have faith. All that enter the chamber shall be saved." Corbin was calm. His faith was unwavering.

From down the street they heard more gun shots.

"We believe you Corbin," The man said with fear in his eyes. "You better get moving. This isn't the safe chamber."

Corbin nodded in agreement and praised God that he was able to lead two of the faithful to safety. He shifted gears and pulled away from the curb.

"Will many people be there?" the old woman asked. "All that believe will be there," he stated. "All that believe and listened to the word of God will survive."

"Everyone else will die?" The man asked. "Can't we try to convince more people to come?"

"The word has been given. We must now enter the chamber," Corbin replied, the houses, full of people, ticked by as he picked up speed.

"I have a phone. I can call. Please Corbin, I know that you have been telling everyone about this for months, but one more try." The man started to shake with emotion. "Please."

"Call everyone you can and convince them to join us in the chamber," Corbin replied. He slammed on the brakes to avoid hitting a car. The couple slid into the dash. "Put on your seat belt. Are you trying to get yourselves killed?"

The dog jumped back onto the seat. The Barton's slid back and put on their seat belts. The old man pulled out his phone and started to call. Corbin looked both ways and started driving.

"Can I turn on the radio?" Mae asked. The mixture of sadness and fear added an edgy undertone to her normally down-to-earth, soulful voice.

"Kelsey. It's Dad." The old man smiled. "I heard honey. Your Mom and I are going to Brother Corbin's farm.

We want you to join us." There was a long pause, "Please honey, we want us to all be together in the chamber. We will survive if we have faith."

Corbin and the Mae listened as the voice on the other side of the phone got louder and louder. "But honey, we love you. All we ever did was the best we could." The yelling stopped and the old man put the phone away.

"What did she say? Will she and the kids be there?" The old woman's eyes pleaded for the answer her heart desired. The old man patted her hand and turned to look out the window.

Corbin saw a house on fire, and people in the street blocking his way. He decided to turn down a side street. "Look out!" he yelled as two children ran from a house and into the street in front of him. They screamed in fear and ran toward his truck. "Help! Stop, please stop."

Corbin stopped and the children jumped into the bed of the truck. "Go! Go! Go!" the children yelled, pounding on the window behind Corbin's head for emphasis.

Corbin pushed down on the accelerator as a man ran from the children's house covered with blood. The knife in his hand seems unnaturally large. The man chased the truck yelling "I love you!" over and over as blood dripped from the end of the knife. The man then stopped and dropped to his knees and began to weep. Corbin wanted to stop and give the man comfort, but he had to think about the safety of the children.

Mae slid the rear window to the side. "Are you ok?" The older child nodded that he was ok. The younger child began to wail. "Daddy hurt Mommy real bad." The older child started to shake.

"You poor things," the she said. "We'll take care of you. Now sit down and we'll be at the farm soon." Banjo pushed his head through the window and tried to get the children to pet him.

"This is madness. What is happening to everyone?" The old man turned away from the children and looked at his phone.

"They're lost." Corbin was sad. God had given him a job and he had failed. "They have lost all hope."

"I told my daughter she would survive if she came to your farm." The old man teared up. "She isn't coming."

"She doesn't believe," he said. "Only those that believe will find salvation."

"That's not good enough!" The man yelled at everyone. "We have to go and get her. We have to save her."

"What do you want me to do?" Corbin raised his voice. "Should I kidnap her? Should I drug them all and drag them underground?"

The old man began to sob as his wife hugged him close. "I should go to them. I should die with them," he sobbed.

"Who will take care of them kids back there? They're going to need us," his wife patted his back as he calmed himself. "God has saved us and brought us these children. We can't abandon them now."

"You should try to call again," Corbin said. We are almost there and there isn't much more time.
The old man pulled the phone out and looked at it. "She hates me. She said she hates me and never wants to talk to me again."

"She didn't mean it," his wife said. "Try again."
The old man dialed and got a recorded message. "It says the system isn't available. The circuits are all busy. What if the last thing I hear from her is that she hates me?"

"We can't dwell on that. You can try again later. Right now, I'm going to need your help moving the animals into the chamber," Corbin said as he turned at a sign that said "Salvation This Way." The unkempt dirt and gravel driveway was an obstacle course of potholes.

"How big is this chamber?" The old man asked as he bounced in his seat. He thought of the children in the back and hoped for the best. "It better be plenty big."

"It's big enough," Corbin responded. The road tracked the rim of deep, bowl like depression. He remembered the day that the depression had filled with light. The vision of the angel was as vivid today as it had been six months ago. He came to a slow stop near a shed nestled against a hillside. A sign on the side states "Salvation Here." I'm going to drop off Mrs. Barton and the kids. They can go on down while we finish up here."

"Where are we going Corbin?" she asked. Her confused eyes darted from Corbin to her husband.
"You need to go into the shed and down the shaft to the chamber. There's a light switch at the top of the stairs." Corbin stepped out of the truck and helped the kids jump down. He pulled out the Barton's bag and laid it on the ground. "Just think of it as home."

"I don't want to leave you," she said to her husband.

"I'll be with you soon. I promise," he answered his wife. "Go, take care of the kids."

The old woman picked up the bag and motioned for the children to follow her. Corbin and the old man turned the truck and headed back down the road toward the barn. The animals had become accustomed to expecting food when they heard his truck and started walking toward the barn. Cows, sheep, and goats jostled for their place in line. Corbin filled the feeding trays and opened the barn door. "Close the doors when the last one is in. Grab that stick. You might need it."

The old man grabbed the stick and walked toward the doors, careful to avoid being hurt. "I worked on a horse farm when I was younger." The old man liked the memory and smiled. The last animal walked past him and headed toward the feed. He closed the door behind them and walked around the outside of the building. Corbin opened a side door and he walked in.

"When they are finished, they will want back out. We need to move them through this door." Corbin pointed to the door he just opened. "They will move through the shoot to the far side of the field where they can enter the chamber and be safe."

"What if they don't want to go in?" The old man asked.

"It has to happen," Corbin replied.

The old man clutched the stick tighter and nodded. The animals moved from the barn and out the door as the feed troughs became empty.

Corbin held out the keys to the old man. "I need you to take the truck along that dirt road. Follow the fence to where it ends at the rock. Open the metal doors and wait for the animals to arrive. I'll walk behind them and shepherd any stragglers." In the distance there was a booming sound that shook the ground around them. They looked toward the sound and a plume of fire brightened the horizon. "That looks like the gas station. We don't have much time. We have to hurry."

The old man raced down Hell's roller coaster disguised as a road. He wanted to get there before the animals, with enough time to try and call his daughter. The rock wall seemed to come out of nowhere. He slammed on the brakes and closed his eyes expecting to wreck at any second. The truck skidded to a stop and he realized that he was still alive. "That was close."

He climbed the fence and opened the metal door as instructed. He found a light switched and flicked it on. The room was filled with tools. Many implements were recognizable. Most were not. "Wow, someone is missing a hardware store." He looked deeper and saw a tunnel leading downward into the darkness. He walked past the equipment and could see flickering light in the distance. The space was cavernous. He stepped from the tool room and walked back outside. He saw the animals in the distance heading his way. With phone in hand he tried his daughter's number. The phone rang without answer. The truck was there. He could go to her. Try to convince her to come back with him.

A goat bounded past him and into the cave. The animals seemed to be moving faster. It was as if they knew what they needed to do. "Corbin trained you good," he said to the next goat as it bounded past and ran down the cave following the other. Each animal came to the threshold and passed through.

Corbin followed the last animal in and down the passage to a chamber that looked like a stable. With few exceptions the animals had selected their own pen and Corbin latched the doors. "That was easier than I thought." He was glad for the luck. "There's a pig pen and chicken coop over there," Corbin pointed. "The pigs go first and then the coop. The coop's on wheels. We can move it with the truck."

"You worked all this out by yourself?" the old man asked in amazement.

"An Angel told me to prepare," Corbin answered as he opened to pen doors and moved the swine toward safety.

"You trained the animals," the old man shook his head.

"I didn't train them," Corbin replied as he walked behind and closed the pen doors.

" With the animals safely in place they moved outside and took apart the metal fencing and stored it inside the cave.

"Let's go get that equipment out of the barn and we should be done."

"I thought about taking your truck and getting my daughter," he said to Corbin.

"That would have been monumentally stupid, and put us all in danger. I'm glad you didn't." He held out his hand for the keys and the old man gave them to him. "Try calling again on the drive to the barn."

The old man got into the cab and dialed his daughter's number. Once again, nobody answered his call. "Let's get that equipment and save what we can. She knows where we are. She'll come. I know she will." The old man was firm, "She doesn't hate me. She loves me."

The ride back to the cavern was quiet. With everything stored, Corbin led the old man through the cavern filled with livestock. They passed an armory, and water storage, and small appliances. There was a kitchen that looked like it had been recently used and the old man smiled. "That smells good," the old man told Corbin. "That smells like my wife's cookin'."

They followed the smell to a dining area. There were people that he recognized and some he didn't. "Corbin, the old woman called. They want to meet you."

"Maybe later after we secure the doors," Corbin responded and walked past the people, down a side tunnel, and past dripping stalactites glittering in the artificial light. With emotions close to overwhelming him he stopped and dropped to his knees. The stalagmite in front of him looked like an altar of silver and diamonds. He thanked God for the mercy that was shown to save him and the people from divine destruction. He thanked the blessed angel for its guidance.

With a final "Amen" he rose from the ground, tears streaming down his face. His knees were wet as he turned to follow the passage back. From down the hall he heard yelling. He wiped the tears from his face and walked faster to find out what was happening. The angry voices led him to a terrible scene.

"Just let the child go," Mae said. The expression on her face belied the exaggerated calmness in her voice.

"I want my children. They're my children." The

man looked familiar and then Corbin remembered. It was the man with the knife that had chased the truck. "I saw you take them in a truck. Where are my children?" He was still covered with blood and now holding a strange child.

"What seems to be the problem?" Corbin asked as he walked into the great chamber. He quickly scanned the crowd of people and didn't see the man's children.

"You have my children. I want them. We have to go and be with their mother." The man stifled a sob.

"You are welcome to join us here and, by God's grace, you and your children will survive the destruction." Corbin held out his hand to the man. "Hand me the knife and we can start again, together."

The man squeezed the child tighter.

"Oh please, please let her go," the old woman pleaded, all semblance of calm now gone.

The child began to cry, "Grandma, Grandma."

"Put down the weapon and let the child go. Believe what God says. Stay here and your family will survive." Corbin took a step forward.

A woman stumbled down the steps. A gash above her head caused a line of blood to drip off of her eyebrow and onto her jacket. "Let my baby go, you bastard!"

"Everyone, calm down," Corbin took another step toward the man. "He doesn't want to hurt anyone. He's scared and wants his family together."

"Give me my kids and I will go," the man with the knife yelled. His head quickly turning left to right. The crazed look in his eyes was barely showing beneath his knitted eyebrows.

"You know we can't do that," Corbin said. "You are distraught and scared. We are all scared."

"I love my family. We are going to stay together."

"You can stay together here." Corbin motioned around him and took another step toward the man. "God has

led you here to save your family. All you need is to believe."
"God's going to fly in and save the day. He's going to stop a
fuckin' chunk of rock the size of a state from destroying the
earth," the bloody man scoffed at Corbin.

The knife pointed at his face did not scare him. "God
isn't some superhero from a comic book," Corbin took another step toward the man. "We…we are the masters of our
fate, and our destruction. All I know is that if we stay here,"
Corbin opened his arms wide, "then we will survive. Trust
the word of God. Open your mind to his promise for just one
night. Put down the knife, for just one night."

"I want my children." The man raised the knife
above his head. Corbin's read the threat and jumped toward
the man.

From behind the man a shot rang out. The sound
echoed through the chamber, and down the unexplored pas-
sageways. The bloody man dropped the knife and fell onto
the ground.

"My baby!" The woman screamed and grabbed her
daughter.
Corbin ran to the man and felt for a pulse. "He's dead." He
said to those around him. "Is the child safe?"

"I had no choice," Barton looked like he was going
to get sick. He looked from the body to the gun in helpless
distress. "He was going to kill my granddaughter."

"Oh Daddy, thank-you," The woman held out her
arms and the old man engulfed both of them in his embrace.

"I love you, Daddy. I didn't mean what I said."

"I know, I didn't believe a word of it." Barton moved
the gun behind his back and away from his daughter. "I'm so
glad you are here."

"I was on my way to the in-laws. I shouldn't even be
here." She looked at her father. "That man jumped into the
car and made me come here. I'm staying here with you and
Mom."

"Get a cart and get this body outside. We need to clean up this mess." Corbin looked around at the terrified faces. "Barton, didn't you say you had three grandkids?" he asked the old man.

The old man turned and looked at his daughter, "Kelsey, where are the others?"

"Only one would come with me. The others wanted to ride with their father. They're going with him to his parent's house."

"The old man nodded and said, "I'll get the cart."

"Quickly, and someone make sure his kids stay out of here until this is taken care of," Corbin ordered to the crowd.

"Do you have a radio?' the woman asked. "I want to know what's happening."

"There's a radio, flashlights, batteries, lanterns and other things in the cot room." Corbin stood and gestured for everyone to follow him. "We'll move the cots to the great chamber. It will be a long night. We should stay together."

"Why does God want to destroy the earth?" a somber looking boy blocked his way and asked. "Why did that man want to hurt that girl?"

"I wasn't given a reason why this is happening," he answered the young boy. "I do know that the earth will not be destroyed. I don't care what the person on the radio says. We are going to survive."

Barton pushed the cart past the crowd and motioned for people to help lift the body.

Corbin turned the child and guided him away from the great room and toward another cave. Corbin turned on the light and revealed a room filled with cots and blankets, "Flashlights, batteries, and radios are on the shelves at the far end. Everyone help move the cots."

Corbin listened as the cart, now heavy, was moving down the tunnel connecting the chamber to the stable.

Corbin grabbed a tote of flashlights and batteries. "I want everyone to carry a flashlight with them at all times. I'm not sure when we will lose the electric, but we will. I want to save the generator for after." Corbin filled several lamps and lanterns with oil and started hanging them from hooks on the cave walls.

"The cots are set up," Kelsey said when she found Corbin in the stable. He had managed to slip away while the beds were being moved. The animals looked up and, finding nothing of interest, resumed their activity. "The radio says that there have been multiple asteroid strikes from what they called the leading edge, but the big one is still on track to hit tonight."

Corbin looked at her and said, "Follow me." Corbin turned and walked down the stone pathway, through the stable, into the storage area, and stopped.

"What are we looking at?" Kelsey asked.

"It is what we are not looking at," replied Corbin. "My truck is missing."

Kelsey smiled and said, "Corbin, a truck is a big thing to lose. Where did you last see it?"

"I last saw it when I was with your father," he turned and looked into her eyes. He saw them widen in horror. "I didn't get the keys back when we moved the coop in."

"Oh, my God, he went to get the children. I have to go after him."

"I need that truck back. We'll need it when this is over." Corbin was frustrated with the turn of events. "Where are they?"

"My husband's parents live about two miles from here," she answered and turned to walk back. "My car is by the other entrance."

Corbin yelled after her, "Do you have the keys?"

She stopped and patted her pockets. "No, that crazy man had them."

Corbin walked to the metal doors and opened them. He looked around for the body and couldn't see it. "You look in the bushes over there and I'll check behind the rocks."

A few minutes later the woman yelled, "Found him, I got the keys."

"Let's go, we need to be back with that truck, before sunset, with or without him." Corbin was serious.

The woman nodded in agreement. They closed the doors and ran through the chamber.

"Mom," she yelled as she passed through. "Dad left to get the kids. We're going after him before he gets hurt."

Outside, the sky was an odd shade of orange and red. The colors seemed to swirl with mystic power. There was a terrifying blackness to the sky and they could see a mass that rivaled the moon. Kelsey screamed in terror.

Corbin pushed her into the car. "Give me the keys," he yelled and took them from her trembling hands. Seconds later they were bouncing down the driveway. "Get your seatbelt on."

"Turn right at the end of the driveway. Take a left on Kettle Hill Road, and turn in the drive with the blue and white mailbox."

Corbin rocketed down the highway, passing out of state vehicles trying to find their way home, only slowing to make the turns as instructed. Corbin parked the car next to his truck and ran to the house, pushed his way through the door, and stopped short. The old man had a gun pointed at his son-in-law. Corbin took a deep breath and said, "Mr. Barton, what are you doing?"

"I need them to listen to me."

"This is not the way, Mr. Barton." Corbin stepped toward the old man.

"Dad!" His daughter screamed at her father. "Put the gun away before someone gets hurt. Corbin, tell him."

"Put the gun away. We need to get back to the chamber before the asteroid hits." Corbin said.

"Tell them about the Angel, Corbin," pleaded the old man. "Make them understand."

Corbin turned to the people in the room. "We've never met. My name is Corbin and six months ago an angel told me to prepare for this day. The angel said that I should bring the faithful to the chamber and they will be saved." Corbin closed his eyes and prayed for strength and guidance. "Please, believe what I am saying. Believe that God will save us."

Corbin turned back to the old man. "You've done all that can be done to save your grandchildren. Give me the gun."

The old man teared up as he handed the weapon to Corbin.

Corbin turned and spoke to the family. "I'm sorry that this happened. It's been a bad day. Please, forgive us." He took the broken old man and led him to the door. "Please, believe the word and join us."

"Please come," Kelsey begged her husband. She dropped the keys on a stand by the door. "Please."

The sky was getting darker the closer they got to the farm. There was a red glow of fire in the distance. It looked as if their small town was an inferno. They stopped at the end of the driveway, took down the sign, and put it in the truck bed. Corbin safely returned the truck to storage and locked the metal doors. He slid a metal bar into place and then rolled down a metal door from above. "Mr. Barton, it's time to feed the animals and then you need to go to your wife. We still need to secure the other door, gather the faithful, and pray for the lost."

"What if they come?" he asked quietly.

"Once the doors are locked, there will be no others. The safety of the faithful is the concern of the chamber."

Corbin sighed and looked at his watch. "They have 30 minutes and no more."

"What's the radio saying?" Mr. Barton asked as they walked into the chamber.

Corbin closed the door to the stable area and followed the old man into the room.

"Most of the radio channels stopped working 10 minutes ago. We can get one national channel, but that is it. Local is all static except for some strange noises. Are the kids coming?" Mrs. Barton asked as she joined her husband. "That was a foolish thing to do."

The old man didn't answer and looked around. The ground shook and dust fell from the ceiling. The lights flickered and came back on. "Is that it?" asked a child. "Is that the end of the earth?"

"No, weren't you listening," her brother said and gave her a shove. "The radio said the asteroid would hit the atmosphere in 2 hours."

Corbin excused himself and walked away. He needed to be alone for a few minutes.

"Can we string some blanket over the cots to keep the dirt off?" Kelsey said as she held her frightened child.

"Yes, good idea. You should do that," he said without really listening. He walked past them and down the tunnel leading to the crystal altar. In a small chamber off the hallway was a library, Corbin sat at what used to be his grandmother's kitchen table. She was the wisest woman he had ever met. Of all the people in the world he wished he could hold at the end of the world, it would be her. "I miss you Grandma," he said as he moved her picture from a small stack of notebooks. He picked up the top book and flipped to an empty page. He dated it and wrote, "Today, one earth ends and another begins. Thank you, Lord, for sending your Angel to save us from destruction." Corbin closed the notebook and returned it to the stack it came from and replaced grandma's picture. He gathered his strength and took what might be his last look at her and walked away.

When Corbin returned, he whistled to the old man. "Help me take down the signs and lock the doors. It's time to think of the safety of the chamber."

"Please, a little longer," the old man implored.

"The time has come," he responded, his voice firm and resolute.

"We've done all we can do," he said to his wife and walked away.

Mae and her daughter hugged as they watched the men climb the steps.

Outside the door the wind was blowing and the sky was dark. A jagged shimmering darkness obliterated the moon and left the landscape in starless black. The temperature had dropped and Corbin wished that he had brought his coat. 'I hoped that there would be more people waiting. I prayed and planned for many people and so few came."

The old man patted his shoulder. "You did all you could. You couldn't make them believe."

Corbin walked to the sign and unhooked it from the base. A flash of lightning lit up the sky enough to see that nobody was coming.

"Let's go inside," the old man said and turned toward the door. "You're right. It's time."

They walked to the door, took one last look around and locked it tight. They slid heavy bars into slots along the wall and then Corbin rolled down a door from above and secured it in place. They were sealed in.

212 steps to safety, he thought to himself. How many people would die when they were so close to salvation? "Who wants popcorn!" He called out. "Lots and lots of butter." He looked down and saw children running for the kitchen.

"There was a chorus of "Me" from below and he smiled. At the bottom of the steps he turned out the lights to the steps and half of the lights in the chamber. He wanted everyone acclimated to the dark before hell rained down on them. God had promised salvation from the devastation above, but he still had the bloody man on his mind. "Everyone, in the kitchen, there's a mess to be made."

"What do we do when the electric goes out," the old man asked.

"I have battery backup for the refrigerator and freezers," he replied. "We'll be ok."

From a room away they heard the radio siren go off. Corbin and several adults broke free of the feast and walked into the room to listen.

"This is just in. NASA is saying that the earth is out of danger. Heroic actions by American astronauts have saved the planet. Officials are encouraging the populace to continue to shelter in place. There will be multiple impacts from the debris and we are not out of danger. We are awaiting more details but as of right now, the planet has been saved."

Everyone looked at each other and smiled, then laughed, then hugged in joy.

"Corbin, you were right," Kelsey said as she joined the group.

"I've never had an angel lie to me," he smiled.

"I'm sorry you spent so much time and effort on the chamber," the old man said.

"The Angel said I needed to gather the faithful here," said Corbin. "Gather them so they survive. The danger has not passed."

The mood in the room changed. The laughter from the kitchen was in stark contrast to the faces around the radio.

"Will NASA give any warning about," Kelsey started when a sonic boom followed by an explosion shook the ground around them.

"Hang on," Barton yelled and dropped to the ground as the lights went out.

The sound of children screaming and adults yelling could be heard above the rumbling in the ground. Corbin turned on his flashlight and ran for the kitchen. Lanterns shaking and banging against the rock wall sent ghost like shadows across the chamber walls. "Turn on your flashlights," he yelled as another sonic boom shook the ground.

Several lights clicked on around him as the ground shuddered and heaved under another impact. Corbin's ears popped as another explosion changed the pressure in the room. Rocks and dust started to fall from the ceiling. "Everyone, take shelter under the tables," his voice seemed muffled.

The next series of sonic booms and impacts became deafening. The sound of rushing water and stalactites crashing to the ground could be heard in the background.

"What's happening," screamed a child as he stood up and ran. Corbin grabbed the child and pulled him under the table. The sound of a thousand freight trains screamed above their heads. The pressure changed again. Corbin's ears popped and he passed out.

Corbin awoke to the sound of movement in the room. He took a deep breath, groaned, and rolled to his side, bumping into the child he pulled under the table. He shook the child and watched his eyes flutter. He picked up a flashlight and used the table to steady himself as he got to his feet. Around him he could see people on the ground. There was movement and Corbin yelled, "Wake up."

He walked over to the wall, relit it, and rolled the lantern's wick up. The light became brighter and Corbin walked from the kitchen. The sound of his steps seemed distant. He opened and closed his mouth trying to get the pressure in his ears to change. Slowly, sounds came back to normal as he moved around the walls, relighting and increasing the light coming from the lamps.

People slowly emerged from hiding and gathered in the great room. Their eyes betrayed their confusion and fear. Corbin could not understand them, "God has saved us from destruction. We have survived," he said with a smile. "Praise God, we have survived."

Mae started to pray and fell to her knees. The others joined in the praise and thanks.

Corbin finished lighting the chamber and followed the hall to the stable. He was concerned that the animals had not survived. The racket from the cave made him smile. The animals looked at him with great displeasure. "I know, it was a rough night," he said to the animals. "You don't know it, but you are the luckiest animals in the world."

Corbin continued down the cave and the heat started to increase. He could see the door to the outside was glowing. "That's not good," he commented to the door and turned around. They weren't going outside today.

Back in the chamber, Corbin approached the adults as they were righting cots and cleaning up the mess. "We're not going outside," he stated.

"Why, what's going on?" asked the old man.

"It's hot as an oven outside," he replied. "The storage room door is glowing red."

"There must be a fire," the old man replied. "We'll have to wait till it burns itself out. I'm gonna bet the fire department is pretty busy."

Kelsey looked at her father and burst into tears. "The boys are out there in that."

Corbin looked sad, "Everyone, not in the safety of the chamber, is in that."

Mae walked up and stood beside them. "They're all dead," she said softly. "The angel said that only those in the chamber will survive."

"We don't know for sure until we can get outside," the old man didn't look like he believed what he said.

"Where's Banjo, I need to find him."

"I saw him in the stable. I think he has adopted a lamb." Corbin said and watched the old man walk away. He could feel his pain through the air and wished there was something more that could have been done. "We may be here for a while. There are games and books in the Library."

"I saw it," Kelsey said looking at her daughter. "I'll go grab some things. Do you want to help?"

"I'll help," a man said from the back of the group. The girl looked happy to stay where she was.

"Great," she said and walked with the man.

Corbin watched them walk away and decided that he needed to get away from the group. He walked down the cave to what was left of the stalagmite altar. His body, no longer fueled by adrenaline and coffee gave out. His knees buckled and he fell back against the damp stone wall, sliding to the ground. Broken icicles of stone cushioned his fall. He was exhausted. "Thank you for saving them. I don't know by what blessing I was chosen but thank you," Corbin inhaled. He wanted to cry but couldn't draw enough energy to shed a tear. "With all reverence, all I have is this farm and my life. They are yours."

Corbin was not a social man. The animals and the farm were all he knew. He tilted his head back with a bump. He slid down into a supine position looking at the ceiling above. "There are at least thirty people depending on me for their safety. What did you see in me? I'm not a preacher. I'm nobody. What do I do now that the cataclysm is over?"

There was no answer from the stone above. The cave did not fill with glorious light to guide him. "Are you tired, too?" Corbin stayed on the wet stone until he started to shiver. He had lost track of time when he was unconscious. "There are no answers in this room. You need to get to work like you always do." Corbin's pants were stuck to his legs and he shook them as he walked back to the great room.

~

In the library, Kelsey found cards, books, and games. She handed them to the man and watched him as he walked away.

"This is a mess," she said as she started picking up books. She righted a shelf and started putting away puzzle pieces and fantasy cards.

The mess was worse than it looked and she moved on to a stand next to a small opening. She righted the stand and picked up plastic totes of office and art supplies. She turned on her flashlight and followed a trail of dice and figures into a narrow opening. There was a lantern on the wall, so she lit it and looked around. It appeared to be a cozy reading room. An old table and chairs and some personal items made her feel like an intruder. She picked up small items from the stone and returned them to the nearest spot. She found a picture of an older woman that looked so much like Corbin it caught her eye.

"You have to be Mom or Grandma," Kelsey said. "Let's get you cleaned up." She removed the picture from the broken frame and looked for paper to wrap the glass in. Nearby, she found notebooks. "We're going to have this mess cleaned up and you'll be looking pretty, Mrs. Corbin."

Kelsey opened the notebook and there was a picture of what looked like a man surrounded by light. "The Angel?" she said with intrigue in her voice. She hadn't realized that she said it out loud and the noise startled her. She felt like a spy discovering a mysterious secret.

She turned the page and started to read.

Melony
Tampa, Florida

Melony's hunger always drove her to the Pilot truck stop to earn money. She knew this would be one of the last times autumn was at its end, and it was getting too cold for her to sleep outside. She wanted to stay here, under the bridge connecting with the park. She knew she would need to leave it soon. Melony disliked the homeless shelter, but this temporary home would be here next year. She may not have much here, but there was peace.

The cars on highway 95 blew her shirt as they went by. She wiped the sweat off her leathered face. It was already 71 degrees in Florida. Her eyes darted from side to side as she waited for her opportunity to cross. The start of the tourist season approached quickly but the truck stop was busier then she had seen it in three months. She walked past the building. People were gathered in the lounge watching TV. Thinking nothing of it she went to the bathroom to wash up. People passed her at a distance not looking in her direction. She was used to this. After all she had been homeless for two years. Melony passed travelers in rushed conversation. She sniffed her armpit and wrinkled her nose. The bathroom was her next stop. She would clean herself and wash her clothes in the sink. She would wear her other set of clothes, a pair of pants, and a button up shirt. After finishing she took them to her cart and laid them out to dry. Jerome hurried outside to throw away trash in the dumpster. Melony took him by surprise,

"Morning Jerome, is there anything you want me to do today?"

Jerome sighed and massaged his temple, "Yes, it's been a crazy morning. My employee just up and quit. I'm finally catching up since his replacement came in."

"That stinks," she said with a chuckle. "Some of them don't last long, do they?"

"No, but it couldn't have been at a worse time. My boss is coming today. He could be here at any minute," he ranted "There was a trucker party. The whole place is a wreck."

"It sounds like you need some help," she said. Jerome lifted his eyes at her. "I'll give you ten dollars if you pick up the trash on the grounds. Melony perked up "I can do it. Is that all you need done?"

"Yes, that will have to do for now. I wish I could do more, but you know I can't," he said.

"OK, I'll see you when I'm done," she said and left.

Even though time passed quickly, she began to feel anxious. She needed the ten dollars. Her constant companion needed a drink. She approached Jerome and said, "I'm finished."

"Here you go," he said and handed her ten dollars. She grabbed the crisp bill from his hand.

"Thanks for being quick. That's one less thing I have to worry about," he said.

"Thanks for letting me do it Jerome. You're always helping me. I wouldn't be able to live here, if it wasn't for you." She smiled and looked at her ten dollars.

She felt a sharp pain in her abdomen. "Man, I'm starving. I haven't eaten since yesterday morning." She took the path to the convenient store and bought a hot dog, and the cheapest liquor on the shelf. She could get twice as much for her money there. The anticipation to scarf down both made her mouth water.

Melony went to her favorite spot behind the truck stop. A slow, trickling creek ran through the back of the property. She sat in a shaded spot, twisted off the cap, and sipped. She devoured her hot dog and generously washed it down. She sat and watched the stream while she enjoyed the next quarter of the bottle. With the shakes gone, she felt normal. She thought of the crowd of people in front of the TV. What had they been so concerned about? She pocketed the bottle and slowly staggered back to the truck stop.

As she got closer, the quiet of the truck stop that she remembered was gone. People rushed to their cars. A man told his wife, "get in the car! We don't have much time. We've got to beat the traffic, or we'll never make it out of Florida." She looked at the highway, there was no traffic. Her heart started to race, there must be something wrong. She hurried back to the truck stop lounge.

She entered, and people were in a panic, she couldn't hear what the newscaster was saying. She asked the lady next to her, "What is going on?"

"The moon was hit by a meteor, and its shards will be hitting the earth in twelve hours," she said.

Her heart sank, they were all going to die. Overwhelmed, she got her bottle out and took a drink. She shook her head in disbelief, the world started to spin. She sat down, and the panicked voices of everyone faded in and out.

"Is this a hoax?" an elderly lady asked.

A middle-aged man, with his arm around his wife asked, "how will they stop it?"

A teenager screamed "We are going to die!"

Melony rubbed the bottle under her jacket, "I need a drink, and some peace and quiet."

Jerome arrived, "Quiet, I'm trying to hear the TV." Everyone in the room turned to look at him. Melony didn't care. She wanted to talk with her son and ex-husband, the only family she had left.

A woman, holding her baby, looked at her husband, "Why have they waited until now to tell us?" He looked speechless, "I'm going to the restroom. Get the things we need and be ready by the time I get back." He said and walked away.

Melony

"Ma'am, can I please use your phone to call my son? He is in New Zealand," Melony asked.

The woman tossed Melony the phone, "Why not? It's the end of the world, right!"

Melony's hand shook that so bad she had a hard time dialing the number. The phone rang for a minute then someone picked up. She exhaled in relief, as she realized it was her husband.

~

Arthur woke up to the phone hitting the ground. Nobody ever called him at this time of night, except Melony. He checked the number, it's was from Florida. He sighed and hastily answered. "Hello?"

Melony was breathing fast, "Arthur, thank goodness you answered. Have you seen the news?"

"No, of course I haven't. I was asleep until you woke me up. I can barely hear you over the commotion. Where are you?"

"Listen, that doesn't matter! A meteor is headed toward earth, they say it will be the end."

Arthur rolled his eyes "Have you called drunk again? We've talked about this Melony!"

Melony snapped, "it's ten a.m. I only just got a bottle. Arthur seriously, turn on the news. Will you wake up Michael, so I can talk with him, this may be my last chance..."

Arthur gritted his teeth. His concern for their safety consumed his thoughts. Was it as bad as Melony said? He put the phone down and went to wake his son. Arthur tapped his shoulder, "Michael, wake up."

Michael woke with a jerk, "What is it dad?"

"Your mom wants to talk with you."

"Do I have to? She's probably drunk again!"

Michael rarely talked with his mom, but this was a terrible situation. Arthur didn't agree with Melony's lifestyle choices and it changed her for the worst.

Arthur reassured Michael, "She's not drunk this time. Please just have a conversation with her." He went and retrieved the phone and turned on his TV. Today's catastrophic news was easily found. He walked back into Michael's room, careful not to show the panic he felt. Arthur handed him the phone and managed to give him a stern look. He left and stood out of sight by Michael's door.

Michael put the phone on speaker and laid back, "Mom?"

"Michael, can you hear me?" she asked.

"Mom, it's 2 am," he said.

"I know It is late, I'm sorry. This was the only opportunity I had to talk with you. How are you doing in school?" She asked.

"I have good grades. It is nice to hear from you. Are you still homeless?" Michael asked.

"Yes. At the end of this season I'll go to the homeless shelter. I'll make some more money then. Things will get better, you will see."

Michael perked up, "does that mean I'll get to see you for Thanksgiving this year?"

"We'll see. I love you son, I'm sorry I can't be there with you right now. Please give the phone back to your dad. I'm borrowing someone's phone to call, I don't have long," Melony said.

"OK. I love you," Michael said.

Arthur waited a moment for Michael to get up before he came in the door. Michael handed Arthur the phone. "She wants to talk with you, Dad."

Arthur turned the speaker phone off and walked in his bedroom. He turned off the TV and he put the phone to his ear "I'm here."

Melony

"What will you do?" She asked the panic in her voice rose.

"What can we do? Other than wait for the inevitable. I'm going to tell Michael there's a tornado and hide in the basement."

"I know, you will do the right thing, you always have."

"We will have fun with our last hours."

"I'm truly sorry for how everything has turned out. I never stopped loving you. I love you both, please take care of our son for us. I've got to go," her voice broke.

"I love you too-" click, his last words trailed off into the distance.

~

Melony wiped her tears and handed the phone back. "Thank you," the room got louder, and she heard people say, "No, my call just dropped." Everyone in the room lost communication.

"You're welcome. I'm glad it all worked out," she turned and walked away.

Melony finished the bottle and wiped her lips, then went to get another. The alcohol was free for her to take, everyone was panicky from the news. She easily put two bottles in her bag. Then effortlessly made her way out and filled her backpack with any food within reach. She was going to eat good tonight, after all it was the end of the world, she had nothing to lose. Arthur would take good care of their son, and there was no way she could get to them before the meteor came. She realized there was nothing she could do from across the world and that gave her a sense of peace. The guilt of the situation made her stomach uneasy. She took another swig, knowing that if she drank enough, she wouldn't feel anything. Melony left the truck stop and made back to the bridge.

November 7th

As she got closer to the highway the noise rising became louder and louder. The honks and shouts pierced her ears. It had been an hour since the tsunamis from the crashing meteorites were predicted and the traffic was starting.

After crossing the highway, she was surrounded by trees on both sides. The landscape reminded her of the park next to the Buddhist monastery, she visited often. The journey back cleared her head and she remembered her cat, Tullia.

The cat was occupied with a mouse and gave Melony no attention. Happiness came over Melony as she felt the fullness of her backpack. She sat down on the ground and pulled out a bottle. Tullia sniffed her while she pushed her way into Melony's lap. "Ahh, that takes the edge off." She shook her head as the whiskey burned on the way down. She twisted the cap back on, then pet her cat, "Tulia, it's the end of the world, what are we going to do?" The cat cocked her head. She paused as the tree line past the bridge started to move. She got up to get a closer view. "Who's there?"

A skinny blonde-haired boy peeked his head out from behind the trees.

"Tullia, you didn't tell me we had visitors. Come out boy, or the boogeyman will get ya." The boy jumped out.

Melony asked, "What's your name?"

He weakly stammered, "Mm-m-my name is... is... Tony, ma'am."

"What are you doing out here? Where's your parents?"

Tony's hand rubbed his eyes, "My parents died in a car crash. I saw the news this morning, everyone in the group home was going crazy. I was scared and ran away. Then I got lost trying to find my aunt's house."

Melony's voice softened, "I'm sorry kid, how long you been in the group home? These are mad times. It's best not to be traveling alone. How did you end up here?"

Melony

Tony pointed to Tullia, "I saw your cat and followed her to here. My mom loved cats. We always would follow cats on our walks. She always said the adventure is the important part, and the destination is a surprise." Tony's gaze fell on the chips and candy.

Melony looked down to her backpack, "Are you hungry, Tony?"

Tony said "Yes ma'am, I haven't eaten since this morning and it was a mighty long walk from there to here. I've been at the group home maybe a week or two. I don't know." He put his head in his hands "I just want my parents back."

Melony handed Tony everything except a couple bags of chips, which she saved for herself. He dived in without another word. "So, what is your plan before the meteor hits?"

"I don't know, I haven't been to a place like this in a long time. What would you do?" he said.

"Oh, I don't know, play some games. That's what my son would want to do when he was your age," she said. Tony perked up, "You have a son? Well then why are you here under the bridge, at this park?"

She took a big gulp of alcohol, "It's a long story. I have made some bad choices in my past, that I regret. Michael is with his father, and he is safe," she said, partly to herself.

"But what about you? What are you going to do?" Tony asked.

Melony slurred as she rubbed her bottle, "I'm going to relax tonight." She was going to try to drink until she passed out. "Hopefully, when I wake up tomorrow, this will all be a bad dream."

"That sounds boring. I want to do something fun," he said.

Melony shrugged "I'm a boring person I guess."

November 7th

"It's the end of the world, I wish I could see my family again. I'm sure your family would love to see you," he said.

Melony wiped the forming tears from her eyes and focused on petting Tullia. "Are you still hungry boy? I have a bag of chips we can share."

Tony's eyes widened "Yes, thank you. If it wasn't for you and your cat, I would still be out on the streets lost."

Melony handed the remainder of the chips to Tony. "You are quite welcome." Then she held up her bottle, "I have my bottle to keep away my hunger pains."

Tullia jumped off Melony's lap as some debris shifted in the sky. "Looks like the light show is starting early. I was skeptical, the world may end after all. I'm glad that one will hit far away though."

Her stomach fell. The world was really going to end. What had she done with her life? She couldn't think of anything notable. She was selfish, and these last few years had been a haze. She didn't want to be here, she wanted to help others. "Get ready, we're going to find your aunt's house. It's better you spend your last moments with family."

"My Aunt Cassandra lives near a baker. He has the best French bread I have ever tasted. We would always have it with my favorite meal, spaghetti," Tony licked his lips. "I don't know if she still lives there because she never came to visit me in the orphanage."

"Tullia, are you coming with us? You may never see us again." The cat came to her and sat down. She packed her bag with all her belongings. The family picture made her halt. It had been taken four years ago when they lived in Ohio. They had chosen a beautiful autumn day to take their picture in front of a dogwood tree. Michael was eight then, and all of them smiled in the photo because of his laughter. The photographer had mustard on his nose and didn't know it the whole time.

Melony

Tony got her attention by asking, "When are we leaving?"

"In a moment," she stuffed her things in the bag and sat down to have one last look. She took a swig, got up then swung the pack on her shoulders. As Tony looked at the landscape, Melony asked, "Are you ready for an adventure?"

The mention of an adventure got his full attention. Tony started to skip, "Yes! I really hope my Aunt still lives there."

"I hope we find her too, kid," Melony said.

The road spilled out on highway 95 headed southbound. As they got closer Melony knew to cup her ears from the deafening honks. The cars lined up on the highway went farther than the eye could see. "We are lucky the direction we need to go is southbound." She said. They looked southbound and saw one car.

On their travels to downtown, they would get whiffs of smoke. The heat rose as the day progressed, "It's hotter than normal today."

They had traveled for forty-five minutes. Tony asked "How much longer until we get there? All we've seen is restaurants and truck stops."

"It's coming up soon, but we got to stop for a bit." She pointed to a shaded place by nearby trees,

"Let's take a break there." She sat down and took a drink.

Tony sat down next to her, "I'm thirsty, do you have any water?"

"No, but we'll get some," she rummaged in the bag and found a piece of gum. "This will tie you over. You said your aunt lives near a baker's shop? Was there anything else you can remember? Like the hospital, library, mall, or a police station?"

"Yeah, it was five blocks from the library. Right after the Dollar General," he said.

"Good I know the area, we'll need to get off on this exit." She got up, "Well, here we go."

They descended the off ramp; Melony's heart sank at her first glimpse of society. The emptiness of the large city was unusual, under normal circumstances this city had a constant hum. There were no children laughing, cars shooting by, constant chatter of people, or construction men banging away. Now there was a nervous quiet. Where they unwilling to accept the newscaster's statement? What do they know anyway? Could earth be saved by some miracle?

They walked through a neighborhood. The random sobs and screams broke the silence. They traveled a block and started to notice that the people who did evacuate northward, left their lawns a mess. Tony pointed at some bikes, barely visible under toys. "Will it be ok if we borrow these bikes to get to my aunt's house? We'll return them like we do books at the library."

Melony chuckled "It will be OK. I don't think they will need them anymore. Did you go to the library a lot?"

Tony replied "Oh yes! We were always going to the library. My parents were teachers, so every weekend I would get to go. I loved to pick out books for school and home to read."

She took her pack off and rummaged the bikes out. Tullia always wandered close by them. Melony chuckled, "Someone was in a hurry, looks like the kids tried to take their belongings." Amongst the toys, there were teddy bears falling out of a briefcase. The bikes were in good condition but too small for her. She figured at least she could stroll, even if she couldn't pedal. Melony said, "Follow me kid, I know right where to go. Things could get hairy before we get to your aunt's house. Whenever lives are at stake people don't think straight. Before we continue, I need your promise that you will listen to me and stay by my side. Can you do that for me?" She handed Tony a bottle of water she found amongst the mess.

Melony

Tony chugged the water and wiped his lips, "I will try to do my best. Why do people not think straight?"

"People do crazy things when they have nothing left to lose. They all think they're going to die. That means, the bad people get worse and the good people sometimes go crazy. We may be lucky and only run into people who want to help us, but I doubt it," she said as they got on their bikes and started cycling down the street.

"My mom always did tell me not to trust strangers," he said.

"I always told my son the same thing."

Tony looked around. "Why are the people sitting outside?"

"They are nervous, scared, and want to see what is going on. With cell phones not working, this is the only news they have. Nobody is good at expecting the unknown," she said.

The sweat rolled off them in beads as the temperature increased. Downtown was a nightmare she wanted to wake from. The streets were littered with trash and the overhead lights were busted out. How can people do this much damage in such little time? They had just heard the news this morning. Half the stores had busted windows. Everything looked vacant, then they turned the corner and saw a long line of people in front of an old drug store.

As they got closer, they could hear a man, "Come get your caffeine pills, only ten dollars a pill. This will keep you awake for twenty-four hours. Don't miss any moments you have left with your loved ones!" The people who waited in line nervously looked at the policeman.

Tony looked at Melony, "Is the police man going to stop them?"

She looked at the policeman, "Not today, kid. They are here to keep order, and to make sure those medications don't go into the wrong hands." She'd seen her fair share of crooked cops on the streets. If they could make a profit from the end of the world, then they would.

The man continued, "Or I got something special that just arrived! You can now decide when to end it on your own terms. Only twenty dollars a pill."

On the next block people were going in and stealing from the tobacco shop. While passing by they noticed a guy with a gun enter the shop. They heard the tall buff man shout, "You'll pay for this in trade, cash, or your life. Which will it be?"

The man's threats motivated Melony to move quicker down the street, "I don't want to stick around, this can get ugly real fast. Let's go!"

After redirecting their course, they could hear a riot in the distance. A policeman stood outside of a library. He told the crowd of people, "Everyone go home, this place is full. Go be with your family and enjoy the last moments you may have with your loved ones." Her fondness grew for the library as she noticed the bomb shelter sign on the wall. They continued.

Her heart sank seeing this block. The building on fire was spreading to the others. Where were the firefighters? Did everyone go home to their loved ones? The street was littered with trash as far as the eye could see. Someone had turned all the cans over. All the windows on this block were busted, and walls were tagged. In the center of the mayhem, was a building that looked like a science lab. Melony said, "Let's turn around," Tony obeyed. Tullia ran to catch up to their quickened pace.

After they traveled some distance away from the disturbed block, they slowed their pace. Tony rubbed his stomach, "I'm thirsty and hungry. Do you have anything?"

"No. We'll have to stop for a break and search this stop and go." The shop was hot, and the pungent smell assaulted their nose. She looked around to locate the smell, and saw chemical bottles lying next to the spill on the floor. This dim store had been picked through many times, but at least there was a canned food and water left on the shelves. She hoped for the possibility that liquor had been left behind. Melony was creatively desperate and looked around the edges of shelves and in the garbage. She found a half bottle of whiskey, in a puke covered bag. Suppressing the urge to vomit, she removed the bag. She un-clipped her multi-tool from her belt and opened a tuna for her cat. As she sat it on the ground a shiny object captured her attention by the cash register. She investigated and found a knife near the register and pocketed it quickly. Best the kid doesn't know I have this, or would a ten-year-old boy be comforted by this? She shrugged and moved on. "We're almost there kid, one more block to go. Are you excited?"

Tony took his time to chew before answering, "Yes! I haven't heard from my Aunt since my parents died. I thought she was going to adopt me," he hung his head. "I really liked staying at my Aunt's house, she was so much fun." He looked off into the distance.

Melony looked over at Tullia to see if she was done. Tullia ate slowly, she was acting like she wasn't a street cat. Melony took another swig of the bottle and pocketed some candy. "Sounds like you really love your Aunt."

"I do. I can't wait to see the big white house with purple shutters again. It's always funny when Uncle Tim makes fun of them." He lowered his voice, "He says they're sissy shutters," he giggled. "One of the first things I'm going to do is swing on the tire swing in the front yard-" Tony went quiet as a man stepped out from the back room, taking them by surprise.

Melony didn't think to scope the place out for others, she kicked herself for her neglect.

The man said, "What are you doing here? This is

my store, and nobody is robbing it. Get out!" The man was sweating and mumbling under his breath to himself.

Tony got behind Melony, "We were just eating, we will leave," she picked up Tullia and the bottle dropped on the floor.

"Give me that back, I know you took it!" he said.

The man stomped toward them and snatched the bottle from the floor. Melony scrambled backward, nearly tripping over Tony.

"No. It's the end of the freakin' world. I could have picked this up anywhere," Melony lied.

The man shook the bottle at them "So what! I'm tired of every Tom, Dick and Harry thinking it's OK to come into my shop to steal or break my stuff." Then he lit the bottle on fire and threw it on the floor. It landed on the spilt chemicals, which made the fire swell to half the size of the man in seconds. The fire licked up the man, as his screams bounced around the room. The smell of burning flesh and hair permeated the room.

"Tony, RUN!" Melony screamed.

They made it out and looked up at the building on fire. The broken moon above them made it seem ominous. The fire had already made it to the door, they had got out just in time. They were both out of breath, but Tony started gasping. Her heart dropped. Something was very wrong. "Tony? What's wrong," she asked. He tried to answer but she couldn't make out a word. She lifted him up and hurried to his Aunt's house. She dreaded what would happen if she couldn't make it.

It felt like hours before she came up on the Dollar General. She located the purple shuttered house quickly. She shifted Tony's weight to one side and pounded on the door, praying someone would answer. Pleading that if she made it out of this, she would never drink again. Not only had she destroyed her life with her son, but she'd almost killed a boy over a bottle of alcohol. Panic stricken she pounded harder.

A tall slender woman with hazel eyes opened the door. Melony could see the resemblance to Tony, the light hair and fair skin. She surveyed Melony briefly, then noticed the boy. Their eyes connecting at the same time. Melony gasped, "HELP! He's not breathing normal."

Cassandra quickly replied, "Follow me. Sit him down on the couch," she pointed to the right, after they had entered the house.

Cassandra ran out and appeared with an inhaler, "He's having an asthma attack." She sat him up and put it in his mouth and pumped. She tried to calm him, "Remember Tony, you have to breathe to the count of three. Let's count together." She pushed the inhaler again, "One, two, three." His breath went back to normal again, "I know I haven't seen you for a couple weeks. I will explain, but first you must get some rest."

"Okay." He weakly smiled. He took her hand and followed along.

When Cassandra returned, Melony started in, "A crazy man set fire to the building we were in. We barely escaped alive! What could have caused his asthma attack?" Cassandra looked out the window, "Maybe the smoke did it. He'll be OK though, I'm thankful I keep a spare inhaler for myself, when things like this happen." Cassandra filled a glass with water and took it in to Tony. Melony overheard her say, "Here drink this and get some rest, water will make you feel better." Her footsteps got louder as she re-entered the room. She turned to Melony, "I'm happy you brought him here, or something bad may have happened."

Melony smiled, "I'm glad I found the right house."

"You were lucky, I just got home from the hospital yesterday. The car accident put me in a coma. After being in the hospital for two weeks, I was shocked to find out this morning that Tony was in a group home. Then this awful

Meteor that's going to hit the earth." She smiled sarcastically, "I have the best of luck."

Melony looked away, "I think I should let him tell you his story about what has happened to him. We just met today. He was lost, and I brought him here."

"Ok, Thank you again. I'll make him his favorite. That should cheer him up. You are welcome to stay for dinner, if you'd like," Cassandra said.

"I'm afraid I must be going, I have something to take care of. It was nice meeting you, thanks again." Melony's heart dropped when she turned to walked away. She couldn't tell Cassandra the reason he almost died was because of her. Melony would no longer be a hero in Tony's eyes. She turned back and said "I'll say goodbye to him. Also, he can keep Tullia, she is the reason he is here. He'll really like that. She's outside in your yard."

Melony looked in, Tony was fast asleep. She walked in and knelt down beside the bed, "You're a great kid, enjoy the last few hours with your Aunt. You said you wanted to be with family, and here you are. I'm truly sorry this happened to you, it won't happen again." Her head sagged down as she whispered, "I will change." Tony was back to normal and it made her feel ten pounds lighter. She expected to feel happy, but all the bad choices she had made resurfaced. She wrapped her arms around herself as she left.

She walked absent minded down the street. She looked back at the house and felt sorry for herself, then realized she didn't want to live amongst people anymore. Greed existed everywhere, and she couldn't accept that. There was nowhere for her to go and she turned into a dark alley. The light flashed directly above and made her stumble. She took a seat next to the trash can before she fell. There was nothing for her to do. She murmured, "This is it. The end of the world, and I'm sitting in a dark alley." She swallowed, "All alone and nobody cares. Everyone is out for themselves," and she didn't want to be a part of it. She reached down for her bottle and took a swig. Then tightened her grip around it, it was reason for the mess. She threw it at the wall and watched the glass shatter in a million pieces. She sobbed at her pitiful life. Her inadequacy led to this. She couldn't be with her family on the last day on earth. She couldn't face Tony after she almost got him killed.

Her egotism made her sick. She got her knife and pressed it down hard on her wrist. Droplets of blood beaded up under the knife's pressure. Melony said, "I should just end it now, spare myself and anyone else." As the tears streamed down, she couldn't see her hand. She remembered one day long ago when she and her husband were together walking in a park. Much like the place she chose to live while homeless. Their son was very young then, Arthur asked, "What would you do if something happened to me and Michael?" Melony confidently replied, "Join a monastery."

He replied, "I didn't think of that. My answer was to become a nomad and travel the world." Screams down the street got her attention. She got up and wiped her tears. People were escaping out of a burning building. The burns that covered their bodies, made her forget about her problems. She saw people sacrifice themselves to help put out the fire. This gave her hope in humanity. She perked up, she could make it through this. After all she promised. If they could go on, she could go on.

What do you do when you know the world is about to end and you have nowhere to go? Should she watch how other people deal with it? People in chaos overwhelmed Melony more than she ever thought possible. She wandered until she heard unhappy voices. The church entrance was crowded with people. The crowd talking overlapped each other. "Repent your sins and God will forgive you." A man held thrusting a sign in the air.

"God take us now! I don't want my family to suffer," a man said with clasped hands.

She felt no peace from this church, her head turned down and she continued. With no place in mind, she found herself close to the park. She entered.

The monks in the park were meditating. How could they be so calm? Then it struck her, they were here every day doing their meditations before nightfall. She sat down and enjoyed the quiet. Why didn't she think to come here? The end of the world gave her the courage to learn more. When would it would feel like, the end? When everyone was about to die? When they watched the meteor enter the atmosphere? Everything felt so surreal, as she sat in the presence of the monks, it helped her accept that this was the end. The best thing she could do was find peace with the person inside. It would not be an easy road, but she was determined in her choice. She got up quickly, "I know what I must do." Not wasting another second, she walked to the monastery.

She walked to the monastery and entered. The long walkway was lined with great white pillars on each side. It emptied into a circular outdoor space with a fountain in the middle. The sand from the floor got in her shoes. She looked up overhead at the bright shards that streaked the black sky. Her stomach fell, the end was near. A monk meditated in front of the water fountain. Every time she thought of meditating, it was in the sitting position like the slender tan monk she saw. Did they all dress alike? Melony broke the silence, "Hello, I don't mean to interrupt you. I would like some information. How can I join this monastery?"

He opened his eyes and looked at her for a minute, "But you did interrupt me. Why do you want to join a monastery?"

Melony lowered her head in defeat, "I am lost and I'm not sure how to fix my problems. The cancer I had destroyed my life, and only bad things have followed since.

I want to know what peace feels like. I don't want to be that person anymore, I want to change for the better."

"Is that why you have come here?"

"Yes and no. The world's end showed me the kind of person I can be. I want to know in my heart that I can change to be a person my son can be proud of."

"Given your circumstances, you can start with ten days. We don't take people in on such short notice, but I think the monastic lifestyle will be a good fit for you. Tonight, I'll have someone show you to your room. You will stay among the nuns; the men and women stay separated for better focus. They will give you the basic details of how things work. Go clean up, eat, and get some rest. Remember, don't be too hard on yourself, you too deserve compassion," the Monk said.

"Thank you. I really appreciate it,"

"I need no thanks. When you find inner peace, that will be my thanks," the monk said.

Another monk came and escorted Melony to her room. Candles guided them down the hallway. A dim light filled the room and cast shadows on a solitary bed roll. He pointed in. "Please stay in your room and keep as quiet as you can. The bathroom is two doors to the left. We wake at 6 am." He left, and Melony started to pace the room. Was it almost 10pm? Surely, they would feel the meteor hit, or would it be quick. Would the news reach this place? Did monks have cell phones? She had never seen a monk with one. There was a knocked on the door.

"Come in," Melony said.

The nun at the door handed Melony some bread, "Here is your food, it will help absorb the alcohol. It is not a normal practice for anyone to eat in the evening, but the head monk made a special request given your situation. I will also need your belongings."

"Thank you for the food," Melony said, then handed

the nun the only thing she owned, her backpack.

The nun took the backpack, "Get some rest, you have a big day tomorrow. If you would like, it is traditional to get your head shaved to sacrifice your vanity for simplicity".

Melony fidgeted, "Yes. I've already lost everything, I have nothing left to lose."

The nun looked at Melony, "You are wrong. You have much left to lose. You have gained a lot by losing what you consider everything. Now you are ready to accept this reality. Maybe in this reality your living, this is the last chance you think you have to do anything," then she walked out. Melony noticed the silence for the first time that evening. The words swirled around in her head and she whispered, "This is the last chance I have."

She sat down on the floor and ate her bread, for being such a small amount, it filled her. The food made her drowsy. She laid down and the silence helped her fall asleep.

Summer
Kansas City, Missouri

The vintage silver phone mounted on the wall rang.

"Liam! Paxton! Turn down volume so I can hear the phone," Summer yelled into the living room.

"Honey, have you been watching the news?" her husband, Wayne, asked.

She glanced around the wall that separated the kitchen from the living room. Their boys were now arguing over the video game controller.

"Haven't had the time," she said trying not to let her annoyance show. She had two rambunctious boys she home schooled, a small business, and a house to keep. Her husband might think she sat around all day eating bon-bons but the reality was she rarely had a spare moment until the boy's bedtime.

"You need to sit down," he said. she hesitated a moment but the tone of his voice convinced her that she needed to listen. She lowered herself into one of the kitchen chairs noting that there was a sticky spot on the tablecloth she'd need to deal with later. How could two children make such a mess?

"Scientists think that the world is going to end sometime today. They saw something in the sky. It's coming towards us," Wayne said.

Summer rolled her eyes.

"Seriously honey, I don't have time for-"

Wayne cut her off. "Summer, I'm serious. The streets are packed and I'm at least sixteen hours away. Call John. Have him come over and bring his gun. You might need protection if people start rioting in the streets."

"Why would they riot? What can they hope to gain if the world is ending today?" she asked.

"Please just do what I ask and don't argue with me," he said. She didn't appreciate the scolding in his voice. He was talking to her as if she was a child.

Her first instinct was to argue. They'd been doing a lot of that recently, but she decided against it. There was no point in arguing with him. Especially if what he said was true. How could it be true? How could the world be ending? How had she woken up this morning worried about the new math curriculum and the load of laundry she'd forgotten to transfer from the washer to the dryer the night before? Why hadn't she known, deep down in her soul, that today wasn't ordinary.

"Summer, you still there?" Wayne asked.

"I'll call John," she whispered.

"Good. I'm trying to make it home. I need to tell the boys I love them. In case I don't get there in time," Wayne said.

"Don't scare them," she said.

"I won't." he said.

"They'll know something is wrong if I let you talk to them. You call at night to say you love them. Not in the afternoon."

"Summer, I don't want to die half way across the continent and not be able to tell my boys I love them one last time," he snapped.

"Fine. Fine," she said.

"Liam, your dad wants to talk to you," she said.

"I'm almost done with this level. Give me five more minutes?" Liam asked.

"I know that game has a pause button," Summer called.

"Can't Paxton go first?" Liam asked.

"I don't care who goes first. One of you come to the phone. Now!" she said.

Paxton took the phone from her a moment later.

Summer

"Hi Daddy. Liam is at the boss. He's a big green snot monster. You'd like him," Paxton said.

Summer walked into the adjacent sunroom and dug through her purse until she found her cell phone.

She held up the phone, trying to find a signal. Cell phone reception in their house was spotty at best which is why Wayne insisted on having a landline even when most of the neighbors had already abandoned such ancient technology. She'd argued with him about the expense and the impracticality but Wayne won that battle.

"John, have you seen the news?" she asked when he answered.

"Yeah, I was trying to call you but it went straight to voicemail. Your other line was busy."

"Wayne is talking to the kids. He told me to ask you to come over and bring your gun, for protection. Do you really think we need that? You know how I feel about having guns in the house with the kids," she said.

"I think Wayne is right about this one," John said. "I'll be over in fifteen minutes."

"Mom, dad wants to talk to you," Liam shouted. Summer rolled her eyes again and then hurried to the kitchen. She grabbed the phone from her son, who headed back into the living room. She watched for a moment as Liam started the next level of his game. Neither of the boys seemed worried or upset. Relieved, she sat down at the kitchen table.

"I called John. He's on his way over," she said.

"Good. I'm glad. I wish I was there. It kills me that I'm so far away," he said.

"We'll be okay," Summer said. She decided not to mention that he was never home anyways. They were used to it. His trucking job meant he was gone five days a week. He missed holidays, anniversaries, and birthday parties. He'd been gone through fevers, chicken pox, and stomach viruses. She'd managed then and she'd manage now. She'd felt resentful the first few years but now she barely noticed his absence.

"Summer I-" Wayne started to say but before he could finish the line went dead.

~

John stood in front of the door to 529 Riverway Drive. It was a two-story home contemporary home with a beige exterior.

It was similar in appearance to his nearby home though notably larger.

He was surprised by the silence that greeted him. There were no elderly ladies walking poodles down the sidewalks nor toddlers on tricycles.

There were also no mobs of people terrified by the recent announcement on the news that the world was about to end.

He'd expected rioting but that was probably reserved for big cities. In this suburb, where everyone was middle class, conservative, and religious, the end of the world was being taken with quiet stoicism.

He supposed people were in their homes praying for God to save their lives and souls, but he hoped that some of them were cooking an amazing last meal or maybe having the most amazing orgasms of their lives.

It was how he thought one should spend their last hours. Not in fear or panic. He would be out enjoying his last day too if he wasn't at his brother's house trying to provide protection and comfort for his nephews and the only woman he'd ever really been in love with.

He opened the front door without knocking and Paxton and Liam ran to the door to greet him. They were smiling, clueless to the significance of the day.

Summer

"Uncle John, come see Liam's game," Paxton said. "He said I can play it next year 'cause I'll be old enough then."

Paxton was five and desperate to mimic everything his seven-year-old brother did.

John followed the boys through the foyer to the living room and sat down on the couch. He was glad utilities were still working here. In some places, they weren't.

Paxton and Liam sat on either side of him. Both boys looked just like he and Wayne had at that age. They were tall and gangly. The boys had dirty blond hair and gray eyes. They had inherited their father's poor vision and both boys had started wearing glasses before their third birthday.

Summer appeared with a tray filled with mugs of hot chocolate and a gigantic plastic pumpkin bowl left over from Halloween. The bowl was filled with popcorn. She sent him a smile that made his knees weak. It was quite the domestic scene. He couldn't help thinking it was the life that should have been his.

"This is great, Mom. You sure it is okay for us to skip our schoolwork today?"

"Dad said it was fine. He thought we could all use a vacation. School work will be there tomorrow," Summer said.

She was wearing a knit mint green sweater and jeans that sculpted to her body. Her chestnut hair was pulled back in a ponytail though a strand had fallen loose, and was hanging at her cheek.

"Yeah, dead presidents ain't getting any deader," Liam said.

"Aren't," John and Summer said in unison.

His eyes rose to hers and the look she gave him made his pulse quicken. It was a look of longing that had been shared again and again in quiet private moments.

Liam and Paxton, oblivious, were back to their game.

Suddenly, the television turned off to the kids' collective groans.

"What happened?" Liam asked.

"When I was a kid our school lost power for a whole day when a squirrel chewed some lines. Seen any squirrels around here?" John asked. Of course they'd seen squirrels in the neighborhood. The suburbs were filled with squirrels, robins, and yappy dogs. He missed life in the big city but he would have followed Summer to the ends of the earth. A few yipping mutts was a small price to pay to be able to join Summer and the boys for barbeques and fishing trips. To feel the warmth of her smile as she joked with him about Liam, Paxton, suburbia, and every other parts of her life. He felt sure he shared in much more of her life than Wayne did. His brother was gone all the time. Summer was left to run the house alone and care for the boys. He'd have never left her alone if she was his. He'd have found a job that allowed him to come home to her every night no matter what the job was. He'd spent more time with Summer in the five years than his brother had in his entire marriage. John pushed the thought away. All of them had made their choices.

"Wonder if it is that big gray one that lives out back," Liam mused.

"Well, if the air starts to smell like overcooked steaks it might be. What do you say we play Monopoly until the power comes back on?" John said.

Summer mouthed "thank you" and he felt a foolish grin overtake his face for a moment. He longed for the moments when he could be her knight in shining armor even when the deeds at hand were only as epic as suggesting a board game to the boys during a power outage.

Paxton disappeared and reappeared a moment later with the game.

"I want to be the car," Liam said.

Summer

"We'll be the dog," Paxton said taking Summer's hand. He wasn't quite old enough to play by himself so he rolled the dice while Summer handled the money and properties.

"I guess I'll be the thimble," John said taking the pieces out of the box. "And the banker."

John barely noticed the passing of time as they moved their pieces around the board. He didn't realize that dusk had fallen until Liam said "It's too dark to see the cards."

"Uncle Johnny is winning anyways," Paxton said with a yawn.

"How about we put the game away and then tell some ghost stories," John suggested.

"Just for little bit. I bet it's at least seven. I'm going to check the time and then find us some flashlights," Summer said.

"Can't we stay up since Uncle John is here?" Paxton asked.

"Nope. Bedtime at nine. If you don't get your sleep you are cranky in the mornings," Summer said disappearing into the kitchen.

"I'll be cranky if the electric isn't back on tomorrow. Why is it taking so long to fix the lines?" Liam asked.

"I'm sure it will be fixed by morning. If it isn't, I'll march straight over to the power company and give 'em what for," John said raising up his fists and punching the air. That sent the boys into fits of giggles. "Start cleaning this up while I go talk to your mom."

John stepped into the kitchen where Summer was looking out the window. His arms ached to reach out and pull her to him but he didn't dare.

He followed her gaze to the moon. A chunk of it was missing. Seeing the chunk of moon missing sent shivers down his spine. This was no false alarm. This wasn't Y2K or any of the other end of earth predictions. This was real and the missing chunk of moon was proof.

November 7th

"You got any power left on your cell?" John asked. He hadn't thought to charge his that morning. It was probably dead by now.

"I'm at ten percent," Summer said.

"Are you still able to connect to the network? I wondered if there was any news," John said.

"I'll check," Summer said.

Paxton peeked his head around the corner.

"Can Uncle John start the stories without you?"

"As long as they aren't too scary. I don't want the boys having nightmares tonight," she cast him a meaningful look before taking her phone into the sunroom.

John picked Paxton up and carried him back to the living room. Liam was messing with the wires of his gaming system as if plugging and unplugging it would work some magic.

"Have I ever told you about the ghost of cowboy Billy?" John asked giving the boys an evil grin. Cowboy and ghosts were their favorite things, next to video games. He immediately had their full attention.

~

Summer sank into the couch beside John and buried her face in her hand. She'd put on a brave face but now that the children were asleep, she wasn't sure she'd be able to hold herself together. Her boys weren't going to grow up. She was never going to have grandchildren. All her hopes and dreams would end tonight.

"I'm glad you're here. I wouldn't have wanted to do this alone," she whispered.

"Come here," he said pulling her against him. She nestled into his side with a sigh.

"Boys are asleep. It's a blessing that they'll miss the actual..." her voice trailed off. If the scientists were right, they didn't have long now.

Summer

She'd spent all day trying to give the boys the best last day possible. It had been a lovely day, all things considered. A lovely day with John by her side lending her his strength when hers faltered.

So much was unsaid between them. So much should remain unsaid.

"I was thinking about Orchard House today," she whispered. He drew in a breath and she almost wished she hadn't said anything.

Orchard House was a quaint little bed and breakfast on Cape Cod. Wayne had invited her there to meet his family. She'd ended up spending most of her time with John. There had been a moment in the garden. A moment where they'd stood too close to one another. Where they'd lost their senses. He leaned forward and their lips almost met. The yowling of a tabby cat broke the spell and snapped them back to reality.

"I think about it too. Almost every night," he whispered.

"Do you think we made the right choice?" she asked. They'd agreed to ignore their budding feelings for each other.

"I think we made the only choice," he said.

"If we'd given into our feelings-"

He cut her off. "Nothing would have changed."

"It might have. I might not have married Wayne."

"You'd have married him. The church was booked and the invitations sent. You needed the security of a husband and I wasn't at a place in my life where I could make that commitment. Wayne was," John said.

"I knew you were my soul mate. Even then." Summer swallowed the lump in her throat. She'd never admitted that to him before.

"I kept telling myself those feelings were just because I was rebounding from Vanessa. In hindsight, I can see I never really loved her."

"I loved Wayne. He was a good guy. Kind. Steadfast. Responsible."

"And nothing at all like you," John said.

"I didn't think any of that mattered. It shouldn't," she said.

"You married for stability. I understand that. Your life wasn't easy. I can't imagine growing up in foster care. Working nights as a waitress while you tried to go to college. My brother must have seemed like a godsend."

"I was scared," Summer admitted. "But that isn't an excuse."

"I don't fault you for that. My brother gave you a good life. A good home. You've got the boys. It didn't turn out so bad," his whisper tickled her earlobe.

"Except that every day I was wishing Wayne was someone else," she said. She still did. Sometimes, when the lights were off and her husband's lips were caressing her, she imagined Wayne was John.

In spite of being identical twins, John and Wayne, were polar opposites. They may have looked alike as boys but these days no one would mistake one for the other. Wayne's sedentary job and truck stop meals had added fifty pounds on him since their wedding day. Not that it looked bad. He and John had both been thin in their twenties. John wasn't the reed he'd once been either but he'd spent his free time at the gym and his body had filled out with sleek muscle.

Both John and Wayne were starting to bald. John kept his dark blond hair on the long side to cover his receding hairline while Wayne had started sporting a buzz cut the year Liam was born.

Both brothers wore glasses with almost identical frames that brought out the gray of their eyes.

In truth, she couldn't say one looked better than the other. She loved that Wayne took great care to keep his face clean shaven while John tended to have several days' worth of scruff. It was the most telling feature of their differences in personality.

Despite her husband's job as a truck driver, he took great care to look and act professional. People usually assumed he was an executive. No one would think that about John. His unkempt appearance and grungy choice in clothes mirrored his free-spirited personality.

John's sigh pulled her from her thoughts. He hugged her tighter as he spoke. "We'd have been a mess, you and me. Dreamers. I'd be down to my last dollar if it wasn't for luck."

"Not luck. You built a company. A thriving company."

"I stumbled upon an idea. I couldn't have done anything with it without my business partner. If he hadn't been there the business would never have gotten off the ground. The minute I could, I sold the company to the highest bidder," John said with a scoff.

"Because we moved here and you didn't want to live so far away from your twin brother," she said.

"That was a lie. I didn't want to live so far away from you."

Summer's heart was pounding. "Do you ever wonder if, in some parallel universe, we ran off together? Maybe right now we are sitting on a beach in Tahiti sipping Mai Tai's as we wait for the world to end."

"More like sitting outside a camper drinking beer," he said.

Summer's heart ached. She would trade everything she had, her whole beautiful life, to live in that camper with John.

No one understood her heart and soul like John did.

"Stop wishing for a crystal ball to show you what that life would be like. We made our choices and they were the right ones," he whispered.

"Tonight, we have the chance to make one last choice," she said leaning forward and pressing her lips to his.

Chris and Kriss
New York, New York

Chris slumped into a nearby chair after hearing the broadcast on the local news channel.

"The world is about to end, and I'm going to die, everyone is going to die, tomorrow," Chris said with despair.

He began to scroll through social media, looking to see what his friends were saying about the meteor strike that would wipe out the entire planet in less than 24 hours. Then he noticed a post from a woman who normally doesn't post all that often, his heart fluttered when he saw her profile picture.

"Kriss..." He said softly as his vision became slightly blurry.

Before he realized what he was doing, he noticed his fingers had begun to type out a private message to her. It read:

'Hey Kriss, I know we haven't talked since graduation, and we had to break up because you went off to college in Kentucky, but I still think about you. Hope you are doing well. Be safe, that meteor is coming to wipe us all out, if you're not too busy prepping for the end of the world, I'd like to see you one last time before the world ends.'

Chris hit the send button. He wasn't thinking clearly and he didn't expect a response. He proceeded to look at the posts on social media, most of which were his idiot friends from college, saying how they were going to rob a place or finally tell their boss what they think of them. Others were posting about the things they were going to be missing out on, one, in particular, was posting repeatedly about how he bought tickets to a concert and now he's going to miss it.

After a while Chris decided to divert his attention from social media and refocus on the real world. He walked out of the small coffee shop and walked solemnly back to his office. People were already rioting and forming gangs to revolt against society; one last defiant act before the end of the world. He reached the top floor, passed off his boss's coffee, and fell into his desk chair.

His phone buzzed in his pocket, he looked at it cheerfully, but he was soon disappointed when it was just junk mail coming to his email inbox. He put his phone down and pretended to work so his boss wouldn't come and bother him. About an hour later he decided to check his phone again, meaningless message after meaningless message, nothing of importance... then he noticed one at the very bottom of his screen, Kriss had replied to him.

He opened up the social media app on his phone and read her message.

'Heyyy! Chris! Hope you're doing well... aside from the world ending tomorrow... anyway, yes, I'd love to see you one last time. Let's meet up at that little diner we always used to go to after school when we were two broke high school kids and we couldn't afford anything other than a small piece of pie that we had to split. xD'

Chris chuckled to himself, and reread the message a few more times, savoring every word she had written, and hearing her voice in his head.

He couldn't focus on his work, not that anyone in his office was actually working anyway. He couldn't even focus on the end of the world. All he could think about was how much money he had in the bank compared to what he wanted to spend on Kriss. The numbers didn't match. He spent nearly an hour punching numbers into his calculator, none of which worked for what he had planned. He wasn't a wealthy man, but he certainly wasn't poor either, he just needed a small loan of a million dollars to make it all work.

He rose from his chair and wondered into his boss's office, and before he knew exactly what he was doing or what he was saying, he realized he had just quit his job. And his boss was very understanding about it all.

~

Chris walked through the crowded streets of New York. He arrived at the bank and applied for a loan. He gave his house and car to the bank and tried to take out a loan. The banker was in a hurry to get back home to her kids so she approved his loan request. Chris then made a few stops on his way to the diner.

Chris approached the diner and saw her through the window. Her hair was still dark brown with faint wisps of golden blonde when the sun shone on it in just the right way. His heart skipped a couple beats and he nearly dropped his bouquet of artfully chopped fruit. He still remembered how much she hated flowers.

He entered the tiny diner. It hadn't changed much since he was in high school, the same waitress still worked there, and she was as scary looking as ever.

"Hello Marge" Chris said.

The woman turned around and grunted in his direction, it sounded like she was asking "what will you have?" She looked like she recognized him but didn't care enough to chit chat. Chris didn't give her the chance anyway, he was a man on a mission, he approached the brunette from behind, hoping to surprise her.

Chris swallowed the lump in his throat and spoke her name. She turned abruptly and their eyes met for the first time in years. She got up and hugged him. Chris sank into her embrace like a person sinks into their bed after a long and horrible day of hard physical labor. She squeezed him tighter.

When they finally released each other's embrace Kriss said, "I've missed you so much!" Chris replied by presenting the bouquet of fruit to her. Her eyes lit up like

Christmas when she saw the colorful fruit, all her favorites, bright red strawberries, pink watermelon, green apple slices, yellow pineapple, vibrant orange slices, purple grapes, all arranged in a beautiful pattern. She couldn't look away from it, and he couldn't look away from her, both admiring the most beautiful thing in the world.

They sat at their booth in the diner that they had always sat in when they were in high school. Marge made her way over and slammed a coffee pot down in front of them. And took out a mangy notebook that was covered in bits of food and drinks   It looked as if she had dunked it into a cup of coffee at least twice.

"What'll it be?" She grunted irritably.

"We'll have the usual," both Chris and Kriss said simultaneously.

"Look here you two love birds!" She nearly choked on the words 'love birds' "I ain't got that good of'a memory no more, so yer gonna have'ta tell me what you want, or yer not getting nothin!" she grumbled.

"Oh, ok we'll have a piece of apple pie with ice cream on top please." Kriss said with an adorable smile, like a little kid given the responsibility to order for herself for the first time. Marge grumbled something under her breath and shuffled away.

When their pie finally came 20 minutes later the ice cream was melted horribly and the pie that was supposed to be hot was cold. Marge slammed it down in front of them like she was angry with them for even existing. Instead of complaining, they stared into each other's eyes and memorized the new features of one another's faces so they wouldn't forget each other in heaven when they died horribly the next day. They also informed each other about how their lives have changed since high school.

After a while of picking at their unsatisfactory pie, Marge returned,slammed the bill on the table, and said, "Alright y'all are makin' me sick with all yer googley eyes. Now get outta my diner. I got stuff I gotta do before this whole place goes kablam!"

She turned and muttered something to herself about a dealer. Chris placed a crisp hundred on the table and they walked out.

They held hands as they took a romantic walk through the chaos of the rioting streets. She noticed how his hand fit around hers, just like old times, and it made her smile despite the world losing its mind around them.

Chris opened a door to a restaurant and gestured for her to go through. She was greeted by a tall man wearing a nice white shirt, tie and a silk vest.

"Good afternoon, right this way."

The tall man led them to a small table in the back where a candle was lit on top of a clean white tablecloth. The man pulled out Kriss' chair and invited her to sit. She looked at Chris with confused excitement.

"How did you? Why is this place so empty? This place is impossible to get into, it's booked all the way out into next year." Chris cleared his throat and looked at her and smiled as he answered.

"I bought out the entire place." She looked around as if someone were listening in on their conversation.

"How did you get that much money?" Kriss asked.

"I took out a loan from the bank," Chris replied.

"I feel so under dressed, this place is so fancy," said Kriss.

"Hey! Waiter!" Chris gestured for the waiter to come back.

"Yes sir? What can I do for you?" The tall waiter asked politely.

"Could you fetch the young lady something a little more suitable to wear while we dine?" Chris said as he slipped the man a crisp hundred-dollar bill.

The waiter bowed and said, "Of course sir, I shall return shortly." The waiter ran into the back and disappeared behind the kitchen doors.

The waiter returned in minutes with a beautiful dress draped over his arms and gestured for Kriss to come and put it on. She changed in the bathroom and returned looking like an Olympian goddess. A blushing and embarrassed goddess. Chris could not take his eyes off of her. He nearly forgot to compliment her new look, but luckily the waiter nudged him and his trance was broken. He was able to pick his jaw up off the floor and tell her how beautiful she looked. The waiter popped open a bottle of champagne and poured two glasses.

"How did you manage all this?" Kriss asked as she sipped her champagne.

"The world treats you better when you have a stack of hundreds in your tuxedo jacket pocket," he said, as he gently patted his breast pocket. She looked at him sternly. She could see the outline of the stack of money.

"Did you rob a bank?" she asked pointing a finger at him. He studied her bright red polished fingertip for a moment as it quivered at him.

"No of course not, I did one better. The loan officer let me get a loan of a million dollars and then she wanted collateral so I sold my beat up car and my little apartment to the bank. She was in a hurry and wanted to get home to her family and when I told her what I had planned, her heart must have melted because she approved the loan. She stamped her approval on the paperwork and made it official." He tucked his napkin into his shirt collar so he wouldn't get food spilled on the expensive tie he was wearing.

The waiter returned and placed a pair of plates on the table in front of them, he removed the silver domes on top of the plates to reveal their steaming entrees, a glorious looking, but very small steak with a diminutive side dish and some edible plant that neither of them wanted to try. But it looked so good nestled up to the tiny bite of steak. Kriss didn't want to think about the cost of this meal.

They tried with surgical precision to cut their steak into even smaller pieces which were barely large enough to stick on the end of a fork but when they finally tasted it they were pleasantly surprised and delighted by the succulent symphony of flavors all mixing beautifully and dancing upon their tastebuds.

"This isn't going to be enough food," Chris said, looking down at his steak which was half gone already, then he glanced over at Kriss' plate which was empty save for the tiny serving of unknown vegetables. Kriss didn't want to say anything but she was still starving. Chris motioned for the waiter to come over.

"Is everything to your satisfaction sir?" the lanky waiter asked politely.

"No." Chris said, feigning anger, "we require more of this delicacy!" He slipped the waiter a few bills from his jacket.

"Of course, sir, they will be out momentarily. Please enjoy a bottle of wine in the meantime." He smiled and walked away briskly into the kitchen and returned shortly with a bottle of wine.

"So you robbed a bank?" Kriss said as though she was proud of him but simultaneously scolding him.

"No, I told you, I got a loan," Chris said defensively.

"That's what you say, but robbing a bank sounds so much cooler! You should say that instead! It's why I fell in love with you in high school," she said.

"Why? Because I robbed a bank?" he asked, slightly worried for her mental health.

"No, silly, because of your rebellious side." She looked him up and down, then said, "it seems like you've been hiding your rebellious side of yourself since high school. Expensive dinners and nice clothes are fun and all but let's actually have some fun!! The world is ending and people are rioting and fighting, they're forgetting how to live so let's spend the rest of our time on this god-forsaken planet living! And living to the fullest!" She thrust her fist into the air and stood up, one foot on her chair and the other on the table top nearly spilling her gross vegetables from her plate just as the waiter returned with a large tray of steaks, steaming with deliciousness.

"I see you've been enjoying the complementary wine." The waiter said as he casually brought over the tray of steaks and placed it down on their table with a gentle clatter.

Kriss hopped off the table and brushed some crumbs off her dress and re-sat herself and tried hard not to acknowledge her behavior, unfortunately for her, her face was so bright red that it was unmistakable that she just did something incredibly stupid. The waiter simply chuckled and nudged Chris.

"She's a keeper, never let her go," he said as he walked away.

Chris and Kriss looked at the minuscule steaks before them. They looked at each other. They both knew what would happen next but they attempted to be civilized, emphasis on 'attempted'. Chris tucked his napkin back in his shirt and Kriss tied her napkin around her neck in a pretty bow. Then they stared into each other's eyes like wolves staring down their prey about to strike. It was an intimate staring contest and when they blinked, they devoured their tiny steak dinners like a pair of wolves. It was a gruesome sight, steak sauce got everywhere.

After their feast they lifted their heads to find a horrific sight before them, their faces were smothered in dripping red and bits of meat. They burst into laughter and wiped their faces clean of their savage murder of their dinner. Chris threw down a stack of hundreds and walked out of the restaurant side-hugging Kriss and brandishing an unopened bottle of wine he had just plucked from the wine rack built into the wall of the establishment.

A cherry red Ferrari nearly crashed into them. The waiter got out.

"Sorry about that. It's got so much power!" he said with so much giddiness you'd have thought he was a school girl.

He tossed the keys to Chris who proceeded to get in the driver's seat while the waiter helped Kriss into the passenger seat. As soon as the waiter slammed the door they were off, speeding dangerously around the tight turns of New York and swerving once in a while to do a donut in the middle of an intersection. After getting too dizzy Chris stopped doing donuts in the car and just let it sit there for a moment, purring like a jungle cat.

"So, what were you saying about me not being rebellious anymore?" Chris asked with a broad toothy grin.

"I take it back, you haven't lost your rebellious side after all," she said as she attempted to do something with her hair after she had stuck her head out the window like a dog.

"Hey guess what!?" Chris said after a couple moments of looking into her dark sky-blue eyes that glinted gold from the store fronts that were ablaze from end-of-the-world rioting.

"What!?" She asked enthusiastically and hopped forward on her seat a little and looked into his eyes.

Chris waited, and didn't say a single word, he just smiled at her and watched the flames dance in her eyes. She was getting impatient. She wanted to know what he was thinking.

"I'll whisper it."

He said it so quietly that she had no other choice than to lean in to hear him, and in that moment, he leaned in and kissed her like his life depended on it. She smiled so hard, that it made it difficult to retaliate the kiss but she tried anyway.

Later they decided stop eating each other's faces and go on an adventure. Chris sped around the city in his fancy car and eventually pulled up to a high school, the high school where they had algebra together. The high school where they passed notes back and forth and got detention together for passing notes, and passed more notes during that detention. The same high school where they fell madly in love and went to prom together.

Chris got out of the car, opened the trunk, and pulled out a pair of backpacks. He slung one backpack over his shoulder and handed the other one to Kriss. She did the same and didn't question anything.

They walked in to the school building it was completely deserted. All the staff had left to attend the world-wide end-of-the-world party and by "that" I mean rioting in the streets. The school was completely abandoned. Chris marched straight into the principal's office, he knew the way by heart, he had been there too many times in his youth to forget the way. The name on the door hadn't changed, which meant he was 'justified' in what he was about to do.

He opened up the backpack and took out some cans of spray paint. He started making "enhancements" to the massive portrait of the principal. The portrait was enormous but it paled in comparison to the man's ego. Chris drew huge glasses over the portrait and a big curly mustache and goatee. Kriss burst out laughing at the addition to the portrait.

"I always hated that cranky old buzzard. But it's missing something," she said. She reached for the can of spray paint and began to draw. She positioned her body so Chris couldn't see what she was drawing, and after a moment she stepped aside to reveal a comically large bow tie on the portrait. Chris nearly fell over with laughter.

After defacing the face of their old principal, they trashed his office and moved on to trash the rest of the school. They also visited rooms where they had class together and reminisced about the good times they had. The rooms where they had good memories they left alone, everything else they trashed.

~

Later in the night, when they were done stomping on their old stomping grounds, they drove around the city again. They parked outside of a sky scraper. They rushed in and rode the elevator to the very top, where they took the exit out onto the roof. There was a helipad on the roof where a man waited for them, he was suited up with a parachute harness strapped to him.

"Are you love birds ready to take flight?" He said with an air of equanimity as he teetered on the ledge of the roof as the wind nearly blew him off.

"Why are we up here?" Kriss asked, hugging her shoulders as the chilling night air tickled her skin and made it goosebump.

"Oh! He didn't tell you!?" the man with the parachute answered. "Well, you certainty are in for a treat then!"

Chris was already putting on a harness. "We're parasailing off the building," he said. "You always wanted to go to someplace and go parasailing, didn't you?"

She shivered a little. "Well yeah, but I always imagined doing it someplace tropical, not on top of a roof in the middle of the night, freezing my face off."

"Don't worry, you'll be all right." Chris said with a puff of visible breath." She folded her arms and scoffed.

"Alright! You guys ready? It's time to go!" the man with parachute said.

Kriss checked her harness to make sure it hadn't fallen off, not that it would, it was way too tight. She was trembling, perhaps from the cold, or perhaps out of pure terror, or maybe it was excitement, she wasn't sure, all she knew was that the world was ending and she was going to jump off this roof top and if she died, at least she would have a choice in the matter.

Chris leaped off the ledge and plummeted several stories before opening his parachute. Kriss stepped up to the ledge, terrified of heights. The guy who helped them into their harnesses gave her a gentle push and shouted something about not forgetting to pull the cord, but she didn't hear him she was too busy screaming in terror and excitement.

After dropping for what felt like an hour, she pulled the cord. Her body lurched upward, a stark contrast from falling and she began to soar over the city. She could see Chris's parachute in front of her and she maneuvered herself so she was following him. She picked up the steering pretty quick.

Chris banked around the corner of a building and so did Kriss. Then he banked around another, she did the same. They flew around the skyscrapers of New York for what felt like hours or maybe it was days, no, couldn't have been days, that asteroid was going to hit in a matter of hours. Kriss didn't care about the end of the world anymore she just wanted to stay in the air. She noticed the feeling of pain in her cheeks, and realized that she had been smiling since she stepped off that ledge and her face hurt. All things in moderation, even smiling.

Chris banked around another building and she followed him and she saw a baseball stadium all lit up like Christmas. Her heart fluttered as she realized they were heading straight for it. Not only were they heading straight for the stadium but it looked as though they were going to land in the very center of the baseball field. With a little finesse of the controls, she managed to land directly on the pitching mound, right next to Chris.

Chris and Kriss

The guy who got them ready for their jump soared over the stadium and dropped something attached to a smaller parachute before flying over the stadium and out of sight. The package drifted down and landed in Chris's hands. It was a backpack. He opened it and pulled out a box of chocolates and a long stem rose and dropped to one knee. He held out a tiny box.

"Kriss, I know this has all happened so fast, but the world is ending and I want to spend what little time we have left together, I hope you feel the same way, will you marry me?"

Kriss took off her parachute harness and let it drop noisily to the ground. Tears streamed down her face, smearing her makeup. She tied to speak but the words hadn't caught up yet. She tried again to speak.

"Yes, yes, of course, I'll marry you! This has been the best day of my life. But you didn't have to organize all this crazy stuff to get me to say yes."

Chris slipped a massive ring on her finger, she could barely look at it, for it was reflecting the stadium lights so brightly that it looked as if it was giving off its own light.

"You're right, I didn't have to do all this, but I wanted to. And I got to do it with the most amazing girl in the world.

She kissed him. And kissed him again, and again. She barely came up for air and neither did he. They kissed for minutes, hours, centuries. After a while, they stopped kissing and Chris dug into the backpack again and pulled out a bottle of champagne, a red and white checkered tablecloth and a candle, and some sandwiches.

It was the perfect little picnic. It wasn't fancy, but it didn't need to be. They both loved the simplicity of the picnic of peanut butter and jelly sandwiches. Chris took all the ones that were just jelly and Kriss took all the peanut butter only sandwiches. Chris and Kriss belonged together like peanut butter and jelly.

They spent the rest of the night, the last night on earth, looking at the stars from the middle of a baseball stadium in New York, eating peanut butter and jelly sandwiches, respectively, and sipping champagne to celebrate their new engagement. They soon fell asleep and dreamt of a complete life together, a life that the asteroid would soon take from them.

Birdie

Idyllwild, CA

The utility closet was cramped, with just enough room for Birdie and Mary to squeeze in among the mops and cleaning products. They hugged each other and listened for any noise that would tell them what was going on outside. Joe, Mary's husband and owner of the small hardware store, was investigating the sound of breaking glass that had come from the back of the store.

A soft, patterned knock on the closet door let them know the coast was clear.

"It was just some young kids. Threw a brick through the back window. I ran 'em off, but they could come back with friends," Joe said.

"Oh, my word," Mary said, wringing her hands. She started to cry again, and Birdie wrapped her arm around the older woman's shoulders.

"It will be okay, Mary. We'll get through this." Birdie heard herself saying the words but wondered if she was telling the truth. Joe set to work, grabbing a hammer, nails, and a piece of wood.

"I'm going to go secure that back window. Stay put," he said gruffly.

As Birdie tried to calm Mary down, she thought herself lucky to be at work when the news reports broke. If there was anyone to face the end of the world with, it would be Joe. He was in great shape for a man in his late fifties, throwing cords of wood around like they weighed nothing. His craggy face and weathered skin reminded Birdie of the guys in old western movies. She remembered being intimidated by him when she interviewed for the cashier job six months ago, but Mary had made quick work of setting her mind at ease.

"Don't you let him get under your skin, sweetheart. He barks a lot, but he's just a big ole' teddy bear once you get past that bulldog exterior", Mary had told her.

Joe returned from the back, dropped the hammer on the counter, and reached underneath a bottom shelf. He pulled out a pistol and quickly tucked it in the back of his waistband.

"Shouldn't we just...go. I mean, if nothings gonna be here and we're all going to...", Mary said tearfully.

Joe cut her off mid-sentence.

"We don't know that, Mary. Somebody probably got some math wrong somewhere. There's just no way that dark matter - stuff we've never even heard of - is gonna wipe out the entire damn planet."

Birdie remained quiet. She was still trying to process the news reports from this morning. They'd listened intently, gathered around a small radio, as a prominent morning newscaster delivered the unbelievable news. In a disconnected haze, Birdie had only processed a fraction of what was said. Words like "matter previously undetected," "extinction event," and "martial law" still didn't seem real. They had thought it was a prank at first. But the calendar date was November 7th, not April 1st.

The power suddenly went off, and Mary tensed under Birdie's arm. It was still early enough in the day that they had plenty of light to see, but in absence of the hum of the A/C unit and background radio chatter, it felt unsettling. Gooseflesh rippled over her body and her sense of hearing heightened, preparing her body for a fight-or-flight response.

"Stay put," Joe whispered and put his hand up in caution. He crept to the front door and looked down the street in both directions. "Looks like everything on the street is off."

In the space of a moment, just long enough for him to add, "It looks fairly calm on the street...", the front of the shop exploded inward as a truck crashed through the window. Joe turned and leapt toward the women, driving his shoulder into Birdie's midsection, and sending them crashing backward against the door of the utility closet.

Birdie came to rest on top of Mary, who was gasping to catch her breath from the having the wind knocked out of her. Birdie coughed, dust and debris clouded around their heads, and she rolled to her side. She raised herself up on her elbow and hovered above Mary's face.

"It's okay, Mary. Try to take deep breaths. Are you hurt?" she asked, wiping tears and dirt from Mary's face with her shirt sleeve. Mary took a few more hard swallows of air and began to gain control of her breathing again. She nodded her head and was able to speak through the last of the spasms, "I'm...okay."

Joe was already standing and had positioned himself in front of the two women. In his hand, his pistol had been retrieved from his waistband and was now pointed at the truck's occupants.

"You've got the expanse of one full second to back that truck up and get the fuck out of my store." he yelled.

The dust from the crash was settling and Birdie could see that two men occupied the truck. They were dressed in camo shirts and ball caps with black stripes painted under their eyes. In the blink of an eye, the passenger of the truck raised and fired a shotgun, and the display case to the right of them exploded from the blast. Joe fired multiple rounds into the truck and hit the ground.

Birdie squeezed her eyes shut and covered Mary with her body. What was likely no more than thirty seconds, she thought felt like an eternity. No other shots were fired, and she heard no movement. She dared a look over her shoulder and saw Joe, face down, unmoving on the floor. No sounds came from the truck. Birdie slowly sat up and saw the driver slumped over the wheel and the passenger slouched against the truck door. The eyes of both men were fixed and wide in permanent stares.

Birdie crawled to Joe and turned him over. His right side was covered in blood and his lips were white.

"Oh God, Joe! Honey, please. No!" Mary scrambled over to them, sobbing, and cradled Joe's head in her lap.

Birdie took off her flannel and balled it up to try to stop the bleeding on Joe's side.

"Hold this here, Mary," said Birdie, firmly planting Mary's hand on the flannel in place of her own. Birdie ran to the back where she knew Joe kept a first-aid kit. By the time she returned, Mary was violently shaking her head back and forth, and she'd removed the flannel from Joe's side.

"Mary, keep the flannel on his..."

"He's gone, Birdie. He's not breathing... and there's no blood pumping," Mary said, holding the balled flannel up in her shaking hand as if it held the proof. Still cradling his head with her other hand, she bent her mouth to his and kissed his lifeless lips.

Birdie watched Mary's expression change from anguish to panicked determination as she leveled her gaze and turned her head to look at Birdie.

"You need to get out of here. Our truck is parked out back," she wiped her eyes on her shoulders and sniffed. "Go up into the mountains. It's where Joe always talked about going if hell broke loose, and I'm pretty sure that Hell is loose now. There're some supplies under the seats, jerky and matches and stuff. It should hold you for a while."

"I'm not gonna leave you, Mary. I know it's hard, but you need to come with me."

"No!" she yelled, startling Birdie. She'd never heard Mary raise her voice before. "I need you to respect my wishes right now and not question me. I've loved this man for thirty-eight years. I will not leave him." She nodded her head toward the truck. "Go get the shotgun from the truck, and you leave Joe's gun with me for protection. I'll be fine."

Birdie obeyed and carefully walked around to the passenger's side of the truck. She tried not to look at the dead men's faces. Her hands were shaking as she reached through the window and grabbed the barrel of the shotgun, resting between the passenger's legs. She opened the glove compartment and found a box of shells.

Walking back around the truck, she could see that Mary had removed the pistol from Joe's hand, and now tightly gripped it in her own. With her free hand, she was mindlessly stroking the hair on his temple, staring expressionless into an unseen void.

"Mary, please...", Birdie whispered.

"Go. Now." Mary sat, still staring, and did not look at her.

Birdie knew she could not convince Mary to leave Joe, and there was no way she would be able to carry the woman out kicking and screaming. Birdie scrambled over the debris to the back of the store. She grabbed the keys to the truck from the hook and removed the metal bar that Joe had used to barricade the door. She paused, hoping she would hear Mary tell her to wait and that she'd changed her mind. Instead, she heard a single shot, confirming the sinking feeling that had been growing in the pit of her stomach since Mary had asked for the gun.

Sobbing uncontrollably, she threw open the back door and jumped in the truck. The truck was older, but the engine roared to life immediately and she shifted into gear harder than necessary. She pushed the gas pedal all the way to the floor and sped down the narrow alley, hitting several trash bins in the process. She took a hard left onto the main road, narrowly missing several cars and two women fist fighting in the street.

The town looked like a scene from a disaster movie. Once, the year before her parents died, they took a family trip to Universal Studios and Birdie had been excited and terrified to see a fake town seemingly blown to bits, set on fire, and flooded, then put back together to do it all over again. But this was not a movie set. The fires, cars abandoned in the street, and the people wandering aimlessly in shock would not be re-set for another take.

Her focus shifted back to trying to figure out how to get up into the mountains. Trying to stop at her apartment for supplies was not a risk worth taking. She didn't need much of anything if there were only a few hours left anyway. If she could find a quiet spot, hidden among the trees, and maybe watch first-hand as the night sky lit up in a fatal, celestial display, it wouldn't be a bad way to go. With her parents gone, and no real extended family that she was close with, she felt no panic to finish any unresolved business, or rush to hold someone close. She only wanted to get safely away from people and the rising violence.

~

She drove until the main road ended, randomly picked a direction, then drove until that road ended too. She drove for a while, mindlessly taking any road that seemed to go in the direction of the mountains and that might take her farther upward and away from town. It was now late afternoon, and the sun blinded her as it broke through the trees. She thought of Joe and Mary and fought to see the road ahead through fresh tears. She thought of her parents and said a silent prayer of gratitude that they were taken instantly, without suffering, in a car accident all those years ago. She thought of her ex-boyfriend, who'd moved to Kentucky to escape the assault charges Birdie had filed and hoped somehow that Karma would be busy collecting debts in these final hours.

Birdie

The road turned to gravel, and the sun was considerably lower in the sky when she finally stopped. The ground was now covered in a light dusting of snow and the tip of her nose had turned cold. She thought the light sweater she put on this morning was not going to cut it for a night on a cold mountain, even if it was just a few hours, and the truck did not have a working heater. Her stomach growled loudly, and she remembered that Mary said there were some supplies under the seat. She looked for a place to pull the truck off, out of sight from the main road. Ahead, the faint outline of road wound through the trees. She inched the truck forward and could see that it curved right, disappearing behind a thick grove.

She drove a few hundred feet, around another turn, and found herself in front of a small gray house with white shutters. Ivy crept through a trellis and up a brick chimney, which was absent of smoke. Birdie stopped the truck and blinked at the sight. It looked like something out of a fairy tale. There were no cars in the driveway, and a detached garage to the back left of the house was closed. There were no lights on inside the house.

Birdie parked the truck, left it unlocked, and pocketed the keys. She watched the house for any movement, but it remained quiet and still. Someone surely would've heard her pull up, she thought. "There could be people inside, just as afraid of me as I am of them," she whispered to herself. But the house looked wonderful. So peaceful. And warm.

She wondered if she should just walk up to the front door and knock. Would she get a shotgun pointed in her face? Maybe the people that lived here were decent folk and they would invite her in, offer her a cup of coffee. She would recount the terror of the morning to them while they played card games and patiently waited for the end of the world.

What were the chances that someone would even be home at this point? Maybe they rushed to be somewhere else with family and they weren't coming back. And if they did come home, could she really get in trouble for breaking and entering when the world was going to end? At most, maybe she would offer her apologies, ask for a warmer coat, and get back in the truck to drive further up into the mountains.

She could put a note on the door to make sure someone knew she was there and that she meant no harm. If someone did return, she certainly didn't want to surprise them. And vice versa. Birdie thought about how she would introduce herself. "Hi, my name is Goldilocks. I would just like a bit of porridge and a chair that's just right. And if you're an evil witch that's made this beautiful house out of gingerbread, please make it quick and as painless as possible before you grind my bones for flour." Birdie was pretty sure she was mixing fables at this point, but it was hard to think with her heart hammering in her chest as she walked toward the house.

She walked around the side of the house to look for someone in the back yard. It was possible that whoever lived here didn't even know what was going on. If they hadn't turned a T.V. on, or didn't get cell service up here, they might be gardening or reading a book without a care in the world as society collapsed around them. She looked through a window and saw an elegant - and empty - kitchen and dining room. Looking though several more windows, she saw a cozy living room and a little library. All the rooms seemed quiet and empty. A sliding door at the back of the house was slid halfway open. She tried the screen and it too was open. It moved soundlessly as Birdie slid it aside. Birdie called out, "Hello? Is anyone home?"

No response.

She tried again. "Hello? I mean no harm!"

Birdie entered and made her way cautiously through the kitchen and living room, calling out as she went. She held the truck keys in her hand, a key sticking out of her clenched fist, just in case someone decided to surprise her. They might get the better of her, but she would at least go down after delivering the key into an eyeball or two. No one in the living room or half bath on the right side of the house. To the left, a small hallway proved the laundry and library were empty as well.

She made her way to the second floor. Most of the doors were open so it was easy to take a cautious and quick peek in them. No one in what looked like a guest bedroom, or the tidy bathroom with the big beautiful claw foot tub. Birdie had paused briefly to imagine the luxurious baths the lucky lady of the house probably enjoyed. She thought of her apartment and the tiny shower with the rotting shower head that she kept asking the landlord to replace. Money made things easier. And provided better bathing options. At the end of the hall, the door was closed. Birdie decided that it must be the master bedroom. She knocked lightly and slowly opened the door.

Birdie felt the color drain from her face.

In the center of the room on top of a beautiful four-poster bed, there lay a very pale, very still woman wearing a long, yellow silk dress. But she was not just very pale. She was very dead. Birdie walked slowly to the end of the bed. She tried hard not to look at the woman's face but couldn't help noticing that she was beautiful. Ivory skin, and a dark neat bob that ended just below her ears. She had no jewelry, but a slim gold band was on the nightstand beside the bed. Also, on the nightstand, an empty pill bottle and a letter. Pretty stationary dotted with little sparrows and periwinkles, and a flowing feminine script:

Dear James,
I know you're on your way here now. I didn't answer the phone, because I didn't know what to say, and if you knew what I was about to do, you would've probably stayed

in the city and made someone miserable in their final hours. It's my hope that by the time you get here, it will be too late for you to make it anywhere else. They're calling it an extinction event. I don't feel panic. I just know that I don't want to spend my last few hours in tears or fearfully looking toward the sky. And I certainly don't want to spend them in your company. I have spent too much time crying and feeling helpless. You've tried to convince me all these years that I am weak, and I can't do anything. I've allowed you to make me your prisoner, catering to your whims and selfish desires. Now, I am in control. I am at peace and I am in the place I loved most in this world. I do want to thank you for Sparrow House. My "silly nature retreat" as you call it. More and more, as you spent those late nights at "work," you didn't seem to mind my extended stays up here, and I was grateful not to have to stay in the city, suffocating under you and the smog.

Now that the world is ending it seems pointless to tell you, but I do wish I could've seen the shock on your face when my attorney delivered divorce papers to you next month. I think you always thought I would be content to be your dutiful, perfect, trophy wife. Up here on this mountain I felt so free, surrounded by nature, finally getting to know who I am. I only wish I would've done it sooner. But now, I'll be truly free. I am not afraid of what comes next. I welcome it with open arms.

- Harper

Birdie exhaled when she'd finished reading the letter. So where was this James? The woman, Harper, has been dead for at least a few hours. Dead bodies did not bother Birdie. What bothered her about this dead body was what, if anything, she should do with her. Did she bury her? Should she leave?

Birdie

Birdie didn't have time to make a decision, because - as if on cue - she heard the skid of tires outside in the gravel driveway. She went to the bedroom window and watched as a man opened the door of a silver Porsche, with what looked like fresh front-end damage. He got out of the car, nearly falling out onto the driveway in the process. An empty bottle of liquor dangled from his left hand. Birdie thought this looked like trouble and decided she should not be in the same room with what was most likely this man's dead wife.

Birdie hurried out of the bedroom and downstairs to the living room, just as the man came stumbling through the front door. He was well dressed, in suit pants and white collared shirt that was half tucked in, arm sleeves rolled up to the elbows and shiny black shoes.

"Who in the hell are you?"

"I'm really sorry."

"That's a funny name. Now, why in the hell are you in my house? Where's Harper?", he slurred and squinted to focus.

"I didn't think anyone was here."

She was stalling. She wasn't ready to tell this very drunk man that his wife, Harper, was dead.

"I'm losing patience very quickly. You don't want to see me lose my patience. I suggest you answer my question now. Where. The. Hell. Is. My. Wife?" The word "wife" was spoken like a cuss word and said as he slowly withdrew a gun from the back of his waistband and pointed it at Birdie. She knew enough about guns that she could tell the safety was off. Did this man really have a loaded gun in his waistband - with the safety off? This man was either stupid or unhinged. Birdie thought the safe bet was on the latter.

This man was not going to be calm or reasonable when he discovered that his wife was dead. She needed to get to her truck and get out of here as quickly as possible. Any sane person could figure out that she had nothing to do with what this Harper had done, but people weren't acting sane now, even the sober ones. She didn't want to give this man the opportunity to take out some last frustrations on the closet target. She tried to calm him down by distracting him.

"I know where your wife is. It's James isn't it? Look James, I was driving up the mountain to get out of the city and stopped at your house. I thought maybe whoever lived here had abandoned it to go be with family. I was just looking for a safe place to stay." His shoulders dropped a little and he lowered the gun.

"Nowhere is safe. Where is my wife?", he asked softly.

"Your wife is in the bedroom sir."

"You're going to go with me and find her."

"I don't want to do that. I would like to just go to my truck now and drive away. You'll never see me again."

"My wife is not within sight and you're a stranger in my house. Do you really think I'm letting you leave until I figure out what the hell is going on?" He smirked. "Now... move."

James grabbed Birdie by the arm and pressed the gun into her shoulder blade. They walked to the stairs and Birdie used the time to try to prepare him for what he was about to see. "Look things are pretty crazy right now. I don't know if the news reports are for real or what, but I really don't mean you or your wife harm and I just want to live out whatever time we have left in peace."

James snorted and stumbled a bit on the top stair, "The world deserves what it gets. There is no mercy or peace..." he trailed off. They reached the end of the hall and Birdie expected him to stop and fear what was behind the closed door as she had, but instead he kicked his foot out beside her to slam the bedroom door open.

He took just a moment to survey the scene and fix his eyes on Harper in the bed.

Birdie

"Christ Harper. Are you kidding me?", he threw his head back and exhaled.

"She left a letter on the nightstand." Birdie offered.

He crossed the room in large angry strides and snatched the letter up. He read quickly, skimmed it really, and angrily crumpled it up in a ball. A stream of cuss words made Birdie cringe as he threw the wadded letter across the room. This was not the reaction she expected out of someone who just found out his wife had committed suicide and whose body lay right next to where he stood. What kind of asshole was this guy? James inhaled sharply through his nose and hissed and exhale. "Well now what the hell to do, hm?" His tone was mocking, and he was waving the gun around as he spoke. "I busted ass to get out of the city and up this stupid mountain, to this stupid cottage, to this stupid woman. I figured I'd been spending so much time with my mistress lately - who decided to be with her stupid family - and Harper would be alone up here. But she didn't even want me here anyway! I would've been better off in the apartment, drinking Johnny Walker, and look down on the city killing itself." He was rambling now.

Birdie shifted slightly, and he snapped his attention back to her, as if he was just remembering that she was there.

"Where you here when she...did this?" he asked her, waving the gun toward Harper's body.

"No. I got here maybe fifteen minutes before you did. It looks like she's been...gone for a few hours." Birdie paused, then offered, "She's very beautiful." She hoped to ease James into a better state of mind, get him to let his guard down so she could maybe make a run for it. But he was smart, and apparently bored or restless because he suddenly straightened and leveled his stare. He now looked at Birdie like a predator that just discovered prey.

"Yes, she is. People like you want to be like her. Don't you?" He walked slowly over to Birdie and put the point of the gun under her chin. "You're not bad. A trip to the salon, maybe dress you up in something that didn't come from a thrift shop. You'd pass." He looked her up and down.

Birdie's senses began to heighten as her adrenaline kicked into high gear. She knew something had shifted in him. Something cold and incredibly dangerous.

"Please. Just let me go. I'm really sorry about your wife. About coming into your house."

"Let's get out of this depressing room and let Harper sleep, shall we? We're gonna go downstairs and have ourselves a nice drink."

Birdie was grateful to get out of the room and didn't need to wait for him to stick the gun in her back to do it. She quickly made it to the stairs and hesitated at the top. Could she throw him down? No, not with a loaded gun in his hand. Earth might be obliterated soon, but Birdie was sure she did not want to be shot.

James pushed her into the living room and Birdie sat down in an overstuffed chair. James put the gun back in his waistband and pulled a bottle of vodka from a glass cabinet. He set the bottle and two glasses on a coffee table and sat on the sofa opposite Birdie. He looked around the room and said, "Damn. This room is a nightmare. Farm chic throw up that women seem to love nowadays." He laughed. He poured vodka into both glasses and slid one toward Birdie.

"You look like I need a drink." He laughed again.

"No, thank you." Birdie said.

"It wasn't a question sweetheart. You aren't worried about your health, are you?" He laughed even harder.

Birdie took a sip of the drink and coughed. James snorted and downed his drink in one gulp. Maybe she could just wait him out and he will pass out.

"What's your name, honey?" He asked without looking up as he poured himself another drink.

Birdie

"Birdie. Jen...Jennifer Byrd. People call me Birdie though."

"Birdie? Alright, Birdie. Drink up."

She took another small sip and he downed his again. The sun was going down. Birdie wondered how much time they had left and if the news reports were saying anything new.

"Do you have a T.V. or a radio or something? Maybe we can find out if there's any new information about what's going on."

"I don't give a shit about what's going on. We're all going to die. What more do you need to know?"

"I don't know. Maybe how much time we have."

"That's just it Birdie. Do we ever really know how much time we have?" He was getting loud again. "I mean, we spend our lives doing what others expect us to do, being the way that others expect us to be, and for what!? Are we ever really doing what WE WANT TO DO?" He slammed his glass down on the table.

Birdie went very still and didn't make a sound. He had escalated very quickly, and Birdie decided not to partici-pate in conversation with him anymore. This time he didn't even bother to pour the drink. He took several big gulps directly from the bottle.

"I have to piss." He looked at Birdie and looked around the room. He giggled and rose unsteadily. He pulled the gun out of his waistband and put it on the coffee table. It was too far away for her to make a grab for it. He slowly walked around the table to stand in front of Birdie and unzipped his pants. Birdie pushed herself back into the chair and turned her head as James urinated on her lap. Birdie gagged, which made James laugh even harder.

He said, "You see Birdie? There are people that get pissed on, and people that do the pissing. Now, the universe is taking a big ole' healthy piss on the Earth. There is no escaping the laws of nature." He took a step back and zipped his pants. Birdie looked him straight in the eye.

"Mister, I don't know what your problem is, but I told you I was looking for a safe place to wait out the rest of our lives. I don't want any trouble with you, but you better think twice before you do something like that again."

"Oooooh. There it is. Little Miss Thrift Shop has a little fire in her shorts! That's something Harper never had. She was weak. Let me smack her around and never said a word back. Pathetic." He plopped down on the sofa and took another gulp from the bottle, which was nearly gone.

Birdie thought about her ex-boyfriend. He had smacked her around too, but when Birdie tried to defend herself, it always got her smacked around more. Harper had not defended herself, and it had still taken a toll.

"Aw shucks, Thrift Shop! Don't you wanna have a little fun? I have a little blow in the car if you need something to help you get in the spirit." He laid his head back on the sofa and pinched the bridge of his nose.

Birdie seized the opportunity and lunged forward to grab the gun on the coffee table. The movement startled James, whose reflexes were almost non-functional at this point. He tried to reach for her but ended up on the floor between the coffee table and the sofa. Birdie pointed the gun at his head.

"Now... you're going to listen to me, you worthless piece of shit!" Birdie hissed. "I told you I just want to go to my truck and get the hell out of here. I'm going to do that, and you're going to stay right there until you don't hear the engine anymore. Got it?"

James was laughing and pushed himself up to sit on the sofa again. All he could manage was to halfway sit on the edge, leaning on his elbow. He kept laughing and a string of drool fell out of the corner of his mouth.

Birdie

In that moment, Birdie thought of Harper laying cold in her bed. Birdie understood why Harper was intent on killing herself before James arrived. Who knew what he would've subjected her to? Running away wasn't an option. Where would she have gone? And Sparrow House was her most favorite place to be. Birdie understood completely. She'd lived with a monster too. But she had survived and lived long enough to be happy again.

"You know, I think I've decided to stay awhile."

James slowed his laugh to a low giggle. "Ahh, Thrift Shop is warming to me! Yes, well I can imagine that even in my current state, I'm a better caliber man than you've had. I'll make you pay for your insolence though."

"James, I really think it's time that you pay."

Birdie relaxed her grip and fired a shot into his knee.

"Arrghh! What the FUCK!?" James doubled over, clutching his knee. He tried to leverage his good leg to lunge at Birdie, but she was standing, and he was sitting, so she used the advantage to kick him in the face. The blow landed, breaking his nose with a satisfying crunch.

"You BITCH!!" He screamed, holding his face.

"Well James, there are those that get kicked in the face, and there are those who do the kicking."

Birdie was outside of herself now. She watched as her hands raised the gun and pointed it at James' chest.

"Men like you don't deserve the love of a woman. You don't know what a gift it is. You behave badly and suffer no consequence. We're a shell of ourselves, believing the lies you've told us, before we realize how much time we've wasted holding on to hope." Tears rolling down her cheeks, she continued as he wiped his mouth of the blood dripping from his nose.

"This morning, I watched a beautiful couple die because of monsters like you. You tell me WHY YOU GET TO WIN!!?? They loved each other? so much and they were robbed of spending their last hours in peace together! YOU DON'T GET TO WIN ANYMORE!!" She screamed and took a step toward him, causing him to sink back into the couch cushions. His face was white with fear and Birdie found it very satisfying.

She squeezed the trigger and smiled at the look of shock on James' face as he looked down and discovered the hole in his chest. She met his eyes and did not look away, even as they looked to the distance and emptied.

She didn't know how long she stood there watching him, but she slowly became aware of her breathing and that the gun was still in her shaking hand. She ran to the kitchen, threw open the back door, and dry-heaved at the ground, her stomach empty from not having eaten all day. She hid the gun in a flower pot on the deck. She didn't know why she was hiding it but felt better now that it was out of sight.

She walked back into the living room and stared at James' body. He had not moved. He was still dead. She went upstairs and entered the master bedroom. She stood over Harper's body and whispered an apology.

"I'm so sorry about what he did to you. I know how it feels. It never goes away, but sometimes you can find a little piece of happiness where you can. I think you had that here in this house, but you deserved so much more. I know it might not matter now, but hopefully you're somewhere where you know what I've done for you. I made him pay, even if it was just for a few moments. But he paid." Birdie left the room and closed the door.

Birdie went to the guest bedroom and found a small T.V. on the dresser. She turned it on, but every channel was broadcasting the same robotic message on a loop,

"Earth is facing an imminent extinction event. Please refrain from violence to ensure all citizens of the world can enjoy peace and order in these final hours."

Birdie

Since the initial report that morning she had listened to with Mary and Joe at the store, so much had happened that Birdie had not even really processed the news. The realization slammed into her chest and it felt like she couldn't breathe. All life was going to end? How was that possible? She had always thought she would die in a nursing home somewhere. But what happens now? Would she see or feel anything? It seemed like days since she'd gone to work this morning and listened to Mary and Joe's playful banter, but it had only been eight hours. It was crazy to think that she'd stocked shelves and taken out the trash after breakfast, then murdered a man by dinner time. She thought about James, oozing blood on the sofa downstairs. Yes, he was a monster. But, she could've gotten away after she shot him in the knee. Hell, he'd been so drunk she probably could've outrun him the moment she picked up the gun. But something made her stay. Was it because she knew in the back of her mind that there would be no consequences? Would she still have done what she did if the world was not coming to an end?

She had no idea how long she sat in the bedroom, but it was completely dark by the time she noticed. She stood up and felt her body protest with the movement after being still for so long. She had run on nothing but adrenaline all day and her stomach now hurt with hunger pangs. She also realized that although they had dried, she was wearing clothes covered in piss.

She went downstairs and paused in the doorway to the living room. "James, you're really ruining the decor in here. And I happen to like farm chic throw-up." She grabbed a blanket draped across the ottoman and covered his body with it.

She made her way into the kitchen, found a bottle of sweet red wine in a rack above the fridge, a glass, and bottle opener. Filling her glass, she leaned against the counter and looked around. Harper kept the kitchen tidy and organized.

November 7th

Everything placed precisely where you think it would be. Her own kitchen, albeit very tiny, had been organized and pristine, so Birdie understood. When you don't have control of your circumstances, at least you can have control of your cupboards. She downed the glass of wine and opened the fridge to find something to eat. The fridge was well stocked. A testament to how much time Harper really spent here. She grabbed a package of cold cuts and some grapes, refilled her glass and went upstairs.

The guest bathroom was done in soft, powder-blue decor and contained a huge claw-foot tub and shower combo. Birdie thought it looked like a spa or something from a magazine. Eating a few slices of the cold cuts, she took a few big gulps of wine, and set everything on the bathroom counter. Avoiding the master bedroom, she went to the guest room closet in search of clothing. Harper was a considerate hostess, leaving a fluffy robe hanging on the back of the closet door and an assortment of soaps and lotions in a basket on the shelf for guests. Birdie took some soap and the robe and shed her soiled clothing.

She turned the shower on as hot as she could stand it and let it beat down on her sore muscles until it turned cold. She felt considerably better stepping out of the shower and was pleasantly warm and fuzzy from the wine. She slipped into the robe and noticed that her hands were still shaking as she wiped the fog from the mirror.

She had no idea how much time was left but was curious what the night sky might look like for a doomed planet. She grabbed her glass, a few more slices of the cold cuts, and quickly headed downstairs. She stopped to grab the half-empty bottle of wine from the kitchen and slipped on a pair of Harper's rain boots by door to the backyard. She peeked her head out and looked around. Surveying the back yard for danger, she thought it unlikely that anyone would investigate even if they did hear the gunshots, but she didn't want to take any chances.

Solar ground lights lit the yard with a soft yellow glow and ended at a tree line several hundred feet back. To her right, a few bird houses and a fire pit led the way to a gazebo with a hot tub. To her left, a huge hammock hung between two enormous oak trees. It was eerily silent. Too quiet. No symphony of crickets, no rustle of raccoons scrounging for food, and no wind blew through the trees.

She sat in the hammock, poured another glass of wine, and set the bottle on the ground underneath her. The hammock gently swayed from the movement, and Birdie lay back in its embrace. The moon shone high and bright in the empty, black sky. She couldn't tell if the stars were covered by clouds or if they were gone, devoured by the mysterious dark matter.

She was startled by a bright flash of light in the sky and dropped her glass on the ground, shattering it. From the right side of the moon, a silent explosion of fireballs sprayed out across the sky like shooting stars. Only they were much larger than any shooting stars that she'd had ever seen. Well, this is it, Birdie thought. It was actually kind of beautiful.

An earthquake shook the ground violently. Normally, she knew that sitting beneath a tree was not the place to be in an earthquake, but there was no safe place to be now. She grabbed the bottle of wine and stumbled to the center of the yard. She threw open her robe and spread her arms to the sky.

"WELCOME TO EARTH, YOU CHUNKS OF SPACE SHIT! I HOPE YOU CHOKE ON THE ROCKY MOUNTAINS, AND WHILE YOUR AT IT, WHY DON'T YOU GO AHEAD AND KISS MY ASTEROID!!" she said, screaming at the top of her lungs. Then everything went dark.

Scott O'Neil
Spacecraft Freedom

A terrifying series of clangs resounded through the airlock. For Commander Scott O'Neil, it was another spacewalk in a long chain of spacewalks. Repeated trips into the void had numbed him to the novelty of weightlessness, of putting clumsy, gloved hands onto handrails and hoisting himself out into the void.

He imagined himself floating off into space, tearful goodbyes from his family crackling into his earpiece as he drifted into oblivion, losing consciousness from lack of clean air, the eyes of a million stars watching without pity or compassion. Now as he tethered himself in, ready for long hours in his spacesuit, he reflected on the strangeness of life, how the human mind can adapt to any situation, so that even the depths of deep space can seem dull. His imagination, once average, had become overactive, often surprising him with strange ideas.

"Can you move, Commander? I can't get out." Fellow astronaut Anton Petrov gave Scott's shoulder a gentle nudge.

Scott knew the impatient Russian probably would have liked to give him a stronger push with his boot, but he didn't dare for fear of damaging Scott's backpack, which contained everything keeping him alive. The smallest misstep was all it took for NASA to scrub a spacewalk, and preparing for a spacewalk and getting into a spacesuit took a few hours too long to be worth any unnecessary risks.

"Sorry," Scott said, pulling himself and his bulky spacesuit out of Anton's way. "Once more into the void," he muttered, playing out his tether just enough that he would be out of Anton's way, but not so far that he wouldn't be close to the ship.

The Freedom was an island of safety amidst infinite opportunities for death. If the tether snapped, Scott could die. Every spacesuit is equipped with small propulsion jets that could guide an astronaut back, but Scott hoped he'd never need them. Too difficult to control. In the simulator he hadn't managed to fly back to the ship until his twelfth and twenty-first tries.

Every other time he'd died.

Out of 84 tries.

Once outside the ship and floating within inches of the Freedom's thin yet reassuring hull, the astronauts gave each other a once-over to ensure there were no leaks or other issues that would ruin their spacewalk. Last of all, they checked the tethers that attached the astronauts to the Freedom, one lifeline for each of them.

"On to the mission," Scott said.

"Hey, just hurry it up out there!" Hinata Tanaka— their pilot— called over the radio. The Japanese astronaut was monitoring the spacewalk from inside.

"Hold the telephone," Anton replied. He'd lived in America for several years but still had a mild Russian accent. "You only want us inside so we can't steal your spacewalk record."

"Seven hours, baby. That record isn't going anywhere."

"There aren't enough space diapers in the world for that," Scott agreed. "You and Jon can keep your record. I know exactly the sacrifices you made to claim it."

"For the record, I held it the whole time," Hinata replied.

"Sure you did, Tanaka, sure you did," Scott replied, smiling to himself. For some reason, he pictured Hinata watching them with a steaming mug of tea in hand, dressed in a cozy, purple sweater. The image made no sense considering he knew she wore a NASA-issued jumpsuit and everything the astronauts drank came through a straw.

"NASA would like me to remind you that you have a job to do," another, far more crackly voice said. Tom Higgins, their ground control liaison.

"Aw, we're enjoying the view, Ground," Anton replied.

"Enjoy the satisfaction of a job well done," Tom replied several seconds later. Coming from Earth, it took time for transmissions to travel the long distance past the moon.

Scott looked to the moon, whose dark side faced the Freedom. "Past the moon" was a phrase Scott had heard almost too often in the last few weeks. Considered a precursor for a voyage to Mars, their expedition was making history, the furthest from Earth any humans had ever traveled.

"This is the last piece of the collider," Hinata said. Scott pictured her blowing on her cup of tea, steam curling through the air as she took a careful sip. "Try not to break it."

"It's ok," Scott replied. "I've got duct tape. Duct tape can fix anything."

"Tell that to Gimpy," Hinata replied.

"Hey, NASA never let me take a crack at Gimpy," Scott replied. "I will coat that bad boy in duct tape."

"You hear that, Ground?" Anton said. "You can save billions here. Just send up a few crates of duct tape."

A few crackles were the only reply.

"Think the moon's in the way," Hinata said after a moment. Scott pictured her drinking tea from a thermos, sitting cross-legged in a park, a red and white checkered blanket beneath her. A picnic.

"Stupid moon," Scott muttered. Anton said something in Russian the moon probably would have found distasteful.

Scott and Anton carefully made their way to the rear of the ship. The doors for the cargo bay already hung open. DMI-7 lay within, a bulky, satellite-like device that would signify the close of the Freedom's long mission.

After DMI-7 was released from its bindings, Scott and Anton floated it out into line with the rest of the DMI satellites, which lay in a hexagon. Held to one another by a cable that conducted electricity, DMI-7 would be hooked into the center of the hexagon— creating a cone shape— and the experiment would begin in earnest.

DMI. The Dark Matter Initiative. A project intended to help NASA— and the scientific community— better understand dark matter. The seven DMI devices were designed to work in conjunction somehow. Scott didn't know the science behind it all, he only knew the scientists back on Earth were trying to figure out dark matter, a mysterious substance thought to underpin the universe.

The cables linking DMI-7 to all the other DMI devices were attached. While Scott tightened every bolt and connection, Anton turned a crank that unfurled a pair of solar panels that would keep DMI-7 going after they left.

Scott gave the big device a thorough once over. The dark depths of space between Earth and Mars were not easily reached. If they missed anything here, it could be years before another expedition was able to travel this far and figure out what went wrong.

"Anything?" Anton asked. "Or did you bring your duct tape for nothing?"

"The 'Quark-Emitting Induction Coil'," Scott said with a frown. He pointed one of his thick gloves at a rounded shape in the center of the machine. "The coil looks... wonky."

"Wonky, hmm..." Anton said, grabbing a rail on the side of DMI-7 and pulling himself closer for a look. "Is that the technical term? "Hinata! Call NASA! DMI-7 is wonky!"

"You're wonky, Anton," she replied with a laugh. Scott pictured himself slicing bread and cheese on a blanket in the park, Hinata smiling as she watched him work. I've got issues, he thought to himself, ignoring the pang of jealousy he felt that Anton had made Hinata laugh and Scott had not. He resolved to make Hinata laugh if he had to die trying.

"It's wonkalicious," Scott said, then winced. Think of something funny to say first. The crew of the Freedom fell silent.

Scott reached for one of the tools strapped to his chest. Unwieldy and uncomfortable, sometimes the spacesuit felt like a small spaceship in its own right. While the arms and legs were flexible, the chest and neck were rigid, and the astronauts had to turn their whole bodies when they needed to see something.

"Looks like a bolt came loose," Scott said. "Shouldn't take long to patch things up."

"Well hurry up with it!" Hinata said. "Not that I'm worried…"

"We could take a wrench to DMI-7," Scott said. "Fixing it would take six, seven hours, maybe longer…"

"You wouldn't dare," Hinata replied. "Your space diaper can't handle it."

"I don't know," Anton cut in. "I think we owe it to NASA to find out just how much these diapers can take."

"Agreed," Scott said. "I'm pretty sick of holding it. I'm ready to begin the experiment."

"Ground Control, we're ready to begin testing our MAGs," Anton said. MAG was the official NASA word for the diaper every astronaut had to wear. Maximum Absorbency Garment. Like the jetpack, they truly hoped never to use it, but you never knew.

If Ground Control heard them, no response came.

"Ew," Hinata said. "Back to work, boys."

Sweat dripped down Scott's forehead and down the middle of his face, making his nose itch. He used a Velcro pad attached to the side of his helmet to scratch it.

"Yep," he muttered. "Back to work."

Scott's prediction proved true. The repair took little time. With a sigh of relief from Scott, the two astronauts reeled themselves back in. The familiar bang resounded in the airlock as machinery pumped precious oxygen back into the room.

"Someday I'm going to find what's making that sound," Scott said. "And take a sledgehammer to it."

"I'll help," Anton said distractedly, sounding tired. "Two sledgehammers are better than one."

Ready for a nap, Scott began the long work of wriggling out of his spacesuit. It took hours just to get ready for a spacewalk, let alone the time spent moving out in space. Moving on Earth is all about the legs, but in space you had to use your arms both for movement and your work, so it was easy to get worn out quick.

Hinata showed up after a few minutes to help the two out of their suits. Scott didn't picture her drinking tea or picnicking. He made a point of not thinking about her doing anything on Earth as she pulled off his helmet and helped him remove the outer layers of his spacesuit.

The crew of the Freedom returned to the cockpit. Scott and Anton wearily pulled themselves into their chairs and strapped in.

"Heard anything from Ground?" Scott asked.

"Just snap, crackle, pop," Hinata replied.

"Speaking of," Anton said. "I'm starving. Do we have time to grab a snack?"

"NASA wanted to get the satellites going as soon as we got DMI-7 plugged in," Scott said. "Try and raise them again," he told Hinata.

"Ground, this is Freedom," Hinata said. "We're ready to begin the experiment."

"We aren't— read you— Freedom," Tom said, his voice cutting in and out. The distance made communication difficult on a good day. Any interference made it almost impossible. A far cry from near-Earth orbit, where Scott could keep in touch with friends and family through the magic of the internet.

"Ok, I'm getting a snack," Anton said, unbuckling himself.

"Stay in your chair," Scott said.

"I'd rather get a snack."

"Fine. Bring me something too. If you eat all the beef jerky again, I'm having you court-martialed."

"Can you do that?" Anton asked, sounding genuinely curious.

"I'm not sure," Scott admitted. "But we can find out."

While Anton left, Hinata and Scott waited in their chairs. Remembering his strange thoughts during the spacewalk, Scott thought it best if he stayed quiet.

Hinata had other ideas. "Think it'll work?" she asked, nodding toward the cockpit window. Beyond the spaceship viewport, they could see the DMI satellites, and the lengths of cable linking them together.

"Probably," Scott said. "Lot of money in this project. Professor Beachum seems like a smart guy."

"Visible dark matter," Hinata mused. "I wonder what it'll look like."

"We'll find out soon enough," Anton said, returning from the rear of the Freedom with a handful of clear plastic bags filled with beef jerky. One of the perks of being an astronaut, Scott thought. On Earth he never bought beef jerky because the good stuff was too expensive. Here in deep space it was on the government dime.

"Freedom, this is Ground," a distorted voice said over the radio. Scott thought it was Tom, but he wasn't certain.

"We copy, Ground. Are we go to launch the experiment?"

"Yes," the voice said, suddenly much clearer. Definitely Tom. "We're activating DMI now."

Everything would be controlled remotely from Earth, but NASA wanted the Freedom close by when the satellite array got flipped on, in case anything went wrong.

One by one, each of the satellites winked to life. A few small LED lights were the only visual clue anything had changed.

Mars here we come, Scott thought. If this experiment worked, it would pave the way for more long-distance missions, missions Scott intended to be a part of. Bored with deep space or not, he couldn't resist the lure of history being made, of a journey into the unknown. Maybe their whole crew could stay together. He'd enjoy another mission with Anton. And Hinata...

"Wonder how long it'll be," Anton said.

"Hopefully just a few minutes," Scott said. "Sooner we begin, the sooner we can test Barsoom."

Named for the fictional Mars in the John Carter novels by Edgar Rice Burroughs, Barsoom was a test engine designed to put more horsepower in a smaller package, the overall intention being to speed up a voyage to the Red Planet.

Extended trips between planets were problematic for the health of the astronauts on board, so anything to reduce travel time would be considered. SpaceX had funded the rocket, part of joint cooperation between the private company and NASA to put men on Mars.

"We should have brought some popcorn," Anton said, nibbling at his beef jerky.

"Mike and Ikes," Hinata corrected. "And a large Coke."

"You Americans and your sugar," Anton said with a laugh.

"Hey, you're an American now, too," Hinata replied. "Nothing wrong with a little sugar."

Hinata and Anton hadn't been born in the US, but both had become citizens years before becoming astronauts. Scott pictured himself sharing a bucket of popcorn and a giant soda with Hinata. She would take a sip, then pass the drink to him, neither of them tearing their eyes away from the movie screen.

"What about you, Scott?"

"Eh? Sorry?" he replied, momentarily lost. "Oh, popcorn and root beer."

"Sensible," Hinata said approvingly.

"Sugar and fat," Anton complained. "I don't think— Whoa, what the hell is that?" He said something in Russian that Scott couldn't understand.

A strange glow had appeared past the satellite array, flashing in multiple colors like a strobe light. Several miles off, at least. Distances were difficult in deep space, with no reference points beyond faraway stars and planets, and no horizon to block your view.

"Are you getting anything, NASA?" Hinata asked.

"Telemetry is coming in now, Freedom," came the reply. "Great job! Scott heard applause and cheering in the background. Serious time and money had been pumped into the Dark Matter Initiative, and no doubt everyone back home felt relieved and excited at the project's success.

"We're getting some strange readings," Tom said. "Are you seeing anything?"

"Yeah, some kind of weird glow," Anton said loudly.

A loud screech sounded over the radio. Scott put his hands to his ears in pain, wincing at the terrible noise. After several minutes, the glow vanished.

"Now it's gone," Hinata reported.

Nothing but static came back to them in reply.

"Well, I'm a little creeped out," Anton said.

A feeling of dread came over Scott. His stomach turned. He pictured Hinata in her spacesuit, tumbling end over end out in the depths of deep space.

"Hinata, prime the engines," he said.

"We're supposed to wait for confirmation from NASA," she objected.

The glow returned. This time the colors changed more slowly. Blue, then green, then gold, then five minutes later the mystery light vanished again.

"We were supposed to wait for them to flip a switch," Scott said. "It's flipped."

"I'm with the Commander," Anton said. "No harm in being ready."

Hinata frowned. "It could be hours till we hear from NASA again…" she said softly, agreeing. With the moon in the way, that was probably true.

Another flash. Blue, green, gold, gone. So unnatural. Scott shivered. What have we done? he thought, still with that sick feeling in his stomach. A veteran of over half a dozen lengthy missions into space, Scott knew better than to doubt his gut.

"We'll wait half an hour," Scott said. "Unless something changes, then we're out of here."

Half an hour came and went, with the flashing glow continuing at intervals. Scott never turned away, mesmerized by the strange light.

"Ground, we're ready to head back to Earth," Hinata said.

"Freedom, standby," Tom said over the radio. "We'll get you out of there in a few minutes."

"Copy that—" Hinata began.

"Negative, Ground." Scott interjected. "We're getting out of here now." The gut knows, Scott thought. And Scott's gut said they'd waited long enough. He'd rather get chewed out for nothing later than die for nothing now.

"Agreed," Anton said. "It's time to go."

Scott couldn't tear his eyes away from the screen. There was another flash. Blue to green to gold and gone again.

And then Scott saw it.

A long, jagged shape like a length of black crystal. Smaller growths sprouted here and there along its length. The otherworldly mass bore down on their ship, a silent monolith. It spun as it moved, the entire pillar-shaped length flipping end over end.

"Ok, I don't know what that is," Scott said. "But I don't want to be anywhere near it." Hinata's fingers clattered over a keyboard. She tugged the joystick as the powerful rockets of the Freedom surged to life.

Blue, green, gold. The gold lingered this time. Scott thought he saw something in the glow. Yellow orbs, something like a writhing tentacle. Scott rubbed dazzled eyes, the afterimage of the asteroid flashing behind his eyelids.

The strange asteroid caught one edge of the array as it spun past, flinging the entire thing like a net. Bits of the DMI exploded as pieces of the satellite array flew in all directions.

"We're not moving fast enough," Scott said. "Whatever that is, it's going to catch up with us." Images of the ship exploding filled Scott's head, of all three astronauts tumbling away from each other in different directions. Talking on the radio to each other till they ran out of air, one by one.

Scott shook the nightmares out of his head. "We have to do something. We have to do more than just run. All that debris could hit the ship."

"If you have an idea, we're listening," Anton said. "For another thirty seconds or so," he added, eyeing the monitor.

"Barsoom." Scott felt a stab of remorse. Not the test he'd envisioned for his baby. "We can use it to get the speed we need to clear out of here."

"Too dangerous," Hinata objected. "There's a reason NASA wanted us to wait till we were closer to Earth."

"We're out of options," Scott replied. "Activate Barsoom." He almost added that's an order but bit his tongue before the words slipped out. He'd found that stating an order was an order undermined his authority as often as not.

"Yes, sir," Hinata said through clenched teeth. Scott couldn't tell if she was upset about Barsoom or just worried about the dark matter.

"It'll work," he said, resisting the urge to pat Hinata on the shoulder. The pilot kept her eyes trained ahead, though now that they'd reoriented the ship, there wasn't much for her to do.

Scott looked to the monitor. Blue, then green. This time the green lingered. Scott saw lightning flash, lighting up a scene of tiny spheres bouncing against each other.

"NASA, do you copy?" Scott asked. "We're not escaping quickly enough, so we're activating Barsoom."

"Snap, crackle, pop," Hinata muttered when no reply came. "Turning on test engine Barsoom-1," she declared, flipping several switches above their heads.

The three astronauts were shoved into their chairs as the spaceship suddenly accelerated to uncomfortable speeds. Despite the heavy centrifugal forces though, it wasn't as bad as Scott had feared. Uncomfortable, but not unbearable. Scott wondered how many hours he could endure on a voyage from Earth to Mars…

"How long do we have to sit like this?" Anton asked through gritted teeth.

"About an hour," Scott replied. "Then three and a half at a slightly lower, more comfortable speed. Beats the three friggin' days this should take! Hey, can you turn on Camera 2?"

"You're worried about your experiment now?" Anton asked.

"I'm worried about my experiment always," Scott replied. "Mars in our lifetime, baby."

"I am not your infant," Anton replied. "But Camera 2 is on."

Scott studied the feed that showed the engine in action, putting it side by side on his screen next to the feed that showed the glowing dark matter.

As the Freedom sped away, one last piece of the array exploded. Scott studied the deadly space rock one last time. What he saw made his breath catch in his chest. White lightning crackled across the surface of a vast blackness. For the first time, he took in the enormous size of the asteroid, nearly a hundred miles long if he had to guess.

"So, they made dark matter visible," Anton said, leaning over to study the same images Scott watched. "But what the heck is it?"

"It better not be what it looks like," Scott said. "Because it looks like a giant asteroid. We got a serious problem on our hands if that thing heads toward Earth."

"Dark matter isn't dangerous," Hinata said, hands resting on the Freedom's flight controls. Scott briefly pictured her with hands on a steering wheel driving through snowy mountains. "It doesn't interact with other matter. We've probably been surrounded by it all our lives."

"Whatever those satellites did changed the dark matter somehow," Scott argued. "And look at what that dark matter did to the DMI satellites. Seems pretty dangerous to me."

"We've created a monster," Anton said, face pallid with horror.

"Bingo," Scott said. "The only question is whether the monster is going to follow us home."

"It destroyed the DMI satellites," Anton replied. "We already know it's following us home!"

"It's pure energy," Hinata said, as though trying to convince herself. "At least, it should be… Even if it does come this way, it'll dissipate before it reaches the Moon, let alone Earth."

"It doesn't look like pure energy," Scott replied. "It looks like a planet killer. "You saw what it did to those satellites, we can't assume anything. We've got to stop it somehow. If it hits Earth, no more Earth."

"What can we do?" Anton asked.

"We made it," Scott replied. "How can we unmake it?"

"Those dark matter gadgets did this," Hinata said, shaking her head. "NASA. We need to know what they want us to do." The image of her driving through the mountains returned. Instead of a jumpsuit, she wore a red flannel shirt and a hoodie. He sat in the passenger seat, a tattered atlas in his lap. Despite their surroundings, it was open to a map of Ohio and Kentucky.

"We'll try again," Scott said. "NASA, can you read us?"

There came a hiss and the crackle of static.

"Snap, crackle—" Hinata began.

"—dom this is Ground. What is your status?"

"Good to hear from you, Tom," Scott said. "The satellites have created some sort of asteroid. Can't tell if it's solid or energy. We're worried it's headed toward Earth."

"We saw it before the cameras on the DMI satellites were taken out. It's definitely headed toward Earth. Judging from what it did to the array, we believe it could wipe out all life on Earth."

"What can we do to stop it?" Scott asked. "Please advise."

"Do?" Tom asked. "There's nothing you can… carry on your present course. May as well come on home."

"That's… that's not very reassuring," Hinata muttered.

"That is the opposite of reassuring," Scott agreed. "There's got to be something we can do, Tom."

"Sorry, Scott. I don't think so."

"A front row seat for the end of the world," Anton said. "Great."

Scott wasn't sure which was worse. Dying down below, or watching everyone die from space, knowing you had mere days left to live. At best the Freedom could keep them alive for a week or two until lack of air, water, or food killed them.

After their three hours were up, the Freedom slowed to its more typical pace.

"Maybe it went the other way," Anton said.

"Fat chance," Scott said.

"The fattest," Hinata agreed, pointing at the monitor. "And speaking of chubby, Earth is a big target. No way that asteroid misses."

"We're the only ones in a position to do anything," Scott said. "How do we fix this?"

"Fix it?" Anton asked. "It's an asteroid! What can we do?"

"Gimpy," Scott said. "What was the problem with Gimpy? Didn't BC tell you why it failed?"

"Well it had issues powering up. And something with the programming. It actually made dark matter harder to detect," Anton said.

"Be more specific, what exactly did NASA tell us about Gimpy?"

"It made dark matter seem fainter and further away," Hinata said.

Scott clapped and pointed at Hinata. "That's it! Maybe… ok, this is a long shot, but we're floating in space. We don't have anything else, and I'm not just going to give up and watch the Earth die."

"What are you thinking, Scott?" Anton asked, raising an eyebrow.

"Maybe we can aim Gimpy at the asteroid and make it fade out again," Scott said.

Hinata made a face. "You weren't kidding when you said long shot. But it's worth a try…"

"Unless we can think of something better," Anton said. "Can we?"

Everyone considered the possibilities in silence for a moment.

"Gimpy it is," Scott said when no one spoke. "Assuming we can even reach it."

"Gimpy's on this side of Earth," Hinata said. "We're lucky about that, but unless you've got another engine experiment up your sleeve, it's going to be tight," Hinata said. "The asteroid is flying at impossible speeds, and we only have so much fuel. One setback could ruin everything."

"A setback like that?" Scott asked, pointing at the computer screen.

The asteroid had struck the moon.

The vast sphere of Earth loomed to the left of the Freedom. They'd been traveling for hours at the best speed the spaceship could manage. Hinata kept a white-knuckled grip on the controls while Scott worked furiously, scrawling messy notes on a pad, trying to consider every possibility, everything that could go wrong. Anton muttered nervously to himself, no doubt also running his own series of calculations.

There is no sound in space, so they couldn't hear it, but Scott imagined terrible sounds bursting through the void as a huge chunk was ground from the moon. Bits of moon flew by them at high speed. A few smaller pieces pinged off the hull, but the larger moon rocks missed.

Gimpy already saved us, Scott thought. By turning right in order to approach the broken satellite array, they'd moved away from the asteroid's angle of approach, and therefore also away from the worst of the moon debris.

"Are you seeing this?" Anton asked, his face once again white. "The moon!"

Scott glanced at the screen. The moon looked as though a mile-wide bite had been taken out of one side. Chunks of rock the size of skyscrapers tumbled toward Earth at terrifying speeds.

"All the more reason to hurry," Scott said.

"How did it hit the moon like that?" Hinata asked.

"Not sure," Scott said. "Moon didn't even seem to slow it down. I can't imagine what kind of damage that thing would do to the planet."

"Giant volcanic eruptions," Anton began. "Ruined atmosphere, terrible tsunamis, general death and destruction, mass extinction, end of all life as we—"

"We get it," Hinata said. "Bad."

"Very bad," Scott agreed.

They were two hours from Gimpy a new voice came on the radio.

"Anton, are you there?" a new, female voice called. Scott glanced at his friend and fellow astronaut, who swallowed hard.

"BC, is that you?" Anton asked. "Hey, Brainy Cakes." Scott rolled his eyes. Anton always had to use his girlfriend's initials for all his pet names.

"Oh honey, it's good to hear your voice," she said.

"You— yours too, Brainy Cakes," Anton stammered. Scott smiled. They hadn't been seeing each other long. Anton still seemed to get a little flustered around his new girlfriend.

A long silence. Neither BC nor Anton seemed to know what to say to broach the terrible distance that separated them from one another.

"I wish I could see you one last time," BC said with a small sigh.

"How are things down there?" Anton asked, smoothing back his hair with a sweaty palm. "What are you doing?"

"I'm still at NASA. It's been chaos. Beachum and I made a program to fix DMI-0. It's just too bad there's no way you can get there in time."

"You made a what? Gimpy's broken?" Anton blurted the words. His shock mirrored the surprise Scott felt. That had never entered his equations. "We're headed there now. Scott figured it was our only hope."

"That changes everything! We shut DMI-0 down because it did the exact opposite of what we wanted. Dark matter becomes even more difficult to detect when 'Gimpy' is turned on. I think if we can turn on DMI-0 and point it at our asteroid—"

"No more asteroid," Scott said. "I had the same thought."

"Nice thinking, Brainy Cakes," Anton said.

"What about me?" Scott muttered.

"Exactly," BC replied. "I mean— yeah, no more asteroid. There are two problems. First, the satellite is currently down, and we can't reach it from here to find out why."

"Happens when you leave a satellite untouched for years," Scott pointed out.

"Second," BC continued as if she hadn't heard, "the blasted thing never worked right in the first place. We've sent you a data file containing a program that might take care of the second problem, but you've got to figure out the first."

"So, repair it, reprogram it, and clear out," Scott said.

"That's what we need. Think you can handle it?" she asked.

"Do we have a choice?" Anton asked.

"No," BC replied. "It's do, or everybody dies."

"Figured," Anton replied. Well, next time you see me I'll either be the astronaut who helped save the world, or I'll be sporting white wings and a halo."

"Ok. We're moving. It'll take some time to get in position," Hinata said.

Tom's voice returned. "Good luck, Freedom. We're counting on you."

~

"You two should start suiting up," Hinata told Scott and Anton.

"Yeah," Scott said. Getting into a spacesuit was a lengthy endeavor on a good day, and this was anything but. The astronauts also had to consider the tools they'd likely need to fix the array. They couldn't just pop back inside if they forgot something.

As the Freedom neared the DMI-0 array, Scott did his best to focus on the mission. The haunting image of the ruined moon kept popping into his head, but there was no time to think about the moon debris, and what its descent might have done to the world below.

"Remind me again what we're looking for," Anton asked as he stepped into the legs of his suit.

"Communications," Scott said, shrugging into the thermal suit that went beneath his spacesuit. "NASA can't talk to the satellite, so there's got to be something wrong with the radio."

"But only one satellite has a radio that needs fixed?" Anton asked.

"Right, the topmost part of Gimpy has the antenna we need to check," Scott confirmed. "We can upload the program to fix Gimpy from here in space, but we need NASA to flip the switches and make it do… whatever it needs to do."

Anton and Scott returned to the airlock. Scott's day had gone full circle. He stepped into the airlock, waiting for the clang that signaled the air being pulled from the room.

Hinata appeared to check over their spacesuits and finish sealing them up. Scott found himself face to face with the pilot as she examined the front of his suit, checking each of the tools strapped to his chest to make sure they were secure.

"No duct tape?" she asked after finishing her examination.

Scott patted his thigh where he'd strapped a gray roll of tape. "Don't be silly. Of course I brought some. Can't save the world without it." Her dark eyes bored into his for a moment.

It's the end of the world, Scott told himself. Say something.

But the moment passed as Hinata took Scott's helmet from his hand and popped it into place. There was no more time to think. Scott had to focus on the job at hand.

Once more into the void. Scott had been bored last time. The thought seemed incredible now. How do you get bored with outer space? There was a lot of moon debris around them. We need to make this quick, he thought. None of it seemed dangerous now, but there was no guarantee that wouldn't change.

Despite having been left to fend for itself for years, the experimental DMI array didn't look half bad. A few pockmarks marred several of the three satellites' metallic surfaces, but the solar panels were all intact, and the tethers securing the array looked as solid as ever.

The two astronauts pulled themselves to the upper tip of DMI-0. A small satellite dish pointed toward Earth. Scott couldn't find any signs of damage, so he moved to check the satellite's internal components.

But everything looked fine.

"Not to rush you," Hinata said, "but the asteroid is getting close to Earth's atmosphere."

"Right, no hurry," Anton said. "No pressure at all."

"Swap me," Scott said, pointing to a tool on Anton's chest. "I need the other wrench to get into the access panel."

Anton did as he was asked, and in a few seconds, Scott had laid bare the delicate inner workings of the satellite's radio. A neat array of cables and metal boxes greeted the two astronauts.

...And everything was fine.

He knew at once there was nothing wrong. Nothing he could see to fix, anyway.

"It's… it looks good," Scott said. "I mean, help me out here. Nothing looks damaged," he said to Anton. "What do you think?"

"It's… fine. It should be working. We could check every circuit board but they're all insulated, there's redundancies in case of burnout…" Even through the tinted glass of his helmet, Scott could see Anton going pale. What now? the Russian mouthed, at a loss.

"Do SOMETHING," Hinata cried. "We're out of time!"

Scott took a deep breath and examined the machine again. "Is that a loose wire?" he said, examining a thickly insulated cable running along one side of the satellite's innards. Two cables, Scott noted. Two cables linked by a coupling that had come loose. Scott tried to snap the wires back together, but they wouldn't stick.

"Loose power supply," Anton said. "Figures."

"Nothing a little duct tape can't fix," he muttered.

"You're seriously going to save the world with duct tape," Anton said. "Congratulations."

"Congratulate me later," Scott replied. "When we're back on Earth drinking beer and playing checkers."

"I don't drink," Hinata said. "And checkers is for two players. I better be invited." He pictured Hinata dropping a red token onto his side of the board with a cheerful "king me!" on a porch somewhere on Earth.

"Root beer, then," Scott said, grabbing the roll of duct tape strapped to his thigh. "Root beer and a deck of cards. We can play Go Fish for all I care."

"Sugary drinks and a silly card game. How American," Anton said. "I'll bring the fireworks."

"I'm going to hold you to that," Scott said, carefully tearing off a strip of duct tape. The gloves made it difficult. As he tore, the roll of tape flipped out of his hands and went spinning into the void.

"Careful," Anton said. "One side always seems to stick to the other when I use duct tape, and that's all we've got now."

"You gotta be a pro," Scott said. He was reaching to slide his duct tape around the wire when several pieces of debris flew toward them. One bounced off Scott's helmet, another off the lower left DMI-0 satellite.

And one cut the tether holding Anton to the Freedom.

Dizzy from the blow to the side of his spacesuit, Scott reeled. The piece of tape floated before his eyes. Where was Anton?

He could see the astronaut floating several feet from the array.

"Scott!" Anton cried. The panic in his voice was palpable. Scott's own worst fears dropping onto his friend and fellow astronaut. Scott's hands grew clammy, his stomach turning.

"The dark matter is breaching the atmosphere!" Hinata yelled, voice rattling Scott's eardrum. "It's too late!"

Save the world, or save Anton.

Scott knew which he had to choose, and it made him sick. Reaching out, he grabbed the duct tape, wrapped it around the wire, and hastily closed the hatch, giving the bolt a few loose turns to keep it from flying away. He could seal it up better later, if enough of the world was left for it to matter.

"Hinata, transmit NASA's program!" Scott said.

"Roger," she confirmed. He could hear keys clatter as she transmitted BC's program.

"Scott!" Anton called again.

"Jetpack, Anton," Scott said. "Use your jetpack. You can do this."

"Ok, I'm coming your way," Anton said.

The quark emitting coils on the three satellites began to glow red hot. Time to get out of here, Scott thought.

Trying not to think about all the failures so common in practice, Scott let go of the DMI array and began to float free. In theory, it should be easy. Anton would angle himself toward Scott, and Scott would angle himself to intercept Anton as he flew toward him.

"NASA needs me to move the Freedom," Hinata said. "We're blocking Gimpy's shot at the dark matter."

"Wait just a second," Scott said, using his jetpack to maneuver slightly. "One second."

"Earth doesn't have a second," she replied. "Sorry."

Scott and Anton were parallel with each other. Anton drifted toward Scott, reaching out his hand. Their fingertips were brushing when the spaceship yanked them away from each other. Scott gave his jetpack a little juice, wincing as his tether strained. Reaching out, he snagged Anton with his right hand. Weightless, it took no effort at all to redirect Anton. The two floated back toward the ship, the tension in their lifeline easing as they followed the Freedom.

"Hang on, buddy," Scott said. "We're not out of this yet."

The glow from the DMI satellites was so intense now it hurt Scott's eyes. The two astronauts were floating between Gimpy and the dark matter. Whatever happened to the dark matter would happen to them, too. He began hauling on the tether, desperately trying to pull himself and Anton back toward the Freedom.

The satellites were activating. A cone of golden light flew toward them. Scott closed his eyes, expecting to be blasted or washed in radiation.

"Watch your toes!" Hinata called. "Moving again so you're out of range."

The light passed in front of him, striking the dark matter asteroid. The huge mass turned blue, then green, then gold.

And then it vanished.

Scott whooped and Anton shouted so loud it rattled Scott's eardrums. Exhausted from their ordeal, the two hauled themselves back into the spaceship.

After the airlock cycled, Scott and Anton were greeted by a smiling Hinata, who swept them both up in a group hug before they began the laborious process of helping the pair out of their spacesuits.

"Nice work, gentlemen," she told them. "You just saved the planet. How does that feel?"

"Hey, you tell me," Scott said. "Couldn't have done it without you."

Hinata turned to regard him. As they locked eyes, the rules suddenly didn't seem so important, both the official NASA ones and all the unspoken rules he'd come to live by, all the little fears and worries he'd built up over decades seemed to slide away.

"Hey, what are you doing December 10th?" Scott asked, breaking the sudden silence that had overcome the airlock.

"We'll be back on Earth," Hinata said. "Why?"

"You want to maybe catch a movie or something?"

She smiled. "Sure. I'll bring the Mike and Ikes."

November 7th

"Movie time?" Anton asked. "I'm in! BC's out of town that weekend."

Scott suppressed a sigh. "For sure." Hinata gave Scott a quizzical look and he shrugged and grinned. There would be time to talk more over the coming weeks. There would be time for everything. Road trips, checkers, movies, root beer. All of it, the good and the bad, all saved. Suddenly, Scott knew this would be his last mission. He would let someone else go to Mars. After coming so close to losing the Earth, leaving again would feel wrong.

"Hey, got a present for you," Anton said. "Caught this floating around. Actually, I found it stuck to my back. Little trophy for you."

Scott grinned at the object in his hand. His lost roll of duct tape. "Hey, told you this stuff could fix anything."

A terrible clang shook the Freedom.

"I guess we're about to find out," Anton said, his face returning to its customary shade of white. "Hinata! What in the world was that?!" he called down the central corridor of the ship.

"The debris from the moon!" the pilot cried. "We've been hit!"

Part 2
November 8th

Scott O'Neil
Spacecraft Freedom

"We're going to land where?" Anton asked.

"The Brazilian rainforest," Scott replied. "If my calculations on trajectory and fuel are right." He took a deep breath. He knew they could do this. The astronauts who had just saved the world weren't going to die over something as simple as a damaged spaceship.

"If your…" Anton rubbed his eyes with thumb and forefinger. "If your calculations are correct. What if they're wrong? Can we land somewhere that won't kill us?"

"Aw, Brazil's not that bad," Hinata said.

"You said Brazilian rainforest," Anton objected. "As in, the Amazon? Land of flesh-eating diseases, jaguars, and giant snakes?"

"Well…" Hinata said, glancing at Scott for help.

The Freedom was doomed. That much had become clear quickly after the dust settled. The moon rock that had struck them had damaged the entire right side of the ship—or starboard as Hinata insisted on calling it— and now life support was failing, and their ability to steer the vessel was compromised.

"It beats fiery crash," Scott said. "We'll be fine. We just have to wait in the ship till NASA can come pick us up."

"If there's any ship left!" Anton shook his fist as though he wanted to bang something. Finding nowhere to vent his fury, he continued. "This thing was designed to land on a runway!"

"Ok, Anton, your concerns are noted," Scott said. "But what else can we do?"

"The ISS," Anton replied. "We make for the space station and use their lander to get where NASA can actually find us."

"We've been over this. It's too far. We'll be out of air and fuel before we get halfway."

"We can suit up to make it the rest of the way."

"It would still be cutting it too close," Scott said. "We'd run out of air five minutes out. That's a long time to hold your breath. Hinata says she can pull off this landing." He glanced at the pilot, hoping it was his head as much as his heart doing the talking. "I trust her."

"Please don't misunderstand, she's a great pilot." Anton eyed Hinata too. "You're a great pilot, but ISS is the safer option."

"Stop trying to butter me up," Hinata said. "I mean, you're not wrong, but seriously. It's getting gross."

"It's ok," Scott said to Anton. "You're going to see BC again. We're going home. It's just going to take a little longer than we'd hoped."

Scott only wished he felt so confident. He knew as commander he had to project strength to his crew. He had to believe it for their sake, even though he knew perfectly well Anton was right about every bit of the danger heading their way. He'd come to rely on the wary Russian's ability to sniff out trouble. It made Anton great at his job. Annoying sometimes, but great at his job.

Anton shrugged, at last relenting. "Well we just saved the world from a giant space crystal with a roll of duct tape. Can't be any harder."

"That's the spirit," he said aloud, clapping Anton on the shoulder and trying not to think about just how wrong the Russian was.

~

The trio began the process of suiting up and preparing for landing. Per usual, they'd be in their pressure suits for the descent in case anything went wrong. Even a normal landing could be dangerous, and this would be its own thing, a feat never attempted.

Pressure suits— or "pumpkin suits" as the astronauts often called them—were thick orange jumpsuits with white helmets. Lighter than a full spacesuit, they were designed to protect the crew during take-offs and landings.

The crew assembled in the cockpit. Earth spread before them outside the cockpit window. Scott drank the sight in. Last time, he thought. If he never left the Earth again, he'd never have this view.

"Have we heard anything from NASA?" Scott asked.

"Haven't heard anything yet," Anton said.

"There's a good chance the radio's as busted as the rest of this wreck," Scott said.

"Hey, don't insult my baby," Hinata said, patting the console with a gloved hand.

"Sorry," Scott said.

"NASA had a long day of terror," Hinata added. "Maybe they're resting."

Scott shrugged, a motion that was mostly lost on his crewmates, strapped in and suited up as they were.

"Any regrets?" he asked, trying not to fidget as he waited for Hinata to move the ship into position.

"Never been to Africa," Anton said. "Always wanted to see a lion."

"They have these things called zoos…" Hinata said.

"It's not the same," Anton said. "Not like in the wild."

"Wait, wait, wait," Scott said. "You're fine with visiting one of the deadliest creatures on Earth, the king of freaking beasts, but you're afraid of a little jungle?"

"Mankind has lived in Africa for thousands of years. We haven't even come close to taming the jungle. Africa's got nothing on poison dart frogs, malaria, spiders the size of dinner plates—"

November 8th

"They have malaria in Africa, actually," Hinata said, not turning from the cockpit. "It's a rough place. Beginning descent."

The Freedom's orbit was decaying, which meant they'd move around the Earth at the same time they drew nearer. It would be several minutes before they entered Earth's atmosphere. Scott pictured them accelerating faster and faster, crashing into the Amazon in a massive fireball that set the trees on fire.

No, he told himself. It's not our time to go. "What about you, Tanaka?" he asked Hinata. "And when did you go to Africa?"

"Peace Corps," she said, "to answer the second question. As to the first... no regrets. Not yet anyway." She turned to Scott and winked. "Ask me again when we're on the ground."

"What about you, Commander?" Anton asked.

"Nada," he replied. "It's been a long strange ride, but you know what? I wouldn't change a thing. We got to save the world. That makes it all worth it." A far cry from the way he'd felt yesterday morning, bored with the magic of deep space and unable to acknowledge his feelings.

Speaking of feelings... He glanced at Hinata. "Might have one regret," he admitted.

"Oh?" Hinata asked, glancing at him.

"Shouldn't you be..." Anton waved his hand toward Earth. "Eyes forward?"

"We should have gone to the movies before we left for space."

Hinata's grin froze in place. "Yep," she said, turning. Scott did the same. He could see Brazil now. Much of it lay swathed in cloud, but sprawling patches of green were visible. Scott still wasn't sure whether he and Hinata were going on an actual date or not.

"Mike and Ikes," she mumbled to herself, so quietly Scott barely heard. "There was nothing good out that week," she said aloud.

"True," Scott said, suppressing a sigh.

"Let's talk about the movies later," Anton said.

The Freedom piled on speed, moving faster as it entered the atmosphere. Her nose glowed red hot. Jungle sprawled before them, endless trees and winding rivers, swamps, and fields. Scott tried to keep his eyes out for a settlement, a logging crew, anyone that would be able to help them, but he didn't see anything but the greens and blues of untamed nature.

"Can you reach that meadow?" Scott asked, pointing to a small field on the edge of the horizon. It lay between the intersection of a swamp, a thick jungle, and a broad river Scott guessed was an offshoot of the Amazon.

"I can aim for it," Hinata said, calm despite the deadly circumstances. "It's too small a target for the Freedom, though."

"You mean the howler monkeys didn't clear out a runway for us?" Anton asked through gritted teeth as the Freedom shook.

The ground was so close now. Scott visualized them hitting the Earth, slamming into the dense jungle trees, their bodies vaporized in the flash of a massive fireball, a bit of one wing pinwheeling into the morning sky. Trees and vines would wind their way through the ruined remains of the Freedom, monkeys and snakes making the fallen vessel their home.

Shaking the vision aside, Scott reached for the parachute controls. "Ready parachute," he told Hinata.

"Stand by," she said. They soared over the jungle at hundreds of miles per hour. The landing point neared at frightening speed as Hinata slowly tilted the ship into a horizontal position.

"Now!" she cried. Scott hit the button, and the three astronauts braced themselves as the ship slowed suddenly, jerking the three of them against their restraints.

The river flashed by below, a broad, brownish expanse. In the distance, Scott thought he saw a silver pillar, but when he glanced down at the console and back up, he could no longer see it.

"We're not going to make the meadow," Hinata said. "Sorry."

And then they crashed.

~

Scott didn't realize he'd blacked out until he woke up. He swung his head left and right. Hinata and Anton slumped in their chairs, unmoving. Outside, all Scott could see was green. Cracks spiderwebbed the cockpit window.

"Hey!" he called, fumbling with his harness. "Everyone ok?"

Anton groaned. A bruise perched under his left eye. "Nothing a few weeks on a beach won't cure..." he mumbled.

"Think you might get your wish, buddy," Scott said. His boots splashed as he got to his feet. His knees wobbled. He hadn't used his leg muscles in over a month, and they weren't ready yet. He sat back down, feeling dizzy and nauseous.

"Not what I meant," Anton replied. "Blah. Bleh. Does anyone else's tongue feel funny?"

Scott nodded. His lips and tongue both felt strange now that they were under gravity's sway once more. This was nothing new for either of them, but Anton always said something.

Scott reached out a hand to Hinata's shoulder and gave it a light shake. "Who needs the beach?" she grumbled. "You've got the all-inclusive NASA vacation package, now with guided river tours."

"Speaking of, think we landed in the river," Scott said, glancing down at his feet. There were several inches of water at his feet, and the water had risen since he'd stood.

"Yep," Hinata confirmed. "I figured it would be softer than the trees."

"You found the trees, too," Anton said, nodding toward the cockpit and its green view as he unbuckled himself.

"That's just the plants on the bank of the river," Scott said.

"There's a lot more Amazon in my spaceship than I normally prefer," Anton said, eyeing the water on the deck of the Freedom.

"We're sinking," Scott said. "At least, I think we're sinking. "We're going to have to evacuate the ship."

"Evacuate?" Anton said with a snort of laughter. "I can't even muster the energy to ridicule that statement properly. We'll be weak as kittens for days!"

"We're going to have to muster the energy," Scott said. "We're going to have to muster a lot of energy. We can't stay here." Scott knew the river couldn't swallow the Freedom completely, but if water continued to enter, the ship would get pretty uncomfortable. It could take days if not weeks for NASA to find them in the Freedom, even if they knew where they'd crashed.

"Where would we even go?" Anton asked.

"We need to get in touch with NASA," Scott said. "The sooner the better, so they can get someone out here to help us."

"How? Radio's out and I don't even want to think about the roaming charges if I turn on my cell phone," Hinata said.

"Are roaming charges still a thing?" Anton asked.

"Doesn't matter," Scott said. "I'd pay you back. We're not going to get reception out here so it's a moot point. Yes, we're all going to be weak, dizzy, and slow. But we're going to be weak, dizzy, slow, and smart. We've got a little time. Pace yourselves, pack what you need, and we're going to very carefully go find some civilization and get ourselves rescued."

"Nice speech," Anton said. "I hope the giant spiders agree." He held out his hands in a shape the size of a dinner plate. "You know how many kinds of giant spiders there are in Brazil? I know of at least three. There's one so big it eats birds."

Hinata stood, using the console to hold herself up. "Well, last time I checked you're not a bird." She winced as her legs shook, then forced a weak smile. "Let's get moving."

"And the frogs, you know there's this yellow frog, you touch it and it can stop your heart. I'm pretty sure they'd agree to leave us alone if—"

"Ok, we get it," Scott said. "The jungle is dangerous. But so is staying here."

"Do you know where to go?" Hinata asked.

"North!" Scott replied. "We'll hit the U.S. eventually!" When no one laughed, he coughed. "I saw something as we went down. A radio tower, maybe. We might be able to use it, or find someone who can help us."

"That's—" Anton began.

"A longshot, I know," Scott admitted. "But it's our shot, and we're taking it."

~

"Well… that's a problem," Scott said, staring at the river swirling at his feet. He had a hand braced against the side of the Freedom. The slight drop made him dizzy, but he managed to keep from throwing up. Barely.

"Well, we are in the river," Hinata replied. She leaned against the other side of the door. "It makes sense we'd have to go through it to get out."

"Through…" Anton muttered, standing a few feet behind them so he could rest against the bulkhead. "You know what swims through the Amazon? Electric eels, piranhas, giant snakes—"

"And astronauts," Scott cut in, ending the discussion. "But don't worry," he said with a smile. I have an idea."

~

Fully ensconced in their spacesuits, the three astronauts returned to the hatch. Hinata shoved the door open, sunlight glaring off her helmet.

"Go ahead," Scott said to Anton, leaning against a bulkhead as his vision swam briefly.

"What?" the Russian asked.

"Tell me what a bad idea this is." Designed for use in zero-g, the suits were heavy, even with much of the life support gear and unnecessary parts removed, each of the suits still weighed nearly a hundred pounds. Backpacks with supplies to help them cross the jungle only added to the strain. On their space-addled frames, the three could barely stand.

"Actually, I'm pretty happy," Anton said. "The jungle can stay out there, I can stay in here."

"Great," Scott said. "As mission commander your happiness is very important to me." Truth be told, Scott would've rather waded across the river in his gym shorts, but all Anton's talk of Amazonian dangers had spooked the trio, giving Scott the idea to use their spacesuits.

"You know, that sounded a lot like sarcasm," Anton said. "But thank you all the same."

"Don't mention it," Scott replied. "Really." He turned to Hinata. "Ready for a swim, Tanaka?"

"Yes sir," she replied, then promptly fell face-first into the river.

"Whoa!" Scott cried. He heaved himself across the ship, grabbing the doorframe seconds before he fell into

183

the water himself. He swayed at the edge like a drunk till his balance came back.

"I'm ok," Hinata said from below. She rose to the surface, her white spacesuit now brown with river silt. "Got a little water in my suit though," she added in a low voice.

Scott leapt down after her, careful to keep his head and shoulders as high as possible. The suits were mostly waterproof, but they hadn't sealed up the hole in the shoulder of the suits that normally fed the astronauts oxygen; they needed to breathe, after all.

The water had a rich living smell, a vast difference from the pool Scott had trained in, which had reeked of chlorine.

Hinata and Scott stood in shoulder deep water and looked back up to Anton. "Come on in, buddy," Scott said. "The water's fine."

"Shut up," Anton replied. "I'm coming."

"You're in a spacesuit. Nothing can get to you," Hinata added.

"It occurs to me water-born parasites could enter through the holes of my suit," Anton replied. "Guinea worms, candiru fish, roundworms…"

"Jump!" Scott cried.

Hinata and Scott both began to chant together, pumping their arms in the air. "Jump! Jump! Jump!"

"Oh fine," he replied, leaping into the water with a splash that sprayed Scott's helmet.

The trio turned and trudged toward shore. Scott's stomach churned from the effort, and he did his best to think about anything else, but the only subject his tired brain willingly supplied him with happened to be the only other thing he was trying not to think about.

Hinata.

The astronaut waded quietly beside him. To an outside observer, it would have looked like three helmets gliding across the water. The opposite shore was close, but no good to them. Scott guided them along the side of the ship, towards the side of the river the Freedom had landed in.

"Did anyone feel that?" Anton asked from a few steps behind.

"What?" Scott asked, not turning to look. Turning took too much energy to bother.

"Something brushed my leg. Could be a titanoboa."

"If it was a titanoboa," Scott said. "I'll buy you a Ferrari when we get back to the States."

"Do I get one?" Hinata asked, seeming to perk up. "Wait, what's a titanoboa?"

"You get two," Scott replied, too tired to worry about giant snakes, or the impact buying three expensive cars would have on his bank account.

"Forty-foot snake," Anton replied.

"That's… big." Hinata said. "Very big."

"They're extinct," Scott said. "Very dead."

"How do you know so much about South America, Petrov?" Hinata asked. "I mean, you have weirdly specific knowledge about the terrors of the Amazonian Jungle."

"Was supposed to honeymoon here once. That was before NASA, before BC, and before America. Fell through. No wedding, no honeymoon, no necrotizing fasciitis."

"I'm sorry," Hinata said. "Well, about the wedding."

"Eh," Anton grunted. "Don't be. I'm better off. Well. I felt better off till we crashed here! Got a gorgeous girlfriend and the best job in the universe. I'm doing fine, really— what is that?"

"What?" Scott asked.

"Swear something's following us," he replied. "Whoa!" Anton cried. He stumbled, whole body falling into the water.

Scott splashed over to help and felt something slap his thigh. He paused. "Anton?" he asked. Could it be a real danger?

Anton shot above the surface. "Careful!" he cried. "We have to get out of here."

"I felt it!" Scott agreed, beginning to panic himself. "Let's get to shore."

Something snuffled to Scott's right, making him jump. Startled, he turned to regard the threat.

The baleful eyes of a small manatee met his.

"A manatee?" Scott asked, baffled.

Hinata's laughter boomed across the canopies of the trees above, echoing out into the jungle.

"Oh yeah, the Amazon has manatees," Anton said, sounding deflated.

"Oh— my— I think I'm—" Hinata gasped, laughing breathlessly. "I think I'm going to die. You were so scared!" Scott didn't think it was quite so funny, but he couldn't help chuckling along.

"And we found the one thing in the Amazon that isn't deadly," Anton said. "Hilarious."

"Ugh, it hurts to laugh," Hinata said. "We've got to get out of these suits. I'm going to collapse."

"Agreed," Scott said. The three staggered on, collapsing onto the shore. The Freedom towered to Scott's right, her nose buried in vegetation. Birds and insect sounds enveloped them, the sounds of early morning in the jungle.

"My poor baby," Hinata said, patting the side of the downed vessel.

"NASA'll get her out," Scott said, pulling off his helmet and letting it fell to the soft dirt. Hinata followed suit, having already tugged off her gloves.

"You sure?" Anton asked. "We're a long way from home."

"The millions of dollars sunk into the most expensive spaceship ever made tell me it's pretty likely," Scott said. "Our spacesuits alone are probably worth coming back for." And Barsoom, Scott added mentally. Setting foot on Earth had only strengthened his conviction he would never leave again, but he still wanted to see a voyage to Mars succeed.

"Can't we wear our suits?" Anton asked. He still hadn't taken his helmet off.

"The jungle's not going to kill you, buddy," Scott said. "Well, probably not. But there's no chance we can make it across the jungle in spacesuits. In our condition, we'll be lucky if we can make it to the pillar without any gear. We'll rest here a bit, then get on our way."

Anton slumped to the ground and seemed to fall asleep in seconds. Scott felt his own eyelids growing heavy. They'd been awake for over 24 hours now and it was catching up with him.

Soon, Scott told himself. He couldn't pass up this opportunity to talk to Hinata. He couldn't wait for the world to nearly end again to tell her how he felt.

"Hey, Hinata?" he asked, resisting the urge to cross his fingers she hadn't fallen asleep.

"Hey Scott," she mumbled, sounding half asleep.

"About our date next month..." he began.

"Yeah, I'm looking forward to it," she said. "You better not let me down, O'Neil."

"I'll, uh you know I'll do my best," Scott said, then winced. Couldn't he think of anything better to say? At least she hadn't denied that it was, in fact, a date.

No response came.

After a moment filled with nothing but jungle sounds, Scott realized Hinata had fallen asleep. He followed seconds later.

~

The quiet woke Scott. The perpetual noise of the Amazon had fallen away.

"Why's at whatsit!" Anton shouted, sitting up suddenly. He scrabbled around on the ground as if looking for a weapon. Giving up, he relaxed. "Sorry. Couldn't remember where we were for a moment."

"Not to mention you've never slept in a helmet before," Scott said.

"You made the right decision," Hinata announced, pulling an alarmingly long bug out of her hair.

Scott squirmed and shook out his own hair with dirty fingers, but felt nothing. "I'm ready for a cup of coffee and a shower," he said, rubbing dirt off his face.

"Counteroffer," Hinata said. "Bottle of water and a sweaty trek across the jungle."

"Why's it so quiet?" Scott asked, then sighed. "Oh. Nobody move."

"Why…" Anton trailed off as he followed Scott's gaze. "Definitely glad I kept my helmet on! Never taking it off again!"

"Shut up," Hinata hissed.

A jaguar crouched on a branch above the astronauts. Its striped tail flicked as it watched them.

"He looks hungry," Anton whispered.

"Shut up," Scott said. "Put on your helmet," he said to Hinata.

Scott reached for his own helmet. Ensconced in their suits, the jaguar would be little threat. He couldn't say for sure his spacesuit was jungle-cat proof, but it had protected him from x-rays, deadly temperature extremes, and chunks of the moon, so it seemed like a reasonable bet.

"Slowly," Scott cautioned as Hinata's slender fingers lifted her helmet. He waited until she'd sealed her helmet, then raised his own into place.

He almost had it latched when the jaguar lunged.

Knocked to his back, the helmet shot skyward like a cannonball, landing in the river with a light splash. The jaguar tore for Scott's neck, its teeth clicking against the metal rim of his spacesuit's collar.

Something bashed the cat in the side of the head. The jaguar stumbled off of Scott, dazed. A black-white blur flashed as it struck again. A brown blur joined the first. In the absence of a weapon, Hinata had ripped off her helmet and struck the cat in the face. Anton had then joined in with his backpack.

Having expected an easy meal and instead gotten a fight, the cat fled, dazed but unharmed.

"Don't worry," Anton called after the jaguar. "We'll be back on the menu later."

When Hinata stared at him for a moment, he squirmed. "What? We will be. As soon as we take our spacesuits off."

Scott lay there for a moment. He could feel shallow cuts bleeding on his neck. His suit had claw marks all down the chest. Hinata glanced at her helmet— which had cracked— and dropped it. Scott thought he heard her murmur something about "A hundred thousand taxpayer dollars" as it rolled through the soft, silty soil.

"We can't make it across the jungle in these things," Scott said. "And we can't stay here."

Despite Anton's reservations, they took the spacesuits off, carefully stashing all the equipment under a tree a few yards inland. Like the ship, the suits would need to be salvaged if at all possible.

Full blown spacesuits removed, the trio donned their pressure suits. The baggy orange suits would keep the plant and bug life of the jungle away from their skin without weighing them down.

"How far is the tower you saw?" Hinata asked when they were ready to depart.

"At least a couple miles," Scott replied, hoping he hadn't gotten anything mixed up during their chaotic landing. You blacked out, he thought to himself. Are you sure you know the way?

Scott pictured the three of them wandering the jungle for years, dressed in clothes made of leaves and wielding homemade spears. Not the worst fate he could imagine.

He decided to trust himself, taking the lead. He still felt dizzy and weak, but it wasn't so bad as before. He didn't want to wear his pressure suit helmet, but the bugs were swarming so bad he quickly found he was more comfortable with it on.

"Just a couple pumpkins walking through the jungle," Anton said, his voice muffled by his own helmet. "What could go wrong?"

"You talk too much," Scott muttered, scanning the treetops. He'd never seen such green. The living jungle enveloped them, so thick they had to press through brush to walk.

One foot in front of the other, Scott thought, trying not to think about how tired and sick he felt.

The trees spun and swayed around him as he walked, using a long branch as a walking stick. After the first mile, the astronauts began to lean on each other. The person in the center had to do the least work, so they took turns resting in this way until the tower Scott had seen at last came into view.

"Where are we?" Anton asked, exhaustion weighing on every word.

Scott studied the tower, which rose above the treetops. At the top, he saw men and women dressed in colorful t-shirts and dresses taking pictures of each other. Tourists.

He let his eyes scan lower down. A row of buildings lay near the tower. Sloped rooftops made of dark wood lay in neat rows, presided over by a taller building with the same slanted roof.

Scott turned to regard his companions, grinning big without realizing they couldn't see his face. "Looks like we really are getting that NASA vacation. It's a resort."

~

The clink of ice cubes in glasses and the murmur of conversation buzzed across the patio as a waiter bustled from table to table. He topped off drinks, delivered condiments, and spoke to patrons. Ceiling fans spun furiously above, keeping the worst of the Amazon heat at bay.

Three astronauts in orange suits stumbled up the steps from the wilderness, supporting each other. Their helmeted heads swiveled as they took in the scene of the restaurant, their faces obscured by black visors. All three suits were ripped and stained green from vegetation. Leaves stuck to their legs.

The waiter stopped between two tables. The dishes and cups atop his tray leaned dangerously toward a suicide leap to the planks below.

Scott murmured something to his companions and staggered across the restaurant. He approached the waiter, ripping off his helmet as he walked and sucking in grateful breaths of cool air.

"Are you— sir, can you help us?" Scott's short, dark hair clung to his scalp. He stank of sweat— both stale and fresh— and his neck was covered in scratches and dried blood.

"Sir?" Scott asked. He swayed, as though about to collapse. "I'm Scott O'Neil. I'm an astronaut. Maybe you've heard of me?"

November 8th

The waiter shook his head. He didn't speak English.

A woman at a nearby table stood up. She said something in Portuguese to the waiter, who nodded. Noting the tray he was about to lose, he carefully righted the dishes and set out to get them to the kitchen and get his boss out here to deal with their uninvited guests.

"You're the astronauts who saved the world!" the woman said to Scott. She spoke with a British accent. "Your faces are all over the news. How on Earth did you wind up here?"

"It's a long story," Scott said, lurching again. Glancing back, he noticed that both Hinata and Anton had laid down right there by the steps to the patio. He couldn't tell if they were awake, but he doubted it. The final mile of the jungle had been uneventful, but far harder than anything else they'd had to endure, as their bodies had grown weak with exhaustion and dehydration.

"I've got time," the woman said. "On holiday and all that."

Scott found himself staring at a half-full glass of water on the woman's table. "Could I trouble for you a drink of water?" he asked before collapsing into her arms.

~

Scott felt he could have slept for days, but he knew he had to get word to NASA. Fighting off sleep, he begged and pleaded for a phone call until someone was able to get him to a landline that could reach the US. They sat him in a small room with a couple computers and a thinly padded leather chair, respecting his request for privacy. Not that it mattered— most of the staff could not speak English. From there, he had to call a directory— he had no idea what number could reach NASA, after all.

And then he got shuffled from one person to the next. No one seemed to know what to do with him, who best to take his call, but they all wanted to talk. Some thanked him, some pleaded for his story. Some even cried. All while his eyelids drooped. His body begged for release. He yearned to join Hinata and Anton in sleeping. They'd long since retreated to empty rooms and been allowed to rest.

The British woman had become their benefactor, insisting on the very best treatment for the trio of astronauts who had just saved the world. He had a sinking suspicion the whole world would soon know where they were. NASA needed to get to them first.

Neil Armstrong and Buzz Aldrin— first men on the moon— had risen to terrifying levels of fame after returning from the moon. Scott had little doubt a similar fate would befall himself and his crew. NASA really needed to get to them first.

He was about to give up and fall asleep in his chair when a familiar voice answered.

"This better be good," someone on the other end of the line grumped. "Dragging me out of bed a quarter to 10 after the worst day the world has ever—"

"Tom?" Scott interrupted, too tired to wait any longer.

"Scott? Is that you? How in the Sam— ok, you know what? Just tell me where you are? Are you safe?"

"Yeah, we're safe. Ready to come home, Tom. Tell NASA it's time to bring us home."

Rachel
Yellow Springs, Ohio

Rachel awoke to the sound of, well, she wasn't sure why her alarm sounded so funny. It almost sounded like crying, like a crying baby. Her sleep deprived and yet not fully awakened self couldn't process the incongruity of the moment until suddenly, with a start, she remembered. That's my child crying. That's Benjamin. Her body responded to his need for food and she pulled him close. This unexpected closeness filled her with a peace she hadn't thought possible. Yet it was a bittersweet moment because she remembered the finality of it all.

Benjamin sated, Rachel tidied up in the bathroom. She and carried him into the kitchen decided she needed a cup of tea. She wondered, how long was it that her life changed? She placed him in his car seat and took him and her tea to the window where, crossing off another item on her to do/bucket list they, at least she, watched the sunrise. The sky was resplendent in reds and yellows, with a tinge of left-over blue from the night before. How she imagined, could things seem to beautiful when it will all be gone soon? Tears again splotched her face as she thought to herself, I never cry, why now? Her mind went first to memories of her childhood, her parents, moments of laughter, times of sadness, occasions where her parents were simply there for her, helping her through them. I wonder if I would have been as good a parent to Benjamin as they were to me? I doubt it she thought, familiar and caustic feelings of inadequacy rising to her throat like bile. It's a good thing the world will be gone. How much can I mess him up in these last few hours?

So now, sunrise having passed into the early morning light, Rachel fixed herself another cup of tea and some toast and wondered, what now? She abruptly came out of her musings when she heard the loud knock at her door. "Rachel, are you there? I saw you leave suddenly yesterday and kept watching for you to come back," her neighbor breathlessly spoke into the closed door. Pausing to make sure Benjamin was Ok, Rachel opened the door for her friend. "Come on in."

Melissa came in, a mixture of relief and confusion on her face when her eyes settled on the car seat with the sleeping Benjamin inside. "Rachel, what happened?" was her stating the obvious yet totally understandable reply.

"I went into labor. This is Benjamin. They let me come home early, considering, well, you know." She and Melissa hadn't had time to speak and process the whole 'world coming to an end scenario.' In what seemed to be a normal thing these last few hours, Rachel began to cry. "Oh, Melissa, he's just wonderful. I decided to keep him. I figured I could handle it for that long. I never knew you could love someone so much in such a short time and now there's such a short time to love him and I can't seem to stop crying."

Melissa put an arm around her sobbing friend, "Oh, Rachel, I'm so happy for you. This is a miracle." "You have a son."

"I do, but it's all going to be over." Rachel's sobbing intensified.

"You haven't heard," understanding dawned on Melissa. "The world's not going to end. We're going to be alright."

"What?!" exclaimed Rachel. "They said we were doomed."

"There was this one plan, an outside hope and it worked. There'll be some clean-up, but we are going to be fine."

"I can't believe it," Rachel whispered as she stumbled to the couch. "Benjamin and I, we will have time?"

"Yes, all the time in the world," her friend reassured her.

195

Rachel didn't know what to think. Her first feeling was adulation. She couldn't believe all the changes in her life and the biggest change, Benjamin. She had resigned herself to making the best of twenty-four24 hours more or less and now, their whole future lay in front of them. Rachel, being Rachel then began to doubt and question. Her friend could see the storm of emotions pass over her face.

"What's wrong Rachel? This is good news, isn't it?"

"Yes, it is, but."

"But what"? Melissa tentatively inquired.

"It's just, I don't know if I can do this? I never planned on being a mother. Wait, maybe I'm not a mother, I mean, maybe Benjamin isn't mine. I had promised him to Ken and Rebecca. They've helped me so much. They were looking forward to him. They had planned and prepared for my baby. What happens now?" A very real fear accompanied by this sinking feeling in the pit of her stomach was rising in Rachel as she began to put voice to the rising dread inside her.

"I was wondering about them," Melissa asked. "Where are they? In all of the excitement I totally forgot. They've been so involved, why weren't they with you when he was born. How did all this happen?"

"Oh, I called and said I thought that if anything happened, I could handle it for the next two days." "They weren't upset. Given what was happening they went home to Kentucky to be with Rebecca's folks. In fact, it was Rebecca who said my back pains might be labor. Good thing she noticed and they told me to go to the hospital. It was close even then."

"You haven't been watching the news. When NASA managed to divert the debris, they couldn't get all of it. There was a major strike. In Kentucky. They say no one survived."

"That's horrible," cried Rachel. Let me try and call them. She dialed and the phone was dead. She then tried to text, no answer. Finally, she turned on the television and for the next few minutes caught up with a lifetime she had missed.

Benjamin stirred and began to cry. "It's probably time to change him. They gave me some diapers at the hospital, and some other things. I was totally unprepared for this, for keeping him." Melissa waited while Rachel changed Benjamin and sat down to nurse him before speaking.

"Let's make a list of what you need. I'll go out and get stuff for you. Do you have something for lunch? Did you eat breakfast?"

"I had tea and toast."

"That will never do." Melissa was in full help mode now and while Rachel fed her son, they created a list of basic things Rachel would need for the next few days. "You should call your doctor, too. Find a doctor for Benjamin." She also went to the refrigerator and made Rachel a sandwich and made sure she ate it.

Rachel started to cry again, "Thanks. I just don't know if I can do this."

Time passed and Rachel sat, holding her newborn son, lost in thoughts dominated by fear and insecurity. Melissa returned, loaded with clothes and diapers and blankets and wash cloths and a bassinette. Rachel, put Benjamin back in the car seat and hugged her friend, overwhelmed. "How much do I owe you for all of this? I might need a couple of months to pay you back."

"Nothing" said Melissa. "I have this rainy-day fund, for emergencies or mad money. I cannot think of a better way to spend it, on this cute little guy here."

Rachel found herself bawling for the 100th time. "I don't know what to say." "Thank you doesn't seem to cut it."

"You are welcome." Just make sure I get to babysit some. Remember, I'm right next door." Melissa cheerfully

left with a hug for Rachel and a soft caress for Benjamin. "You two are going to be fine."

Benjamin clamored to be fed again. Rachel
marveled at the way her body had risen to the occasion. Just
barely managing to keep the doubts and fears at bay, Rachel
put the sleeping Benjamin in his new bassinet and sighed and
began to think. The room had an eerie stillness, punctuated
by little baby noises from time to time. She sat, absent-mind-
edly petting Vincent who had come to cuddle next to her. At
some point after maybe minutes or perhaps hours, Rachel began to think, but as was usual for her when it was important,
she thought not in words, but in images.

First, she pictured striations of black and gray, dark
hues which spoke of her fears and doubts, her insecurities
over not being good enough. Then the image grew as the
colors lightened and the canvas in her mind became patches
of neutral colors, ambiguity and indecision, places where she
was stuck in her thoughts. And then there was the sunrise
of this morning, the dark blues becoming azure and then
the beginnings of yellow, orange and red. The angularity
and almost stark quality of the dark colors of the beginning
of her mental portrait gave way to some curves and muted
edges. Then there were brilliant greens and purples, fuchsia
and turquoise spreading out like ripples caused by a stone in
still waters.

She was totally caught up in the picture her mind was
creating. She noticed with a start that throughout the entire
scene there were dots of yellow, tentative at first, bursts of
color breaking through the landscape of her emotions made
visible. With her new mother's heart, she knew those bursts
were Benjamin. Benjamin when she first realized she was
pregnant. Benjamin when he moved. Benjamin's ultrasound
which showed a healthy child but was unclear as to his
gender. As her picture progressed Benjamin became bigger
and brighter until the entire top of her mental landscape was

this brilliant yellow made not of a solid color, but of bits and pieces, hues of yellow and she realized that the bursts of color were not only Benjamin. They were hope and joy and the possibility and love. Suddenly she realized that even though it would be difficult, she could be a good mother to Benjamin. She had a lot to learn, but they would learn it together. The world had been given a second chance and so had she.

Drained, but filled in a way she wouldn't have believed possible forty-eight hours ago, Rachel gathered up her sleeping son and went into her studio. She set him near where she could see him and she put a fresh, clean canvas, full of possibility on the easel. And then, with tears of joy this time, she began to paint.

Robert
Indiana

Robert awoke to the honking of car horns out on the street. It sounded like someone had just gotten married or something. His neck felt stiff as he sat up. Sunlight was streaming in, and he squinted to look out the window. Wait a minute…the world didn't end after all? He checked his watch—almost 7 a.m. The asteroid was supposed to wipe out the earth hours ago.

Suddenly, Robert noticed he was not alone in the room. Nora was standing on the far side looking at him. She was wearing an Elsa backpack.

"Hi," said Robert.

"Do we still get to go on the rocket?" asked Nora.

"I don't know," said Robert. "We better see what's going on."

He turned on the TV. CNN was reporting that the asteroid had safely passed by the earth. Some debris from the moon had destroyed part of Kentucky, but everywhere else the danger had largely passed.

Cheryl came running down the stairs. "It's a miracle!" She knelt down and hugged Nora.

"But Mommy, I want to go on the rocket."

"Someday, when you're a grownup, you can go on a rocket. But right now, let's just be happy that the earth's OK." She kissed Nora on the forehead.

Robert glanced back at the TV. Apparently, the President had commandeered the SpaceX rocket and blasted off before midnight. It was unknown if Elon

Musk was aboard or not. There had been no plan to return to earth, so it could be a one-way trip out into space.

Heather and Ben came down the stairs. "What's going on?" asked Heather.

"Looks like it was all a false alarm," said Robert. "The asteroid somehow missed the earth."

"Are you kidding? That's great!" said Ben.

They all hugged one another, laughing and crying. Robert heard more commotion outside. It sounded like a celebration was in full swing.

"I'm hungry, Mommy," said Nora.

"OK, honey, let's get you some Frosted Flakes." Cheryl motioned for them to follow into the kitchen. They had a breakfast of cold cereal and toast. To Robert everything tasted wonderful. They recounted their adventures from the day before, especially the part about smashing through the police barricade.

After breakfast, Robert and Ben went out front to check the car. The euphoric mood continued out on the street. People driving past honked and waved as they went. Robert's car looked slightly damaged; one headlight was cracked and there were some dents in the grill. "Not too bad," said Robert. "Do you want me to drive you back down to Bloomington later?"

"Actually, Heather and I are going to stay here with Cheryl and Nora for a couple days. But after that it would be great to get a ride with you, if you don't have to be at work or anything."

"I'll be glad to take you," said Robert. "Some things are more important than work. And anyway, I decided that my research is pretty much complete."

"You mean for that new medicine you were working on?"

"Yes, I've done enough. If it needs more testing and development, there are others who can handle it."

"That's great. Oh, and Dad, I should mention something."

"What's that?" asked Robert.

"Well, you know, last night with the earth about to end…it didn't really seem necessary for us to…you know…"

"I'm not sure I follow you, Ben."

"Well, Heather and I kind of threw caution to the wind. So, there's a chance you could become a grandfather."

Robert smiled. "Ben, I would love to be a grandfather."

They went back inside and talked a bit more. Then, after Robert had a chance to say goodbye to everyone, he walked out to his car. He started the engine and checked the gas gauge. It was almost on empty, but he didn't have far to go to get home. After his Mad Max performance the day before, he knew there was nothing that could stop him. As he drove away, he laughed and said to himself, "And the Road Warrior? That was the last we ever saw of him. He lives now only in my memories."

Videl Corbin

near Leitchfield, Kentucky

"What time is it? I'm hungry," Corbin said as he walked toward the kitchen.

"My watch says it's about 6 a.m.," someone answered.

"Has anyone checked the radio?" someone asked.

Corbin replied, "It probably isn't going to work. I had wired the antenna through the door. It probably melted away in the fire."

"It can't hurt to try. I'll see if it works," Mae said as she put down her cards. "I'm losing anyway."

Corbin smiled at her and went to the kitchen. He poured some cereal, ate, and went to check the door.

The door was no longer red and he was able to walk into the room. He found a hammer and heavy gloves. The door was still hot but rolled up. The door to the outside was too hot to touch but looked in good shape.

Corbin grabbed an egg basket and went to feed the chickens. "Same routine," he told the chickens.

"Kelsey, where are you," Barton yelled. Banjo dashed ahead of him sniffing and exploring the cave.

"I'm in here Dad," she yelled. Banjo took off at a sprint and skidded past the entrance to the library. A quick recovery and he disappeared. Barton followed the sound of a happy dog.

"What are you doing down here?" he asked and sat down at the table. "Everyone is looking for you."

Kelsey looked at her father over the top of her glasses. "Dad, you have to read these," She slid a notebook across the table.

Barton stopped the notebook with a hard slap. "What is it?"

"I think that it is Corbin's diary."

"I can't read a man's diary," Barton sniffed and pushed his chair away from the table. "I can't even read a woman's diary. Women get angry when you do that."

"Seriously, Dad," she smirked and couldn't help but smile. "It tells everything that happened in the last six months."

Barton was intrigued, but not enough to risk bodily injury, "Everything?"

"Including what the Angel said, word for word, and a sketch," Kelsey was in awe. "The angel appeared to Corbin by the entrance where I came in. It told him what was coming."

Barton pushed in his chair and pulled the notebook toward him, "What else does it say."

"The Angel told him the only safe place was beneath him. It told Corbin that he had to find the chamber and bring the believers to safety." Kelsey was excited. "What happened yesterday," she paused. "It's exactly what he said when he was preaching in town."

Barton opened the cover and looked at the Angel. The dark-haired figure on the lined sheet of paper looked nothing like the angels from the movies. "This isn't an angel. Angel's wings are white. This guy has dark hair and the shadow things around him look like they might be wings but they're black."

"Are you racist? Why can't an Angel have dark hair and dark wings?" She raised an eyebrow over the top of her glasses, "Look at the eyes. They look movie angel worthy."

"They are full of energy."

"Dad, Corbin built this shelter all by himself. He dug it out, he filled it, he prepared all of this," a tear started to course down her cheek as she swept her arms out in a widening arc. "Nobody believed him, but he did it anyway. He built all of this to save our lives."

Barton looked up from the notebook and tried to imagine the magnitude of the work.

"He didn't know if the Angel was real. He didn't know if the end would happen. He didn't question that this was a message from God. He only believed." Kelsey wiped the tear from her face.

"You know what this is?" Barton asked.

"It's a miracle." She answered. "He was visited by an Angel and given a message. Corbin is a prophet."

"We were told that the world was going to end and he said that it wasn't. What do you think it's like outside?"

Kelsey sat back in her chair and pondered the fate of the world. "It has to be bad. Corbin's cavern is filled like a prepper. There's enough in here to last six months."

"We need to get back to the group and listen to the radio," Barton said and stood up.

"We need to get outside," Kelsey stood up and gathered the notebooks and moved them to a shelf. "We need to see what happened."

With the notebooks back where they belonged, they walked out of the room.

"There you are," Corbin smiled in surprise. "We were getting worried."

"We were exploring," Barton responded.

"The radio didn't work," Mae said and smiled. "We followed the wire to the door and it isn't hot. Can we fix it?"

Everyone was smiling.

"I need to call my wife," said a man from the back. "I can call her if we can get the door open."

"I'm not sure if a cell phone will work. That explosion and fire probably took out the cell towers. I have a ham radio in storage, but we need to put up an antenna outside when we fix the radio wire," Corbin said.

"Can we go outside?" asked Kelsey.

"The doors were hot earlier but we can check again," said Corbin as he jumped to his feet and started walking toward the stairs. There was a new energy and lightness to his gait. The weight of the world was lifting and he was happy for the second wind. His long stride soon had him moving up the stairs.

Kelsey jogged behind him and couldn't catch up. Halfway up the stairs she heard the sound of metal moving. She was out of breath as she finally topped the stairs and saw Corbin quickly tap, tap on the door, and then put his hand against it.

Corbin turned and smiled at her. He seemed so much younger than he did the day prior. "It's warm, but not hot. I think we can try to open it." He slid the bars away from the door. He scowled and said, "It won't open." Corbin pushed without affect. The door would not open. "We'll have to try the other door."

Kelsey followed him down the stairs and toward the stable. This time more people followed and a small crowd stood looking at the storage room door.

Corbin tapped the door, put his hand against the door, then turned and smiled at the group. He started lifting the bars away from the door and many hands reached out to help. "Here goes," Corbin said as he pushed against the door. It wouldn't move. "Damn it, next time the earth is going to end, we make the doors open inward," Corbin said and leaned against the door.

"We'll have to use the truck to open it," Barton said.

Corbin nodded and said, "We do this and we will not be able to seal the door shut again."

"The door is cool, so I think we're safe," responded Barton.

"We're safe from fire, but what if there is something else," said a voice from the crowd.

"Like what," snapped another voice. "Do you think that demons are waiting for us right outside that door? Umph!" Someone had elbowed the man in the ribs.

"There's something blocking the door. That's all," said a woman holding her elbow.

Corbin looked around at the frightened faces and made a decision. "Everyone get back in the stable. I'm opening the door."

"I'm helping," said Barton as he walked to the passenger side. He watched as the crowd fell back to the relative safety of the stable.

Corbin opened the truck door and looked back at the sealed exit that held back the unknown. Be it demons lurking just beyond, or not, they were going to find out. He slid behind the wheel and closed the door. "I built this place to keep people in. I didn't plan on anything after," he said as he gripped the steering wheel. The anxiety in his voice was in contrast to the determination in his eyes. "I believe that we will be safe," he said and started to slowly back the truck against the door.

Barton closed his eyes and crossed his fingers. "God, protect us from what lies beyond that door."

The truck bumped against the door and stopped. Corbin pressed down on the accelerator and the tires started to spin against the smooth stone surface. Barton continued the prayers as Corbin shifted gears and pulled forward. "Shut up Barton. The prayers aren't working," he said and shifted the truck into reverse and slammed the accelerator against the floor. The tires began to spin, catch, and the truck slammed against the door. The doors groaned in metallic pain and slammed open. The truck accelerated out of the door and through the branches of ash and dust, that had once been a tree. Corbin braked to a stop and looked at the hole the truck had made through the tree. Slowly, the tree disintegrated in front of him. "Look at that," he said and punched Barton's arm.

Barton opened his eyes in time to see the tree become dust. "What the hell?"

Corbin looked around in horror. Through the smoke and ash in the air he could see that the barn was gone. The house was gone. "Everything is gone." He coughed and covered his mouth with a rag.

Barton looked around. There wasn't anything as far as he could see. "Where is everything?"

"Gone," answered Corbin. "It's just…gone." The wind kicked up and lifted ash from the ground and deposited it on the truck. "We need to get the truck inside and cover that door. There'll be ash and smoke in everything."

"The kids are gone." Barton said without emotion. "There's no way that they survived."

Corbin switched gears to pull back into the storage room and saw the crowd of people emerging in stunned awe. He honked the horn and the sound seemed to travel forever without an echo. He pulled forward and watched as they slowly moved out of the way and he coasted by. He parked the truck and walked over to join the others. Awe had changed to shock. Dusty tears rolled down their faces. Eyes darted around to landmarks that were once so familiar. They could not find a match to their destroyed memories. "Everyone inside," he said.

"I've got no bars," said the man as he held his phone above his head.

The crowd didn't move. A woman trembled and sat down in the ash. A man pulled her back up and said, "I'll help you."

"Everyone inside," Corbin said with a much sterner voice. He knew it would be bad, but he had no idea of how bad it would really be. He expected tree stumps and remnants of houses. There was nothing. The land itself seemed to have changed.

The crowd seemed relieved to have any reason to go inside. "Is the whole world like this?" asked a woman in the crowd. There was no response.

Corbin rolled the internal door down and leaned his back against it. "We have to remember that we are safe here. We need to join the others and say a prayer for the ones that didn't survive."

"We can pray while we work, Corbin. Where's that radio and antenna?'" asked Barton. "We still need to get that put up."

"I'll go get it," Corbin said and walked away. The crowd followed.

"We should find out what's blocking the other door," Barton said.

"One thing at a time," Corbin said.

"You and the big guy can take care of the ham radio. A few of us can go around the hill and clear the door."

"Okay," Corbin agreed. He wanted to do everything himself, but knew he couldn't. "If you can't find it in an hour, come back."

"We'll be fine," he said and motioned for the others to follow.

Everything was covered with ash. Barton returned to the storage room and retrieved long poles and a shovel for the group to carry. It soon became apparent that the danger would be falling into a hole and swallowed up by the thick and ever-present remnant of their former lives. It was a miserable hike with the blowing glass like dust from above and the ground radiated heat from below. They coughed and hiked until they found cars piled on one another. "That's mine," said the man. "I wonder if that is covered by insurance."

"Good question," someone else said. "I don't know if asteroid damage coverage is part of my package."

"The entrance has to be here somewhere," said Barton. "There was a building around it, but it's got to be gone. Look along that hillside," he said to the group.

The group broke apart and the men started pushing their posts through the ash that had drifted against the hillside, hoping for a metallic response. "I have something over here." A voice called out. "It's the door. It's blocked by something big. I think it's a car." The group gathered and helped shovel away the ash and found the door.

"We need to move this car and we should be able to open it," said Barton.

"I tried to push it, but there are no tires," someone said. "We're going to have to flip it away from the door."

"You're right. Alright, everyone on this side," said Barton. "On three, lift with your legs," he said, out of habit. "One, twooo, three, lift."

The ash fell away from the car and the metal hulk flipped over without much effort. Barton turned and then looked back, "That's my daughter's car."

Barton ran over and looked inside, "My grandkids, I left this with Kelsey's husband and kids. They came, but it was too late." There was nothing in the car. He looked down at the ash below his feet and jumped as far away from the car as he could.

A man walked over and put his hand on Barton's shoulders, "We're sorry Barton. We'll flip this thing over with the other cars and hope your daughter doesn't see. You can tell her later."

"Yes, yes, that's a good idea," Barton stuttered and recovered his composure.

The group flipped the car over with the other cars and walked back to the door. They finished clearing the door and, with a whoop of victory, they yanked it open.

"Find that wire and see if we can get the radio to work," a man said. "I don't plan on being incommunicado." He stopped and looked around. "Barton, pull it together. We need you."

Barton turned from the car and walked to the opening. "Incommunicado, what kind of word is that? What the hell does that even mean?" Barton smacked his pole against the door in anger. "I think we can tie the wire to the metal door until we can secure it," Barton started pounding the door. Anger and pain fueled his attempt at destruction. "We'll have to lean," Bam, "this thing," Bam, "against the door frame until later." Bam, Bam, Bam.

Barton looked up at the hill and contemplated climbing it but realized they were all in danger. "Guys, we need a shelter around the doors. If we get any rain, all that ash is going to end up in the chamber."

"Oh, shit," said one of the men. "You better stop banging that pole against the door. You'll bury us in ash. I saw some sheet metal and 2x4's. C'mon guys."

"Tell Corbin to look at the other door. It's probably the same," Barton called after them. He wanted to hit the door again. "Try the radio now," he yelled and walked down the steps. He was exhausted and filled with guilt. "How do I tell them," he asked himself.

At the bottom of the steps, he followed the sound of radio static to his wife. He needed to be near her. "Anything?" he asked when he found her. "Where's Kelsey?"

Kelsey said she was taking Sarah to the library," She said as she slowly turned the dial on the radio.

Out of the static came a voice. Mae pulled her hand away with a start, then smiled and turned the dial back. Through the static and sparks they heard the announcer checking off a list of places impacted by asteroids. "We still do not have any information about Kentucky. As previously reported, Kentucky took the largest hit from the asteroid impacts. Witnesses that have flown over the area describe it as a wasteland. Planes have only gone so far before turning back. Ash is clogging engines and it may be weeks before the area can be surveyed. Please keep the citizens of Kentucky in your thoughts and prayers tonight. They will need it. Now, back to your regularly scheduled programming."

"Kentucky is a wasteland. That describes what we saw outside." Barton said. "I'll check to see if Corbin has that ham radio up."

"How's it going," Barton asked.

"We finally have the antenna wire up. We're about to connect it to the unit and see if it works," one of the men said.

Corbin walked in trailed by a thick wire, "Hey Barton, I heard you found the door. We'll get the roofs over the doors after we get this running."

"According to the radio, Kentucky is a wasteland," Barton told them.

"Kentucky, as in all of Kentucky?" asked the man.

"It's possible that we are the only people alive for miles."

Corbin didn't look at them. He attached the wire to the connector and screwed it into the back of the set. "That should do it,"

Corbin flipped a switch and listened to the hum of the machine. He reached for the tuner and pressed the lever on the microphone. "Hello, Is anyone there?" There was no response. He reached out and turned the knob. "Hello, Is anyone there?"

"This book says you need to say CQ," said the tattooed man holding an instruction manual.

"Oh, Okay," Corbin turned the knob and said, "CQ, is anyone there?" He repeated this over and over until finally, a response. "CQ this is WX7QLF, Whisky X-Ray Seven Quebec Lima Foxtrot, WX7QLF in Montana calling, copy now. Who am I talking to?" The storage room was filled the sound of cheer. Corbin hushed them and pressed the button on the mic. "This is Corbin, Videl Corbin, from Kentucky. We're here. We're alive."

"Holy Shit Balls, Kentucky. My name is Frank from Montana and I've never been so happy to hear a voice through my set before," yelled an excited Frank from Montana. "It sounds like you've never been on air before. Here's my training. Don't touch anything. I've got your band and I'll be back. I'm going to pass the word and be right back."

The set went silent and the group of survivors sat around in stunned silence waiting for Montana to return. The set crackled and Montana returned. "You there, Kentucky? Everyone is tuning in to listen. Where are you?"

"We're in a cave in west central Kentucky, near Leitchfield," Corbin responded. "We have a few people that want their family to know they are alive," Barton started to name them off.

"How many are you?" a different man interrupted and asked.

"I don't know. We didn't do a head count. About 30, I think," Corbin said feeling the anxiety of the moment start to take over. "I'm going to give you to Barton. I have to take care of our entrance." Corbin stood up and made sure Barton was in place.

"Corbin, don't go," Frank snapped, but Corbin was gone.

Corbin waved most of the people to follow him and moved toward the building materials. "Wood, sheet metal, nails and tools over there, we need to make sure the entrance has a roof and that any runoff is diverted away." Corbin made sure they knew what they were doing and went through the tunnel to the main chamber.

"This is Barton," Barton said a little too loud into the microphone.

"Barton, stay on mic," commanded Frank. "How did you survive? The whole state is dust," Montana asked. There was a moment of static and Frank came back on, "Sorry, that was rude."

'I don't know about the whole state, but everything around us is ash." Barton released the mic as the group knocked over a stack of metal sheets. Barton clicked the mic and continued. "Now, I know you won't believe me, but how we came to be here and survive is a miracle. Six months ago, an Angel appeared before Corbin and told him that a great calamity was upon the world. He must dig below and find the chamber that will protect the believers…"

Corbin walked into the kitchen and poured himself some water. Mae walked in behind him and asked, "Do you want me to make you something?"

Corbin shook his head. "I needed a drink."

"The kids are fed and there's some soup in the pot on the stove," she said. "You can get some when you're hungry."

The radio chatter stopped and an announcement was made that, by some miracle, there were people in central Kentucky that had survived.

In the library, Kelsey put down the last notebook. She picked up a new notebook and a pencil. On page one she wrote,

"THE BOOK OF CORBIN by Videl Corbin"

Melony
Tampa, Florida

The next morning, Melony woke to a gong. Startled, she lumbered out of bed and forgot temporarily where she was. Then the importance of the day hit her. The world didn't end. Wait, the world didn't end! She was still alive! Everyone was still alive! She had to get a letter out to her family. She was happy, happy to stay in this monastery for the next ten days. She wanted alcohol but wasn't going to tell them in fear they wouldn't think her serious about her decision.

A nun knocked and peeked her head in, "Are you ready?" It was a different nun than yesterday; this nun was pale with blue eyes.

Melony looked at the nun "I am."

"We will go to the fountain and meet with the head nun, Rosmerta. Everything will be explained there. You can call me Kahlie," she said.

Melony asked, "Why didn't the world end?"

"I do not know. We are still here. We go about our daily life; the outside changes affect our routine very little. This practice keeps us mindful of the present moment," Kahlie replied.

She followed nun Kahlie down to the fountain. The path seemed long, but the simple beauty of the walk was peaceful. Her stomach panged as she walked. Melony was weak from lack of sleep and the alcohol she consumed. "This monastery didn't look this big from the outside," Melony said.

"Yes, I suppose so. Buddhist's practice minimalism. So, we only have what we need," Kahlie said.

They entered the courtyard. The nuns meditated around the fountain. A nun got up and greeted them, "Hello, are you ready to begin, Melony?" The caring in her voice

215

caught Melony off guard. Nun Rosmerta handed her a paper with the daily schedule, a list of rules, and some suggestions. "Once you read this and you accept our ways of living, then we shall continue. Not all Buddhist are like us in their ways." Melony skimmed through the paper, it was straight forward.

She would be focusing on meditating, cleaning. Also, a list of items that would be prohibited during her stay; she read No: talking, cell phones, media, video cameras, writing, and reading. The people in the introductory phase were not allowed to talk?

"No new input is the goal, you must clear your mind then the real learning begins," sister Rosmerta answered her unspoken question. Melony owned none of the items listed. "We would like you to check in with our doctor, given your circumstances," Rosmerta said. After agreeing, they handed her the white long-sleeved shirt, and matching pants that she would change into afterwards.

Rosmerta approached her with a razor blade in one hand," Do you want your head shaved?"

"Yes," Melony ran her hand through her medium length brown hair as a goodbye.

Rosmerta used an old straight blade. She poured water on Melony's head and patted it dry with a towel. The head Nun looked at Melony, "This is your family now, please stay as long as you like. Breakfast is after this. Please follow Nun Kahlie for three days to understand the routine."

Kahlie looked at Melony, "I remember feeling tranquil after that."

Tranquil was an understatement, Melony wanted to jump up and down. She had chosen mindfulness over mindlessness! She felt the need for a drink surface, and she knew this would be a hard day. She wanted to scream, but she held it in. She would keep the battle inside of her. If she didn't obey its command, then hopefully it wouldn't have any power over her. After all she wasn't supposed to talk. Maybe that was partly the point. She wanted to leave and buy alcohol, but she couldn't give in. She needed to deal with her negative companion.

She got bored of meditation fast, but she really liked the results. Her new family offered encouragement at every turn. Buddhist ways were different, yet simple in nature. The path ahead would be long, but she was ready to change her life. She thought a lot of her marriage and could see she wasn't ever happy with who she was. So how could she be happy in a married life?

~

A day of meditation had exhausted her, it was nine pm and time to go to bed. She had plenty of time to think about how her mistakes affected her in ways she never considered.

Her mind and body would be affected for weeks by the alcohol abuse, but today she took charge. She never thought that one day would make a difference. She had more control over her emotions. She wanted to drink, but knew she was making the right choice for her and her family.

She got into her bed and looked up at the moon, they were very similar now. Everyone had a piece missing after today, but just like the moon she also made do with what was left. She let the knowledge and acceptance of that fill her. She could finally be the mom that Michael could be proud of. That night she had peaceful dreams.

Summer

Kansas City, Missouri

"Get your damned clothes on before the kids find you," Wayne growled. John decided it was better than his shouting, but his menacing glare made John unsure what to do next.

"Wayne, what happened?" Summer asked sitting up and rubbing her eyes in confusion.

"Some heroes saved our lives. I almost wish they hadn't after coming home to find you naked in bed with my brother."

"I can explain," Summer said.

"You were scared and the world was ending so it seemed like a good time to screw around on your husband?" Wayne asked.

"It wasn't like that," John said.

"Wasn't it? Her I can almost understand. But, you, my twin brother, how could you do this to me?"

"If you have to ask that then you've been blind this whole time," John said quietly.

"You need to get out of my house, brother, before I shoot you with your own gun." John doubted Wayne would do it but he wasn't about to test him in that moment. He got up and grabbed his clothes off the floor.

"I'll be by later to check on you," John said to Summer.

"I think you'd better plan to leave my wife alone," Wayne said.

John hesitated by the door. He wanted to scoop Summer up and take her away. But what would happen if he did? He could never offer her the financial stability his brother did. He barely had anything left from the sales of the company. He'd never managed to stay at any job longer than a few months. Hell, he'd barely shown up at his own company. He wasn't like Wayne. He'd never been the responsible one.

Instead of stealing Summer away, as every instinct in him wanted to do, he walked through the door and into a new day. The world looked much the same as it had the day before. The neighborhood houses were still standing. Birds were chirping in the sky. Only the damaged moon showed how close they'd come to the end. The moon, like him, would never be whole again. John wondered what he should do now.

~

Wayne sunk down on the side of the bed. All his blustering was gone. He covered his eyes with the palm of his hand and they sat in silence for a long moment.

"I can forgive you for this. It won't be easy for me to do it, but I know I can. Lots of people did things last night they weren't proud of because they didn't think they'd ever see another day. You were scared and lonely. John was here protecting you and the children. I'm not saying it was right. Our wedding vows didn't have an end of the world exceptions clause. But it is understandable."

"Wayne, I..."

"Don't tell me you love him. Please. I don't think I could bear that. I know you've always admired him. I've been the dull practical brother and he's been the bad boy dreamer and schemer. You might think you want that. Who wouldn't want a life of adventure? That is, until the bill collectors are on the phone and you can't afford food."

"Even you have to admit things have been difficult between us for some time," she said. He'd have to be blind not to realize that she'd been going through the motions in their marriage. She couldn't remember the last time she'd told him she loved him and meant it.

"I work too much. I realized that on my way home. I spend too much time away from you and the boys. I wanted to provide a good life for us. But, if you'll stay and try to fix the life we have, I'll give up my trucking job. I'll find something where I can come home every night."

"I don't know if that will be enough," Summer admitted. His absence made living the lie of their love easier. If he'd been home more it was possible that they wouldn't have lasted as long as they had. When they argued she could always shrug her shoulders and remind herself that in another day or so he would be gone and their argument would be meaningless. When he returned a week later their argument would be forgotten. They would again go through the motions of being married until he returned to his truck and the open road as she managed the household alone.

"Running off with my brother isn't going to fix our marriage. You want to put the boys through that? You want us to go to court and battle over child support and visitation schedules? You aren't happy in your life now? Well, I can promise it will be much worse if you leave me for my brother." She thought he meant for his tone to be threatening but she could feel the fear emanating from him. Had he truly been oblivious to the deterioration of their marriage?

"I don't know if I love you anymore," Summer said. It was a relief to admit the truth that had been hiding under the surface for at least the past three years. She wasn't sure when the love had gone but three years before she'd been hospitalized with pneumonia. Wayne had spent a week in the hospital by her side and she'd spent the whole week wishing he'd leave.

"I know that I love you. Ever since the day I came into the cafe and saw you waiting tables I knew I wanted to marry you. I can't explain it. My eyes fell on you and my heart said that's the girl you're gonna marry."

Summer

She remembered that day too, though a bit differently than he did. When Wayne had paid for his meal, he'd asked for her number. She hadn't given it to him. So, he'd come in every day that week and ask to be seated at her table. When he paid his bill, he asked for her number again and again until she finally relented. When he called to ask her on a date she accepted because she was sure he would keep calling until she did.

"You were very persistent," Summer said.

"If John had wanted you bad enough, he'd have wooed you away from me before the wedding," Wayne said.

"He was just getting over Vanessa and he didn't want to hurt you."

"I'd have walked to the ends of the earth to have the woman I loved. My whole life has been about taking care of you and the boys. Making sure you are comfortable."

"You always took care of us," she agreed. Wayne had always been a good provider. He'd been kind and caring since their first date. But there was an impenetrable wall that he kept around his heart and soul. A wall she'd long since given up ever scaling.

"John is fun. I get that. He's spontaneous and he goes through life like it's a game. He's done well for himself despite that but he isn't the type of man you want when the cards are down."

"He was here for me tonight," she said.

"I'd have been here if I could. I went through hell to get here. You have no idea how difficult-"

"I suppose you want me to be grateful that you did that," she said.

"A little gratitude would certainly be appreciated considering all that I do for you."

"It isn't that I'm not grateful, Wayne. I'm very grateful. I'm just not happy."

"Who is happy? Name me one grown up who is handling their business that is really happy. There isn't one. If they say they are then they're a liar. You are a grown woman and a mother. Start acting like it," Wayne said.

"Wayne, I slept with your brother," she whispered. She was still trying to wrap her mind around the fact that it had finally happened. Years of longing had culminated into one night she'd never be able to forget.

"Yeah, and if the world hadn't been ending, I wouldn't be so quick to forgive you. Considering the circumstances, I can understand your lapse in judgment. Now, go tell John that you never want to see him again. He isn't welcome in our house anymore."

"You can forgive me so easily but not your own flesh and blood?"

"He should have known better," Wayne snapped.

They both should have. If there had been an inkling in their minds that a new day would dawn, they would both had held back their longing as they had all these years. But, after they'd come together, she knew there was no returning to a life apart.

~

John opened the door. Summer was on the other side. He wasn't surprised to see her. In fact, he'd been expecting her. "Wayne send you?"

She nodded.

"Wants you to tell me to go fuck off?"

Summer nodded again.

"Well?" John asked steeling himself. He couldn't stay here. He'd have to sell his house. He couldn't be so close to Summer and not see her. And, if he saw her, he'd take her in his arms again. He'd made a mess of things when he'd let her marry his brother. He'd told himself he wasn't ready and that his feelings for Summer had only emerged because of his break up with Vanessa. He'd toasted Wayne and Summer at their wedding all the while trying to push away the unsettling whisper that he should have been the groom. After the wedding, those feelings never really went away. He tried throwing his heart and soul into his company. He dated dozens of women, hoping to feel the same for them as he did for his sister-in-law. But, like a caterpillar to milkweed, he'd been drawn to her and he didn't think, even now, that he could stay away.

"What do you think of a little house on the beach? I know beachfront property usually costs a fortune but maybe we can find a place that was damaged by falling galactic debris. Nothing too severe. Just a crater or two in the back-yard."

"What are you talking about?" John asked, confused. She was supposed to be breaking his heart.

"I'm leaving Wayne," she said. Her eyes caught his and he stared deep inside those pools into the depths of her soul.

"That's crazy," John said. It was crazy. Summer had the American dream complete with a white picket fence.

"I know. But I realized I was never going to be truly happy if I stayed with Wayne. I want to be happy. I deserve to be happy."

A hundred thoughts ran through his mind. "What about the boys? What about-"

She put her finger on his lips to silence him.

"We'll figure all that out later. The world isn't ending today. We still have time. Time to live. Time to love," she said. She stepped forward and wrapped her arms around his waist. He could feel her heart beating against his chest.

"You're crazy. You know that, right," he said.

"Yeah, but at least I get to be crazy with you," she said.

Chris and Kriss
New York, New York

Kriss awoke the next morning, despite the fact that the world was supposed to end.

"None of this should have happened," she thought to herself as she looked around at the baseball stadium where Chris, her new fiancée, was still sleeping through the end of the world.

The stadium lights were too bright, they didn't seem real. She noticed her left hand felling a little heavier, she looked at the ring. She smiled at the ring, but that smile soon became a frown, she shouldn't have said yes, she had a whole life in Kentucky a life she was proud of building for herself, she had a medium sized apartment and a little dog that she missed. She shouldn't have come to New York.

Chris stirred in his sleep and woke up with a start. "What happened? I thought we weren't supposed to be alive today?" He rubbed the sleep out of his eyes.

"I dunno, and I, um, Chris…" she said, but he wasn't listening. He was busy getting to his feet and looking at the moon. Kris looked up.

The moon was missing a large chunk and there was a streak of debris and smoke trails that looked like an ugly scar that stretched across the entire sky. The sun was rising and the smoke trail was lit up with bright orange. It looked like the sky was on fire.

"I don't think that was supposed to happen," Chris said.

Kriss looked down at her ring. "Chris, we need to—" she was cut off by the sound of sirens in the distance.

They made their way into the stands of the stadium and soon they were at the top, looking down upon a smoldering city. Every building was perfectly intact, no damage from an asteroid but plenty of damage from the previous day and night of rioting in the streets. Thick columns of smoke billowed from cars still ablaze, and buildings smoldered. People milled about, not really knowing where to go or what to do.

"We gotta find out what happened. Why are we still standing here? The planet was supposed to be destroyed today." Chris said. He pulled out his phone, it was out of battery, he couldn't check the news.

"Chris! We need to talk," she said.

"Yeah, we should talk to somebody about what happened last night," Chris said distractedly.

"No Chris, I mean about us. We need to talk about what happened last night. I think we made a mistake. I shouldn't have —" She paused and buried her face in her hands, tears streaming down her face, her hands getting soaking wet.

"What are you saying?" Chris asked as he stepped closer to comfort her.

"You took advantage of me. We haven't seen each other in years and suddenly you message me out of nowhere and want to catch up. I happened to be in New York because I had an interview. It didn't go well, and I thought it would be nice to see a familiar face, and it was, but I have a life in Kentucky, a happy one. I can't just up and leave my home. I didn't tell you earlier, but I'm seeing someone, and he makes me so happy. What we had in high school was fun but we aren't kids anymore. I've moved on, not that this wasn't fun but it's not a life. Eating a fortune of food from one of the most expensive restaurants in the city, speeding around the streets in a supercar, committing criminal acts of vandalism in a school, and jumping off a building are all fun, but nobody lives like that. Yesterday was fun and it helped me get my mind off the interview that went horribly, and the news of the end of the world, but when you proposed last night, I had just had the most terrifying and awesome experience of my life, and I was pretty drunk, and I didn't think we would actually wake up today. So, I thought what the heck, sure I'll say yes and I'll spend the last few hours being engaged to my high school sweetheart. But we don't live in a fantasy, we live in the real world, and the real world isn't all sunshine and rainbows. But we persevere and we make the best of it. Life is a roller coaster of ups and downs. Last night was a very high up but today we have to come back down to reality. What goes up must come down. Look around, the world didn't end and we have to pick up the pieces and go back to our lives," Kriss said solemnly.

The sparkle in her eyes had left and Chris watched it leave. He had no reply, she was right, he did take advantage of her. He played on her emotions and made her say yes even though she truly didn't want to. Chris dropped to his knees.

"I'm so sorry Chris, but I have a boyfriend and a dog to go back to in Kentucky. I truly do love you but I can't abandon my life and be your wife," Kriss said. She realized that her words didn't help the situation.

After a while, Chris recovered and began to speak. "I gave up my whole life for you, I quit my job and robbed a bank, you were right to suspect that I did, I robbed the bank of all the money I could carry. I shot somebody!" He sobbed suddenly and startled Kriss. "I lost everything, I even sold my house to have more money so I could make everything happen for you last night. I'm sorry it didn't work the way I thought it would. I wish the world did end last night because to me, this, this right here feels like it's the end of the world."

"Chris, don't talk like that, it's not the end of the world, you survived! We both survived! This is a new beginning and you can finally work a job you love instead of fetching coffee for your boss and paying out of your own pocket for it and you can follow your dreams!" Kriss said, feigning excitement.

Chris and Kriss

Chris looked up and met her gaze "How? I have no money and no house. I lost everything because the world didn't end. I'm going to do the only thing that a reasonable and responsible member of society should do." Chris said while never breaking eye contact with Kriss.

"And what's that?" she asked.

"I'm going to turn myself in. I robbed a bank and shot someone. I should pay for those crimes," Chris said with hopeless determination.

"That's the dumbest thing I've ever heard!" Kriss said.

"Dumber than jumping off a building and landing in a stadium before the world ends?" Chris said trying to stifle a smile.

Kriss looked dumbfounded for a moment then attempted to feign anger to mask her bewilderment.

"Well, no, that's dumber, but still!"

They walked out of the stadium, still wearing the tuxedo and the dress, looking like a fashionable mess, both feeling an overwhelming amount of emotions. Happy the world didn't end. Sad that the world didn't end. Happiness for the world almost ending. Regret. Pity. Pain. Uncertainty. Love.

As they walked, the streets that were filled with greed and selfishness and rioting, were replaced with cheering and generosity, a sense of friendship, and compassion. A random stranger came up and told them how happy he was to be alive. They didn't know how to respond since they were struggling to grasp reality and its harshness.

They arrived at the police station and Chris walked, tripped, and stumbled, courageously up to the mean looking cop who seemed to be at least a hundred years old and told him that he robbed a bank.

"Did'ja rob more than a million?" He said unenthused.

"Um, no? I didn't really have time to count it, I just grabbed as much as I could," Chris said, gesturing with his arms like he was holding a pile of something invisible.

"Then it wasn't enough for us to care. Do you know how many robberies happened yesterday with this whole 'end of the world business? You probably don't, it was a lot! A whole heap of a lot! And a bigger heap of paperwork! Your robbery is small potatoes and more paperwork than it's worth. Enjoy the money and don't spend it all in one go!" he said wagging his finger in Chris's face.

"Well, I did kinda spend it all in one go... and I shot somebody." Chris said as though he was offering a counter offer in a haggling deal.

"You shot somebody? You're not the brightest bulb in the box are ya?" The officer begrudgingly pulled out a piece of paper and a pen. "Well did'ja kill them?" He asked with more enthusiasm.

"No...? I shot them in the leg." Chris said with a little embarrassment.

"So they bled out, I'm guessing. That's pretty serious. What caliber bullet? And what type of gun? Rifle? Pistol? You seem like a pistol kinda guy," the officer said, leaning to the front of his chair.

"Yeah, it was a pistol," Chris said trying not to look the officer in the eye.

"Well, what's the make? And what size were the bullets?" he asked, as if the answer were the next play in an exciting football game.

"I, I um don't know much about guns, it was black...? And the size of the bullets... well, it, uh it shot BB's."

The slap was heard throughout the police station and reverberated around the walls. Chris looked up, the officer's forehead was turning red in the shape of a handprint.

"You came all the way in here to confess to a meaningless crime you committed with a BB gun?!? Well! I better lock you up! And believe you me, you'll be locked up for as long as you deserve for your crimes!" the officer said.

Kriss's laughter died down as the officer waddled around the desk, nearly knocking it over with his girth, probably too many years on the force or eating doughnuts. He grabbed Chris by the arm and walked him down the hall to the small cell and pushed him in and slammed the door so hard that it bounced and swung ajar. He didn't lock the door, nor did he bother closing the door completely. He just stood there with his arms folded across his chest and tapped his foot.

"Idiot," The officer said. "Get out of here! I needed a laugh after all this end of the world garbage, we've got bigger fish to fry, and you're just small potatoes. I gotta get back to work and I gotta go shred the forms I was filling out about your BB gun assault. You're free to go. Moron." The officer laughed, and his rotund belly jiggled like jelly filling in a jelly-filled doughnut. Kriss laughed so hard she had to steady herself against the wall.

"Come on Chris, let's get out of here!" Kriss said when her laughter died down a little.

"Where will we go? I don't have a place to stay anymore?" Chris said.

"My place! We're going to Kentucky!" Kriss said.

They walked out of the police station. They say prison changes a man, but I suppose you'd have to be there more than half a second for that to really take effect, because Chris felt the exact same as before being a "hardened criminal". They stepped on a bus heading out of state.

"Does this bus go to Kentucky?" Kriss asked the bus driver.

"Um, I don't think any bus is going to Kentucky. Didn't you hear the news?" the bus driver said.

"No. My phone is dead I haven't been able to check the news," Kriss said, holding up her phone as if the driver wouldn't believe her.

November 8th

"That asteroid thing that was supposed to hit us and wipe us all off the map missed its target, the moon got in the way. Saved the world. But it hit the moon, and a big chunk broke off and hit Kentucky. Nothin' left in that whole state. Weird that it only hit Kentucky and nothing else if ya ask me," the bus driver said.

"Kentucky is gone? What will I do? It's like the end of the world!" Kriss said over-dramatically. The emotional roller coaster made her nauseous. Her knees buckled and she dropped to her knees and began to cry. The bus driver offered to charge her phone.

After rebooting it displayed several messages on the screen. Most were from her boyfriend in Kentucky. Twenty-seven missed calls, one hundred and nine missed texts, and a bunch of spam emails she never even looked at. She read the texts.

Her boyfriend said there was some crazy person talking about angels and a shelter of some kind and that he would be safe if he stayed, but he thought it sounded like a hoax. The texts seemed to be cut off in the middle of a sentence. She called him, the phone was no longer in service. She called again and again. The phone was dead, and so was he.

"Kriss, a very wise woman once said, 'this isn't the end of the world, it's just the beginning,'" Chris said. "You survived the end of the world. You can have a fresh start in life."

"Chris, I love you. Sometimes I hate you, but it's only because you're too good for me. I guess I'm stuck with you until the next apocalypse," Kriss said, conflicted, not knowing which emotion to feel. She stood and hugged Chris, she sobbed into his shoulder with a smile on her face. Apparently, her eyes decided to be sad while her mouth decided to be happy. Life is whatever you decide it to be.

:(:

Happiness is a perspective.
It just depends on how you spin it.

Birdie
Idyllwild, California

Birdie woke up in the yard, as the sun rose over the mountain ridge and shined its way through the trees, directly into her face. She first noticed that she was freezing. She noticed second that she was half-naked, which was probably why she was freezing. She covered her face with her hands and sat up. "Good god my head is pounding!" She looked around, and thankfully, still seemed to be alone.

"Holy, crap. I'm still here. Everything is still here."

Birdie ran into the house and turned on a T.V., but it was still the same emergency message. She ran back to the yard and carefully picked her way through the trees and brush to the edge of the ridge line. A sharp drop-off led to a river about a hundred feet below. She could see the town in the distance, and it looked like hell had broken loose. About a dozen large fires sent black smoke into the sky, and she could see no flashing lights to indicate they were being attended to. Half of the town was flooded from what looked like massive flooding coming inward from the Pacific Ocean. There were a few cars on the road and it looked like they were headed to the highway, away from Fleming.

Birdie hugged the robe tighter around her body and slowly made her way back to the house. What now? Should she go into town to try to help? Leave Harper and James for someone else to find - eventually? James could rot in his own putrid filth for all Birdie cared, but Harper was a different story. She deserved better. Birdie knew she needed to bury Harper, and she had enough time on her hands, but she needed to find better burying attire. She examined the guest bedroom closet again, but there were no clothes. She did find some aspirin and took two along with a quick breakfast of fruit from a basket on the kitchen counter. She wasn't quite

231

ready to face the master bedroom yet, so a quick look in the basement was rewarded with a box marked "Donate". She found a worn tee shirt promoting a band she'd never heard of and a pair of shorts with paint on them. Both were a decent fit and once she put the garden boots back on, Birdie decided she was work-ready.

A shed at the far back of the property was unlocked. Birdie imagined that since the nearest neighbor was easily a half of a mile away, Harper had trusted that anything inside would not be disturbed. From the looks of the shed, Harper appeared correct in that assumption since every tool and gardening item was clean, well-organized, and present. It was filled with any yard gadget you could imagine and they each seemed to have an intended place. She quickly found a shovel and a pair of pink gardening gloves.

Birdie surveyed the property and found a spot about twenty feet inside the forest, straight back from where the biggest bird house was installed. She knew it was silly, but she wanted Harper to have a view of the birds she seemed to love so much since they appeared everywhere in the house. Birdie had found them embroidered on hand towels, on the comforter in the guest room, and even on the paper towels in the kitchen. She felt a strange sense of connection and duty to Harper that she, someone named Birdie, should be the one to lay her to rest. It took Birdie a few hours to dig, stopping for the occasional water break, and she estimated she could only manage about four feet down, because the soil was a bit loose and the sides were starting to come down a little. It was deep enough to protect her from animals and prevent the smell from escaping. Birdie wiped her brow and put the shovel to the side of the hole. She decided she should eat something, she's spent most of her energy digging and still had a huge task ahead of her. because she didn't think she would have much appetite after dealing with Harper's body.

Birdie

She found lunch meat in the fridge and bread in a cupboard. Harper seemed to keep somewhat healthy food on hand. Birdie was used to either fast food or microwave meals. She found some wheat crackers, and paired with another piece of fruit, rounded out a decent lunch. As she ate, Birdie contemplated what she would do after she buried Harper. This seemed as safe a place as any. It had been a quiet refuge - well, after she'd dealt with James. But what the hell was going on out there? Why was the Earth still intact? It was frustrating to not have contact with the outside world to know what was going on, but Birdie thought she should probably enjoy whatever peace she could get, for as long as she could get it. She wasn't looking forward to what came next but thought it best to just get it over and done with.

She paused at the bottom of the stairs and gave herself a small pep talk. "C'mon Bird. You can do this. You're brave and you're strong. There is no time for sadness now." She willed herself to the master bedroom door and opened it. There was a smell, and even though it had made her gag, it was not too bad yet. But it was obvious she needed to get Harper in the ground as soon as possible. She decided that rolling her up in the bed sheets was probably best to contain her and drag her easily through the house. Untucking the comforter and sheets, she rotated Harper cross-wise on the bed and tightly rolled her to the end. Birdie tied the ends as tightly as could and started pulling from the end head of the Harper burrito. Harper's feet hit the floor with a heavy thump. "Oh god. I am so sorry!", Birdie said. "I know you don't mind but I'm trying my best here and I really don't want to hurt you." She pulled Harper through the bedroom and down the hallway without incident but paused at the top of the stairs. "Ok. So. This is gonna smart. I'll try to be easy." Cradling the head end as tightly as she could, Birdie worked her way down the stairs, an apology following every resounding thud as the feet end hit each step. When she made it to the bottom, she paused to catch her breath. Birdie threw a shout toward the living room to Dead James. "Typical that you would sit down on the job when there's work to be done!" Then she muttered to herself, "Best that you never lay a finger on this woman again though. I'd kill you twice."

"You're talking to dead people Birdie. You do realize that, don't you?", she laughed to herself. "Well, sure," she answered as she lifted Harper's head and began pulling, "These are my friends now. They've opened their lovely home and been so hospitable. It would be rude of me not to make conversation." A few more thuds and apologies later and Birdie had made it through the yard and to the hole. She tried to lay Harper down in the hole as gently and as reverently as possible with a last push of energy. She covered her with the soil and packed it down as tightly as she could. A small ceramic bird sculpture she found in the shed served as a marker. Birdie had never given a eulogy but wanted to say a little something for the woman that she never met, but somehow knew. "I know it wasn't easy, or fair. What he did to you. I've learned that monsters disguise themselves with charm and pretty words that cast, like a spell over those people that just want to always try to see the good in people. It wasn't your fault for picking him." Birdie choked back a sob and for the first time said out loud what she had not been able to say to herself yet. "We have to forgive ourselves, because it's them that need to pay a price. Not us. Not you. I hope you're somewhere real nice and at peace." Birdie wiped her eyes and brow with the bottom of her tee shirt and blew a kiss at Harper's grave.

After putting the shovel and gloves back in their place in the shed, Birdie went to the kitchen for some cleaning supplies. She quickly wiped down the furniture in the master bedroom with wood polish and sprayed the mattress with fabric refresher. Harper's body had not begun to leak fluids yet, but the smell still lingered in the air. It was already greatly improved by the time Birdie was done. She opened the master bedroom closet to find sheets to put on the bed. It was a huge closet. Full of beautiful blouses and dresses, a floor-to-ceiling shelf of shoes, and pretty purses lining the entire upper shelf. There were a few men's suits and shirts that occupied a small corner, but otherwise it was a closet that every little girl dreams of playing in. Birdie ran her hands over the silky textures and long lines of the gowns and imagined going to a symphony in one of them or attending a gardener's club in one of the smart pastel suits. Birdie laughed at the thought.

The fanciest place she'd ever been in was a restaurant attached to the mall where her ex-boyfriend had taken her as an apology after one particularly nasty night he'd used Birdie as an ashtray, extinguishing his lit cigarette on her arm. She shook the memory and went about locating the sheets.

She found them neatly folded in large wicker basket on the floor at the back of the closet. As she pulled them out, a scented sachet dropped down into the basket and Birdie saw that there was a large manila envelope that had been concealed at the bottom, under the sheets. Birdie felt guilty for snooping but was curious what Harper had wanted to hide, even in a house that James was apparently not at very often. She took the envelope and the sheets and sat down on the edge of the bed. Nothing on the outside. She undid the clasp and slid a stack of crisp white papers out. A cover letter on the top read Malcolm & Associates, Legal Attorneys. Further down, Harper Yvonne Phillips Benson vs. James Edward Benson III. These were the divorce papers Harper mentioned in her suicide note.

Birdie went on to read that of the couple's substantial holdings, which were all in James' name, Harper was only asking for Sparrow House. They had no children, and Harper wanted no alimony. Only the house and her car, a

1959 Volkswagen Beetle convertible, both the only things in Harper's name. A house that James detested anyway and a car he probably wouldn't be caught dead riding in. Birdie had a feeling that he would've fought her for them anyway. A man like that would hold on to every ounce of his pride and needed to "win" without mercy.

Birdie felt something hard in the bottom of the envelope and tipped it upside down. A little silver key slid out. Birdie looked around the room but couldn't see anything that might require a key. "What else did you have up your sleeve Harper?", she asked the room. She had not seen anything in the house that looked like a safe or a lock box, but then again, her inspection of the house had been mostly under duress and she certainly wasn't taking an inventory. She had noticed a desk. It was in a small room that looked like it served as an office/library. The shelves were filled with books, and the desk had caught her eye because it looked like one she'd seen in the window of an antique store in town. She took the key downstairs and examined the desk. Nothing but what you'd expect to find in a desk, some old receipts, an unopened letter from the Fleming Arts Council.

Birdie's "desk", which was the edge of her kitchen counter, was stacked with the electric bill or past-due medical bills from previous trips to various emergency rooms in Colorado. Birdie knew this house likely had no such thing as an electric bill. The roof was covered in solar panels, and she could tell from the water she drew from the faucet that it was drawn from a well.

Almost at an end with the exploration of the desk, Birdie noticed that the bottom right drawer was shallower than the rest. She pulled several magazines out and saw a small lock opening at the back. The key fit perfectly, and a quick turn released a spring-loaded panel at the bottom. Birdie lifted the panel out and nearly fell over. Stacks of hundred-dollar bills neatly filled the entire bottom of the drawer.

Birdie

A quick count told Birdie there were ten stacks. A hundred-thousand dollars in cash. A white envelope tucked at the side contained Harper's birth certificate, social security card, and driver's license. It also contained the deed to Sparrow House and the title to the vintage beetle in Harper's name.

"Holy Christ Harper. You go girl. I wish we both could've seen the look on his face when you dropped the bomb on his arrogant head." This was a game-changer. Birdie couldn't help but instantly think of all the things she could do with the money. Was money even relevant anymore? What would the world be like after - whatever it was had happened? "Even if the world doesn't use money anymore, it's a helluva souvenir that I don't mind keeping," she said to herself. Harper certainly didn't need it anymore.

Birdie went to the garage, the only room she had not been in by now and there sat the shiny red beetle, keys dangling on a hook by the door. Birdie went back to the office, locked the secret panel back up, and sat at the desk to think about the next steps. Was it stealing? Harper had no kids, and apparently no family, since there were no photos in the house and she'd isolated herself at Sparrow House. Was it wrong? Well not anymore wrong than, I don't know, murder, she thought to herself. Who would know? Birdie ran to a T.V. and turned it on to see if there were any updates. A grainy picture appeared, apparently some signal was getting out now. A tired looking junior reporter several counties over was reporting mass chaos and casualties. Electric and phone service outages were reported to be nationwide and martial law had been instituted.

The next hour Birdie spent disposing of James. The bullet had not gone through, and because he had been sitting up, most of the blood was contained to his clothing. She turned the cushion over that did have a little blood on it and placed the throw blanket across the splatter on the arm of the couch. It was a quick cleanup and if anyone did come

to the door or look in the window, they wouldn't be able to
tell that a man had died there recently. She wiped the gun
clean and put it along with the bullets behind the bread in
the cupboard. She thought it best to keep it close by in case
someone did wander onto the property. Hell, she did, and
even had peaceful intentions but she still managed to kill
someone. You never know what can happen.

She dragged James to his Porsche and wrestled him
into the driver's seat. She threw the empty liquor bottles on
the floor and pocketed the spare bullets to the gun that she
found in the glove box. She found the cocaine he'd mentioned and emptied the entire packet as far back in his throat
as she could. She put the car in neutral and lined the wheels
up to point them at the drop off. She used one of the empty
bottles to wedge under the gas pedal and turned the car on.
"Have a good flight, you sorry bastard."
She threw the car into drive and watched with satisfaction
as the car accelerated through the brush and over the edge.
Birdie ran to the cliff just in time to see the car crunch, head-
on into the rocks below. It teetered vertically for a moment
then fell, top-down, into the water. The current was strong,
and the water had risen from the floodwaters, so the car was
quickly carried downstream and out into the Pacific.

Birdie was exhausted and after finishing the job of
putting the sheets on Harper's bed. She took a long hot bath
in the guest bathroom. The robe was dirty from her tossing it on the ground the night before and she forgot to go
to the basement to look for clean clothes in the donate box.
Wrapped in a towel, she went to Harper's closet and chose
a simple gray cotton tee and black leggings. "Thank you for
the outfit Harper. Lucky for me, we seem to be similar in
size, although you had considerably better taste than I do."

She looked in the master bedroom for a ponytail
holder since hers had been soaked in sweat. She found
several unopened boxes of hair color. "You had grays you

wanted hide too, huh?" She caught her reflection in the mirror. It could work. Birdie had fuller cheeks and bags under her eyes, but what person wouldn't look a little different after surviving an extinction event? She found scissors in a shaving kit and cut her hair into a short, neat bob - ending just below her ears. Yes, it could work. She practiced in the mirror, "My name is Harper Benson, and I have no idea what happened to my dear husband James."

BC Winters
NASA, Goddard Space Center, Maryland

"Miss Winter?"

The words barely penetrated into the void that passed as BC's sleep.

"Sorry to wake you."

She groaned and rubbed at her face. Her hand came away sticky and damp. She opened her eyes and frowned at the puddle of drool she had left next to someone's keyboard. BC sat up and turned toward the door and the source of the noise that had woken her. Tom gave her a wry smile. He looked like death warmed over.

"What's —" BC cleared her throat and tried again. "What's going on?" The last thing she remembered was watching the scattered news stories later into the night, or morning, depending on how you looked at it.

"Director Justus is on site. He is asking for you."

BC looked around as the fog slowly lifted from her brain. There were no windows and no clock. Who had an office without a clock?

"What time is it?"

"Mid-morning," Tom said. "I, uh, I wasn't sure there would be one. A morning that is. Thank you. You saved us all." The intensity of his expression made BC uncomfortable.

"All I did was write a program with Beachum's help," she said. "The crew of Freedom are the ones who saved us." She couldn't suppress the tremor in her voice as she asked the next question. "Is Anton … Are they still all right?"

Tom looked down at his shoes. "The ship was pretty severely battered. We tried to get them into an orbit that avoids the majority of the debris." Tom looked back up and BC's heart sank at his expression. "There's been no contact with them since the maneuver." He fought to get a smile back on his face. "That doesn't mean anything. We know their antenna was damaged. They can wait out the next few days and make repairs while the meteor storm dies down. With luck, they will be hungry, but none the worse for wear."

"With luck." BC shuddered at the mention of the meteor storm. The news had shifted from the rioting to the devastation across the American southeast as the moon debris rained down on the Earth. The dark matter might have disappeared, but its destruction continued. Her heart ached, but she refused to believe anything other than Anton was all right.

"He'll be fine," Tom said. "They all will, and you are right. They are heroes. NASA will do everything possible to get them home safely. Besides, Musk is already tweeting about some kind of rescue ship idea he had, not that we will need it. Director Justus is determined to get them home."

BC nodded. She needed to believe that. She stood and stretched, then followed Tom to the director's office. She was not surprised to find Beachum already there. What did surprise her was the state of the Director. He was filthy. His clothing was torn and he sported a split lip and purpling bruise on one cheekbone.

"The commute last night was — interesting," he said in response to her stare. "Rioters filled the streets" He brushed his fingertips across his cheek and winced. "And NASA employees weren't too popular. I shouldn't have left the car." He smiled, and his lip began to bleed. "I believe I have you to thank for helping change that a bit."

"Yes," Beachum said. "Some of us remained here to continue our efforts last night."

BC's jaw dropped at the sheer audacity of the man. The Director froze in the act of dabbing at his bleeding lip. He made a visible effort at relaxing his shoulders.

241

"And bravo to you, sir," he said. "But I won't apologize. I spent what I thought were my last hours in this life with my family. I would do it again in a heartbeat." His jaw muscles jumped as he ground his teeth. BC stepped in before Beachum could make a fool of himself.

"I'm glad you are all right, Director," she said. "But I assume you had a reason for calling for us?"

Justus folded his handkerchief and directed BC to the seat next to Beachum.

"Please, Ms. Winter, have a seat." He waited for BC to settle in. "I'll cut right to the chase. We need damage control. We need to have our feet beneath us before the media gets their collective acts together." He sighed and leaned back in his chair. "Look," he said, "the fact is, as far as the world is concerned, the Professor's experiment unleashed hell on the planet. Right now, everyone is numb or rejoicing the fact that they are still alive. But, anytime now, they are going to look for someone to blame." He stared straight at Beachum.

"That's preposterous!" Beachum shouted. "There was no indication -" Justus held up a hand and waved him to a halt. No mean task, but his swollen cheek gave him a look that wasn't to be trifled with.

"That is neither here nor there, Professor. We have been incommunicado since declaring the planet a lost cause. People are already wanting answers. I beat my phone into pieces last night just to have an excuse to avoid speaking to the president." He turned his attention to BC. "I need to know what happened. I need to know why it happened. And more importantly, I need to know that it won't happen again."

It was a long meeting. BC was amazed at the Director's restraint as Beachum kept interrupting the debriefing to argue his innocence. As the morning dragged on, the Professor became more and more agitated and verbally combative.

At first BC dismissed it as his normal behavior, but then she noticed a desperate undercurrent to his outbursts. He was feeling guilty. The thought was an epiphany, and her attitude toward him immediately changed. For what may have been the first time in his life, Beachum was feeling responsibility for his actions, and it was beginning to eat him alive. The irony was that this time he really was innocent of anything other than hubris.

"Director," BC said. "Where is this going? You understand that whatever happened was completely unintended, right? There was no way for Professor Beachum to anticipate this. No one could have anticipated dark matter changing state. This is something entirely new. Beachum can't be blamed for this."

"He can, and he will."

"What?" Beachum came up out of his chair. "Have you not been listening, you administrative idiot? This is an entirely new branch to the field of particle physics and astrophysics combined. I should get a Nobel for this."

"But you won't," Justus said. He sighed and motioned to the chair. "Sit down and listen, Beachum. This isn't personal, this is human nature and Public Relations." He turned to BC and fixed her with a stern gaze. "This is off the record." BC opened her mouth to protest, but he shook his head. "No compromise. Just listen." Justus stood and began pacing behind his desk.

"There has been a catastrophe, damn near an apocalypse. The entire world lost its collective mind as suddenly, out of the blue, they found out it was their last day alive. Humanity showed its best and its worst as it tried to cope. Then, just as suddenly, poof - it's over." Justus stopped and shrugged. "Just like that. Everything is going to be fine. Right now, people are elated, or they are dealing with the ramifications of their bad decisions. Either way, all of that stress and adrenaline has nowhere to go." He tapped the surface of his desk with a finger. "I've seen this before, though. That stress must go somewhere, and that somewhere is usually anger. People will want answers, they will want reassurances, but most importantly, they will want someone to blame."

"But it was not my fault," Beachum said. The defeat in his voice was something BC had never heard before.

Justus nodded. "You see my point, don't you? They can blame you, or they can blame NASA, or they can blame the science. I intend to show them the NASA heroes of last night, the crew of The Freedom. Fighting impossible odds to save all of mankind. We will either get them home safely, or they will have died for the cause. Either way, NASA will not go down with this calamity." He pointed at BC. "I can also give them Dr. Winter, here. The hero on the ground that figured out how to stop your runaway experiment. The science should escape with only minor setbacks. But for that to work," Justus pointed at Beachum, "you need to be the villain."

"That's not right!" BC couldn't believe what he was suggesting. "Professor Beachum and I worked on the solution together. I couldn't have done it without him."

Justus nodded. "And that may be what keeps him out of jail."

"Jail?" The word was a startled squeak from Beachum's throat. "That's preposterous!"

"No, that's reality." Justus leaned forward, placing his elbows on his desk. He rested his chin on his clasped hands as he studied Beachum. "You really don't see the whole picture, do you? There will be congressional inquiries. All research experiments into dark matter will be halted. A censure will be placed on all government grants currently in the works. NASA's budget will be audited and most likely cut as the loss of equipment is tallied." He shrugged. "The list goes on. The same thing happened in the late 1980's when the Space Shuttle Challenger exploded. It took years for NASA to recover funding and to win back people's confidence. This will be worse. You will be blamed, Professor, deservedly or not."

Beachum stood up, an odd expression on his face, and headed toward the door. "Excuse me," he mumbled, "I … I need to clear my head."

"I should make sure he's all right," BC said, but the Director waved her back to her seat.

"He will be fine," Justus said. "We need to talk about the story you are going to give to the press."

BC felt her ears begin to burn. "I'll tell them what happened. I was here to report on the project. I've already sent my copy to my editor. There's no changing it."

"Settle down! I didn't say you would change anything," Justus said. "It's a matter of tone, of focus. Concentrating your story more on the heroics of the astronauts and your own contributions would go a long way toward damage control. No one needs to hear about the lack of NASA personnel or Beachum's involvement in your plan."

"You can't just make your own reality!"

Justus sat back and steepled his fingers in front of his lips. His expression had gone cold and he looked at her like he had looked at Beachum the day before.

"Do you like your access to NASA, Ms. Winter?"

BC was surprised at the fire that burst to life inside of her. "Don't you threaten me!" She stood, leaned over the Director's desk, and met his cool gaze with one of fire. "You can't intimidate me, Justus. I might have a history as a pushover, but that ended last night." She shoved herself upright and stalked toward the door. "Do what you have to do, but don't expect me to lie for you."

She was through the adjoining secretary's office and into the hall before her legs began to tremble. She leaned against the wall and gathered herself. What was the man thinking? He couldn't just spin this into a win and the hell with everyone else. Could he? The chill that ran down her spine told her he could.

"Well, only one thing to do," she muttered. BC reached for her phone and dialed.

"Hi Rebecca. Have I got a story for you."

$\sim$

"Ma'am? I'm afraid the facility is on lock-down."

BC whirled at the sound of the security guard's voice.

"Why?" BC demanded. "I've been here all night. I need to go home."

"Director's order's, Ma'am." The guard motioned for her to step back from the door. "If you will come with me …"

His tone left no doubt that it was not a request. BC took a deep breath and shrugged.

"Why not?" she muttered. The guard, Toby, according to his name tag, indicated she should precede him down the hallway. "Where are we going?" She turned and frowned at him over her shoulder. "When did you get here? And shouldn't you be out celebrating?" The morning news stories had been of riots turned to celebrations when the fiery destruction from the heavens had disappeared. The destruction in Kentucky was barely mentioned, at least so far.

The guard's cheeks flushed pink. "I, uh, did my celebrating last night." He cleared his throat and squared his shoulders. "Besides, I've got bills to pay and a job to do." He motioned to the intersection ahead. "We will go left here. The Director has a room set up for you."

BC tried not to stew as she was led through the maze of hallways. How on earth had Justus managed to get things back together so quickly? She knew he was good at his job, but she had been amazed at how quickly he had acted. She barely had time to discuss the basics of her plan with Rebecca when her phone died. No signal. Obviously, he had activated the cell phone jammers in the facility. After that, she made a run for the exits and found a guard at each one. It was less than half an hour since she stormed out of his office and he already had more security in place than there were engineers and technicians. She didn't understand what he was trying to accomplish. She had sent her story last night. It was in her editor's hands.

With that thought a chill ran down her spine. It wasn't published yet. Could he stop it? She knew the answer. With enough pressure and politics her editor would hold the story. All it would take was a request from the Director of NASA for her editor to validate her sources. It would give him time to pressure her.

"In here, Ma'am."

BC looked around, startled. She had been lost in thought and had not realized the guard had stopped. Toby was holding open a door and motioning her inside. She forced a smile onto her face.

"Thanks for the tour, Toby. You can go back to your desk now." It came out as sarcastic as she hoped

He grinned back with genuine humor. "I'll be right outside if you need anything, Ma'am."

"Great," she muttered. "I'll let you know."

Toby chuckled as he closed and locked the door behind her. BC hoped he choked on it. What was she going to do now? She dropped her bag beside the door and appraised the room, too angry to just give up.

The room was fairly large, but not a conference room. The lighting was more subdued and the color scheme not as stark white as most of the facility. There were no windows, but a very large television screen was centered on one wall, silently showing a montage of the events of the previous twenty-four hours. A small table and four chairs were across the room from it. Between them, a variety of overstuffed recliners and couches filled the space. The only door was the one she had come through. A waiting room of some sort, perhaps for the families of NASA astronauts?

Beachum lay on the couch farthest from the door, an arm across his eyes and the other dangling onto the floor. His mouth was wide open, and BC couldn't believe he wasn't snoring, he really seemed the type to rattle the rafters. There was no special treatment this time around. They were both prisoners. Though she admired his ability to relax, this wasn't the time for a nap. They needed a plan or Justus would be throwing them both under the bus of public opinion. From the images on the TV and the headlines crawling across the news ticker, the public's opinion was not good. There was still no word from NASA or the White House. Angry Congressmen and Senators were demanding answers. BC rubbed at her aching head. The politicians had certainly recovered quickly. She needed to do something now, before things got worse.

"Sorry to wake you, but we need to talk, Professor." BC dropped into the nearest chair. "We need a plan." Beachum didn't move. She leaned forward to give him a shake and her eyes fell on the small prescription bottle lying on the floor just past his fingertips. "Oh, no!"

BC crossed to the couch and took Beachum by the shoulders. "Professor? Wake up, damn it." She shook him, but there was no response. He was completely limp. She took his wrist to check for a pulse and checked again at his throat. Nothing, and his skin was cooler than it should be. Panic welled up in her chest as BC leaned over his face, listening for breath as she watched his chest for movement. He wasn't breathing. She stood and stared down at her former mentor. He had done it. The bastard couldn't take the heat. Her eyes flicked to the television and the scenes of destruction caused by the moon rock meteors and she felt sick. Maybe it was remorse that drove him to do it. They would never know.

She sagged into the chair leaned her face into her hands. There wasn't anything left to fight about. Beachum's suicide played right into Justus' plan to blame him. With Beachum no longer around to refute anything, the only one who could argue was herself. BC shuddered. If she did, Justus would bring her reputation into question and blackball her from NASA. He had her right where he wanted her. BC wiped her eyes and looked at the bottle on the floor. It was completely empty. True to form till the end, Beachum hadn't left anything for her. Not even scraps. She laughed at the dark humor. She didn't quite understand why she felt so bad at the old man's passing. What had changed? Was it her? She had been rooting for him to have a heart attack when he flipped out in the control room the previous day, so why was she crying?

BC stopped cold as a series of thoughts ran through her head. Was she insane? She looked from the pill bottle to Beachum and back and knew what she had to do. She knelt back beside Beachum and shook him again while palming the bottle and its cap. BC didn't know if there were cameras in the room or not, but best to be careful. She surged to her feet and crossed the room to hammer on the door.

"Help! We need help. Beachum's had a heart attack!"

She tucked the bottle into her pocket as Toby opened the door. "What?" The security guard's face showed genuine concern.

"It's Beachum! I think he's dead!" Her tears from earlier must have been convincing. Toby didn't even question her sincerity.

"Where is he?" BC pointed to the couch and Toby shot across the room, talking quickly into his radio. "We have a medical emergency in room one twenty-seven." As he dropped to one knee beside the couch, BC grabbed her bag and slipped out of the room.

November 8th

An hour later she practically fell into Rebecca's arms. The release of the tension she had been carrying throughout her escape made her knees weak with relief. The chaos of Beachum's death, and some very timely help from Tom, her only ally, had allowed her to slip from between Justus' fingers. She had been looking over her shoulder the entire time, but no one had followed her. Thank God Rebecca had been waiting.

"Are you all right?" Rebecca held her as BC fought to maintain her composure. "What happened? I've been worried sick ever since we were cut off."

"It's a long story," BC said. She followed Rebecca to the network's waiting car. "And it's one that I'm ready for you to tell."

~

"Thank you for your time, Dr. Winter. I am sure Professor Beachum's loss will be felt throughout the field."

"Thank you, Rebecca."

A red light shone on a camera off to the side, and Rebecca turned to look into its lens.

"The crew of the spaceship Freedom. You just heard of their heroic effort to save the world, but it nearly came at a terrible price. Their crash landing and ultimate rescue is a story for the ages. Rob has the details after this break."

"And cut! That was great, ladies."

BC let out a pent-up breath and sagged in her chair as a studio engineer removed her microphone and sending unit. Rebecca chatted with the director, elated at the promotion she had negotiated with the exclusive story, but BC tuned her out. Anton was alive! The breaking news story during this last interview had nearly sent her into tears of relief. She had been on the air three times this evening and had been too worried to really think straight.

"Are you all right?" Rebecca reached over and placed a hand on her knee.

"Just wrung out, BC said. "It's been long two days." She wanted to rub her eyes, but knew she would smudge the mascara the network's makeup artist had applied. She heaved another sigh, instead. "Was this the right thing to do?"

"Of course it was." Rebecca led BC through the studio and into her new office. She closed the door behind them. "You're a natural at this. You are smart, easy on the camera lens, and come across as a genuine person and not some talking head. People understand you. They can relate to you, and I think telling your story is the best shot you've got at protecting Beachum's reputation." She cocked her head and gave BC a quizzical look. "I just don't understand why you care. I pictured you celebrating when he finally kicked the bucket. I mean, it's a tragedy his heart failed due to the stress, but after what he did —"

"That was years ago, Rebecca. And given what we all just went through, it just seems so petty, now. Is it so hard to believe I might have finally forgiven him?"

"I guess not." Rebecca nodded, half to herself. "Okay. That's over. How about that late dinner I promised you, now that it's well past dinner time? I know I'm not Anton, but since he is safe," Rebecca grinned and gave BC's knee a pat, "but thousands of miles away, I'm afraid I will have to do."

"Sounds great. I'm famished."

"Great. Just give me a couple of minutes to check on things, then I'm good to go." Rebecca patted BC's shoulder on the way across the room and closed the door behind her. BC sagged in the chair and stared unseeing into the corner.

When she had first called Rebecca, it was with the intent of giving the interview with Beachum alongside of her, but that changed when she finally found him in the lounge. He was dead. She hadn't expected to take it so hard, but then again, she hadn't expected the note she found in the pill bottle. She pulled the crumpled piece of paper from her pocket and read it again.

Winter, I accept responsibility for what I have done, both now and in the past. However, I am too much of a coward to see it through properly. The future of our work is now yours alone. I have every confidence you will exceed even me. Carry on.

BC wiped her eyes. To hell with the mascara. To hell with Justus and his plans for a scapegoat. This was what the world needed. A story of hope, a story of teamwork, a story of a man whose heart burst saving the world. Who was she to say otherwise.

Our Authors

BC Winter's Story by Mike Ghere

Mike Ghere has written three novels in the Broken Worlds trilogy, and is currently working on another episode in the series. His Sci-Fi/Western will be out in early 2019.

An engineer by trade, Mike is patiently waiting for his writing to begin paying the bills. When he is not working or writing, he enjoys reading, hiking, camping, collecting and repairing fountain pens, and catching up on his sleep.

Mike can be reached at:

www.MikeGhere.com

mikeghere@mikeghere.com

www.facebook.com/mikeghere

Rachel's Story by Diana Gugel

Diana Gugel lives in Ohio. She has been a parish pastor for over 30 years and has written over 1500 sermons. This is her first published short story and she is almost finished with her first book. She is married and has two grown children.

"Writing in this cooperative has been one of the most unexpected and wonderful gifts of grace."

Robert's Story by David L. Hoffmann

David L. Hoffmann is a professor of history at The Ohio State University. His most recent book is The Stalinist Era (Cambridge University Press, 2018). He lives in Lancaster, Ohio.

Videl Corbin's Story by Julia Burnside

Julia Burnside is a writer from the deep dark wilds of Ohio. Her writing style incorporates realism, humor, and visual writing to connect the story to the reader. This is Julia's second published short story. You can find her first, The Early Christmas Gift, in Legacy Quarterly, October 2018.

Melony's Story by Tarence Bright

Tarence Bright has a certificate in Mindfulness and Meditation. She is a nature enthusiast who enjoys regular hiking and canoe trips with her husband and son. She lives in Ohio.

For more information please contact her at:

TarenceBright@gmail.com

Tarence Bright on Facebook https://www.facebook.com/TarenceBright/

Her Website is https://tarencebright.home.blog/

Come along on with her on her writing journey.

Summer's Story by Jane B. Night

Jane B. Night published her first novel in 2013. Since then she has written a variety of romance novels. She is a blogger, ghostwriter, and YouTuber.

www.janebnight.webs.com

Chris and Kriss' Story by Cory Overmeyer

Cory has been a writer, officially, for about two years now, though he's been creating super-powered characters since he was five years old. In 2017 he participated in National Novel Writing Month and completed the challenge, which is a minimum of 50,000 words within thirty days. As of right now, he has approximately twenty-six books planned.

Birdie's Story by Lily Griffen

Lily Griffen lives in Pickerington, Ohio with her two children, The Hubs, a lazy bird-dog, and the incomparable Miles the Cat. A technical writer by trade, she works from home, which allows her to wear pajamas every day and frequently stare out the window into imaginary worlds waiting to be written into existence. This is her debut publication and she is pleased as punch (however pleased punch could possibly be) to be here. Find her on Twitter @lilybynature.

Scott O'Neil's Story by Leuke Ender

Leuke Ender has been writing stories since he was 15. Portal World is his first published novel. He was born in Ohio, then moved to Colorado, then returned to Ohio, where he currently lives with an unruly dog. Ender has worked as a dishwasher, a beef jerky labeler, a warehouse worker, a shelf stocker, a greeter, a traveling technician, a laser engraver, a package handler, a sales writer, and a virtual assistant. In his spare time he hosts a YouTube show called Coffee Nerds and writes novels. He hopes to one day be able to write full time so that he can devote more of his life to the stories he enjoys creating.

Social Media:

Website: http://www.leuke.net

Twitter: Leuke0

Facebook: @writerleuke

Made in the USA
Lexington, KY
20 December 2018